BANISHED TO BROOKLYN

BANISHED TO BROOKLYN

Volume II of the Bucceroni Series
By
W. J. Reeves,
Author of *Betrayal in Brooklyn*

Acknowledgments

● ●

I'd like to thank my wife, Cathie, for her support. I'd also like to thank Rebecca Swift for creating the cover, Karen Carter for the editing, and 52Novels.com for the formatting.

Introduction

· ·

The Urban U. in Brooklyn had become a dumping ground for down-and-out professors. Within the less-than-cozy confines of the college were the young and the incompetent and the old and over the hill. The young were supposed to quit and ply a new trade while the old, well, they were to die.

Preface

· ·

"Teaching…here…sucks," gasped Professor Rudolf Randle, clutching his chest and slumping forward, his head clipping the edge of his desk.

The portly Ph.D. slid from his chair to the floor, knocking over a coffee cup during his descent.

In the small office he'd shared with two colleagues, the professor lay, stone-cold dead, on a never-very-clean navy blue rug.

Outside the college, business in Brooklyn went on as usual. Subway riders swore and elbowed each other while drivers honked and passed on the right.

The sun did its best to beautify Brooklyn, but beauty must come from within, and within was one dead professor.

Chapter One

. . . .

It was in the time I call A.D. that all of this happened. A.D. is not *Anno Domini,* and it isn't Attention Deficit. A.D. in my book stands for "After Dom," after I'd blown to hell and gone my best friend because he had me lined up for the cold meat slab. Even thinking about it now made my temperature rise. Me, the old buddy buddy from Bensonhurst, the pal of pals, me he'd gone after. I counted to ten. In Brooklyn, it was bad enough getting pissed off at the living; putting on a head of steam about the dead is nutzy. Which sometimes I think I am.

The day this all started was a day like most days—life was up to no good with me. I was on my way to see the Dean at the Urban U. The Dean liked me as little as the former Dean had. The former Dean, D. Douglas Fenner, had been fired for "conduct unbecoming", which in his case was for banging his Assistant Dean, an activity that had come to the attention of his wife, who'd shot the offending, lustful Assistant Dean, twice, in the caboose. Now Fenner's no doubt in Florida, at Century Village, gulping Viagra by the fistful and going on the prowl after the Blue-Hairs. Wherever he is, he isn't here and that's OK with me. He and I didn't see eye to eye, and it had nothing to do with height. He was a scum-turtle, while yours truly is the Prince of Prospect Park, the type of individual who makes the pope's short list, an all-around swell fella—even if I do kill someone now and then.

At the office of my current supervisor, I noticed something different. While Fenner had splashed his full name on the gold plate on the door of the Dean's office, this one just used "Dean". Which made sense. Hitler hadn't signed his name as Führer Hitler, yet everybody knew he was the only tyrant in town. Fenner had been an academic clown, a poster professor for the Peter Principle. This one was different. Not necessarily better—just different.

The Dean's secretary, who'd probably been around when there were dinosaurs, said, "Your appointment was at nine."

Her voice sounded like she'd chain-sucked on one too many unfiltered cigarettes.

I looked at the large clock in the room, which read 9:01. I could see this clear as day, even through my dark Armani sunglasses. I looked down at her. I searched for words of wisdom.

"There was a problem with the elevator—it was going sideways," I said.

"Have a seat," she croaked. Never cracked a smile at my Henny Youngman.

It was quiet and peaceful in the room, making it different from the rest of the Urban U., which was largely nine floors of messy mayhem. It had not taken long to change a brand new building into a dirty dump. The Dean did not stray from here. Who'd blame him? Outside, there was mayhem, and sometimes murder; here there was peace and quiet. I looked at the reading material, which included the *Chronicle of Higher Education* and magazines on how to teach and how to manage. The people who wrote those articles should come here—I'd introduce them to one of my students, a Mr. Barry "Three-Balls" Ashby, see if they could get through to him. If not, I was sure he could get through to them, like with a switchblade to the throat. My classes were exercises in survival, especially with the changes that had come about. Our motto should be "Trouble is our Business"— whoever couldn't be taught in Brooklyn was sent to us. We were supposed to civilize these students and do so without pistols. Lucky us.

Time passed. I stopped staring at what I wouldn't read and examined the walls, which were spotless. The furniture had been dusted, and the carpet cleaned. I stretched out my legs. I was beginning to enjoy it here.

The inner sanctum door opened, and Winston Wiant, HEO, appeared. He looked like he usually looked, which was creepy; fish-belly white skin contrasted with a deep black suit. He smiled at me. I smiled back. He motioned for me to come in.

"He's here, Professor Bucceroni is finally here," Wiant said, stepping aside to give me just enough room to enter. I eased past him; up close, I could tell he was a guy who didn't waste a lot of time showering. Next time, I'll bring my Drakkar and give him a squirt or two, or three.

I walked in and took a seat in a small, green plastic chair which was no doubt not greatly pleased with having to support my girth. Even though I ran, my weight stayed at 250, which might had been the result of my exercising little control over calorie intake. If it didn't move or wasn't a vegetable, I ate it. Plus dessert.

Wiant took up a position to the Dean's right. Like Goebbels had stood next to Hitler.

"Professor, do you know Natasha Natooska?" said the Dean, a short plump man not given to smiling and well known for nastiness, getting right to the point. There were no inquiries about my health and well-being. This guy was no academic. I had no idea where the university had dredged to find him, but he was a total administrator, which made him an absolute asshole.

He had before him on his desk a legal pad and a manila folder bulging with documents. To his right, on another desk, were a CPU and a 20-inch monitor. The Dean's office had a musty smell, like a basement with a water problem, and Wiant wasn't helping with the smell factor. Lucky for me, I'd put cologne behind my ears before I came. I smelled swell.

"Like in the Bible?" I said, adjusting my ample rear quarters to fit in the small chair. I kept my sunglasses on. The chair placed me at eye level with the five-foot-tall Dean. I wondered if the chair were on loan from

Attica, where prisoners maybe had been "sweated" in it. Maybe I'd ask my students, who probably had lots of relatives there.

"Excuse me?" said the short fat ass.

"You know, like Adam knew Eve."

"I do not think you understand me. I meant, have you ever had Ms. Natooska in your class?"

"Nope."

"So, you do not know Natasha Natooska?"

"In the biblical sense?"

"Professor! This is a serious matter; I am conducting an investigation," said the Dean, his voice rising, his chins quivering.

"Good for you."

"Yes, 'good for me' and if you know what's good for you...."

"You seem a little hung up on Bible-talk."

"Professor! This must stop! I am the Dean of this college, and it is my...."

"And might I say you're the best Dean we've had since the last one was canned," I put in.

"Thank you, but really, this is a very serious matter. Ms. Natooska has claimed she was sexually harassed by your office partner, and I am directing you to help in the investigation."

"You're kiddin' me."

"No, I am not."

"Randle is old and fat and unwell and couldn't harass himself."

"That's not what Ms. Natooska said to me."

"You do know, of course, that he failed your Ms. Natooska for plagiarism. He showed me the essay. He was dead-on correct."

The Dean did not reply. Wiant just cold-stared at me. The two of them were probably wondering how big a stick they'd need to roast me on a spit. I smiled a winning smile at them.

I took a small leather carrying case from the inside pocket of my dark blue jacket. I removed a cigar; I put the cigar into my mouth. I now knew why I'd been summoned. An unjust case was being made against my office partner, Randle, and the Dean, as administrators too often do, was looking for "evidence" to bury him. The lack thereof would not stop this overly dutiful Dean from sharpening his knife and sticking it in the innocent. I'd seen this scene before. The misuse of the sexual harassment charge by students who were trying to get back at their professors was not an uncommon occurrence. The Dean also knew this, but he wanted Randle out, and this "charge" was convenient. The Brooklyn branch of the Urban U. was where the professors who couldn't cut it were sent. Randle was a good example of one who had lingered too long. He'd been told to quit, but he'd refused; now he'd be made to twist in the wind. This brilliant idea of sending burn-outs and incompetents to Brooklyn was the brainchild of the President, which meant we now had an evil combo— students who didn't know from Adam about academics and professors who couldn't teach. It made for a wonderful job. I could no longer leave here, for my department had transferred me. Also, I had reasons for staying that had nothing to do with academics.

"Professor, smoking is not allowed in this office, or in this building."

"Is gnawing allowed in this office or in this building?"

"What?"

"Gnawing. You know, rollin' around in one's mouth in a disgusting fashion a known carcinogen."

"I guess so."

"You're a Dean, you shouldn't guess," I said, staring at the Dean from the safety of my dark glasses. A smile twitched over Wiant's features, exposing one of his yellow teeth. He was quite a sight to see. The Nosferatu of Nostrand Avene was Candy's moniker for him, and she was dead on, just like he was dead looking. The Dean had kept him on from the previous administration, no doubt because Wiant had a file on everyone, including me. This guy knew more about me than me. Whatever the Dean had ever done, Wiant would have a handle on it, and he'd use this info to worm his way into a position of power.

"Yes, you can 'gnaw,' but you cannot smoke," said the Dean, opting to sound happy.

"That's kind of like sloshin' beer over your teeth but not swallowing, or takin' off your pants but not…." Wiant's smile got bigger; whee, I was a hit with the undead.

"Professor, we seem to be getting off the point."

"How 'unseemly' of us."

"Professor, let us return to the matter at hand, shall we?"

"Sure."

"You share an office with Dr. Randle, correct?"

"Yes, indeedy."

"Professor, let us now focus. Have you observed the relationship between Professor Randle and his students?"

"I have."

"What is their relationship?"

"They hate one another."

"Hate?" said the Dean, bending over his large desk, writing quickly with his red pen, getting ready to copy down some negativity.

"Loathe. Despise. Hold in contempt. That kind of hate."

"You have witnessed these…exchanges?"

"I most certainly have."

"Can you describe one of them?"

"I very definitely can. A student comes in. She, or he, or it, sits down by Randle's desk. The 'exchange' usually goes somethin' like this:

"'Why'd you give me an F?'

"'Because you did not answer the question, because you did not write in sentences, because you did not understand the meanings of the words you misused.'

"'I don' need this fuckin' shit....'

"'Next.'

"If no one is next, he tells me that teachin' down here sucks."

"Have you ever observed his behavior with female students?"

"Well, some of them complain about the bright-red blinking 'HARASSMENT IN SESSION' sign outside our office."

"That was a serious question," said the Dean, still not smiling.

"Oh well, then, speaking seriously, he does object about girls in his classes, sittin' in the front row, wearin' short skirts, with their legs crossed, thus eliminating any secrets about their victorias."

There was a knock at the door of the Dean's office.

"Enter," said the Dean, who seemed glad to be doing something other than questioning me.

I turned my head to see the wizened, slightly younger-than-dirt secretary step into the room.

"Yes?" said the Dean.

"It's Professor Randle," said the secretary in her Marlboro soon-to-die voice.

"Yes?"

"EMTs are in his office."

"Is he ill?" said the Dean, his voice rising for the second time in an hour.

"They said he's dead," she rasped.

I was up and out the door before the Dean was up and out of his chair. Wiant never moved. I was surprised, for I would've thought a chance to be near a recently deceased corpse would be up his sick-ass alley.

My haste earned me a final look at my colleague. Dr. Rudolf Randle, age 67, author of thirteen articles on Hemingway (published in the last century), recipient of four Urban U. Research Grants (the most recent two decades ago), lay on a stretcher, blank-staring at a somewhat soiled ceiling.

What a way to go. Die on this crummy job with your boots on. Your last glimpse would be of your shitty office, where you had to meet the shitty students and tell them their work was shit. I finished that burst of crappy thinking and watched the EMT crew as they removed the dead professor from the office. Both of Randle's arms were sweat stained, which meant he'd been stewing before he croaked. He'd done a great deal of that in my presence—bitch, moan, and make himself miserable. And this is how he ended up—back down on a dirty floor.

I took out a butane lighter. I lit the Robusto I'd been gnawing on, taking care not to let the flame touch the end of the cigar. I checked my watch. It usually took me thirty minutes to smoke a Robusto. I had time. I did not think the Dean would be interested in further directing me to help in the investigation of bogus sexual harassment charges against the late Dr. Randle. Even the administrators of the Urban U. would not pursue a case against the dead. They had their standards, after all.

I drew on the cigar. I had a class to teach. Someone would tell Randle's students to go home. The next day another professor would be assigned to teach the classes. Life at the Urban U. would lurch onward. It was a truism that all of us were just cogs in a wheel. No one gave a rat's ass how or what we taught as long as we showed up and faced the great, unwashed masses. That was the hallmark of our place—keep the process plodding along, and keep replacing those who dropped by the wayside.

It had been said that only the dead know Brooklyn. I looked over at my dead colleague's desk. What did he now know?

I saw something under the desk. I put my cigar in an ashtray. I bent over, picked the something up, saw that it was a coffee cup. Why I did what I did next, I haven't a clue. As a kid, I'd always been curious. My mother had thought that was cute; my father, a.k.a. "The Butcher", thought I was a pain in the ass. I have the sneaking suspicion my father had been right. There was some liquid still in the cup. A thought flashed across my mind. I dipped my finger in the liquid and took a tiny taste. It didn't take long for an old, unpleasant feeling to occur. My heart started to race. I sat down.

Weakness surged over me. My face felt hot.

This was not good. Randle was dead, supposedly of a heart attack, but I now knew better. He'd been drugged. I now even knew the drug. I stared out the window. This was all supposed to be over. The killing of Dom Mancini by yours truly should've put me in the clear, but here again was murder on my doorstep. I drew on the cigar. It tasted foul. I put it out. Outside, rain was coming down. Even at this time of day, Brooklyn was dark.

Chapter Two

· ·

I observed my office, which had three metal desks.

The gray desk closest to the gray door had on it a 20-inch monitor and a DeskJet printer, over it a picture of a literary critic whom I'd been told by Mac McClure was a nasty bastard, beside it two bookcases with books mostly about literary theory, and under it a red Oriental rug that hadn't been bought on eBay. This was a well cared-for area. Whoever was placing his can on this seat was trying to make a go of it here. Good luck to him.

The second desk had on it a 14-inch monitor, a printer which was not a DeskJet, and a phone. Over it was a picture of Hemingway, beside it one all-Hemingway bookcase and one small table supporting a German coffee machine, and under it a navy blue rug spotted with food droppings of all colors. This was the place of a loser who'd gone to meet his maker.

My desk was by the window. On it was nothing, over it was nothing, beside it was nothing, and under it were ashes flicked from cigars. This was the spot of R.V. Bucceroni, the Mr. Chips of the Urban U. I wouldn't call myself a burn-out; I was just a little torched at the edges.

I looked out the window at an apartment building. Facing me in one of the apartments, looking out of a bathroom window through the slowing rain, was an old man seated on a toilet. Not exactly a million-dollar view. I looked away before the old guy took a dump.

My office door opened.

I turned away from the window and picked up my Robusto.

"Today's Thursday," I said to my other office partner, who had a Monday/Wednesday schedule, which meant he never appeared on Tuesday/Thursday. This was a good job I had.

"I came in because of what happened," said the other, older-than-me-by-a-lot professor who wore a bow tie. He placed books on the desk closest to the door. He was a short old man with all-gray hair. His name was Winston Bath, and he had been the first in the boatloads of burn-outs coming to us. He was like Randle, a loser.

"Why?"

"Well, I thought, it seemed to me, I…have you, did someone, I just heard. Quite a shock, wasn't it?"

"To whom?"

"Excuse me?"

"He had no friends, the students hated him, the administration was after him, you never saw him because you teach on Monday/Wednesday and he taught Tuesday/Thursday. Who's shocked?" I asked.

"But we were colleagues."

"You ever invited to his home?"

"No."

"You ever eat lunch with him?"

"No."

"You know his wife?"

"No."

"She died last fall," I said, keeping my eyes fixed on the old man.

"Oh," he said, not meeting my gaze.

"Why're you here?"

"I just told you, I came in because of what happened."

"How'd you know anything happened?"

"I had a call into the Dean's office. He wanted to talk to me about sexual harassment."

"Who'd you harass?"

"No, no, not me, him," said Bath, nodding toward Randle's desk. Randle was no longer a person; he was just a pronoun.

I drew on my cigar. It didn't taste so good.

Someone knocked on the door. Bath opened it.

"Is Doctor Bucceroni here?" said a voice I recognized.

"Come in, Pat," I called.

A stocky, well-put together young man entered the room. His name was Detective Pat Reagan.

"Need to talk with you," he said.

"I'll go check my mail," said Bath, who left the office.

"Professor, want to give you a head's up," said Reagan, sitting in the chair of the departed Professor Randle.

"About?" I said, looking at the cop, remembering when I'd had him in class. I also remembered talking to another cop about deaths at the college. As it had turned out, I'd been talking to a killer.

"The prof who died, Randle, we gotta investigate him."

"This a homicide?" I said, feeling tension work its way into my voice.

"The ME said it looks like he had a heart attack, but I'm still checkin' it out. Fill me in about him."

"He taught Tuesday and Thursday from 10-3. He had an office hour from 3-4. I start teaching at 4:30. Sometimes when I came in, he was in here with students."

"The ME said he'd been dead for about a half hour before the EMTs got to him, so he musta come back here and died right after his class. The EMTs told me someone called them, said for them to come to this office."

"Oh."

"You know, this is some place down here. This Dean of yours, he told me Randle was accused of makin' a pass at some Russian broad. These Russians are nutballs, fuckin' Wild West cowboys. You think he was poppin' her?"

"He'd have to do it before 10 a.m. or after 4:30 p.m."

"You think he did?"

"I don't know."

"Lots of profs go in for that?"

"Some do, most don't," I said, thinking of my pal Mac McClure, who used his office as a love nest. This would all start again. My colleagues would become suspects. Around every corner, I'd see danger. I had done that before with very little success, playing at being a detective while I got deeper and deeper into hot water.

"This Randle, he a doer?" said Reagan, who had a gentle high voice which didn't fit his job. My voice is like my old man's, a deep rumble, making me sound like Louie "Take Your Thumbs" Loriano.

"He was 67, he had bad breath, and he farted a lot."

"Not exactly a stallion."

"Not exactly."

"The girl, her name is Natasha Natooska. Anything on her?"

"A while ago, Randle told me about the trouble he was havin' with her."

"Fill me in."

"She's got an attitude. She speaks Russian-English, which means understanding her isn't easy, so Randle gave her the grade she deserved." Which was true. She was a little troublemaker who Randle should've bought off with a grade. Not him. He'd been a hard ass until the end.

"Which she didn't like."

"Right. Randle told me her writing outside class was passing because it was plagiarized, but her work done in class was F level. So, she apparently went to the Dean to bitch about it, and the result was a case bein' made against him."

"Who made the case?"

I took a coffee cup from my desk drawer.

"Want a cup? I'll make us some."

"No thanks, I don't sleep so good. My doc, he tells me to cut back on the caffeine."

"The Dean made the case."

"You don't think anything happened, why would he?"

"He wanted Randle out of here."

"So why didn't he go?"

"Stubborn. He wasn't going to be run out of town, that's what he told me."

"He have any other trouble with the students?" Reagan wasn't letting up with the questions. I felt like telling him to do some work on his own. Caught myself. Getting pissy with a cop just buys more trouble. So I made like a good boy and provided answers.

"He flunked everyone, black, yellow, brown, made no difference."

"So the One-Percenters, the Seoul Brothers, they could've had it in for him?"

"What'd they do, scare him to death? He wasn't shot, knifed, or beaten up, and that's their stock in trade. Your medical examiner said it was a heart attack," I said, looking closely at the cop, my eyes hidden as usual behind my dark sunglasses. These help me a lot, keep me of being accused of being shifty.

"That was his quickie opinion."

"I see."

"You never know what's what until you look. In the meantime, you watch your back, OK?"

"For?"

"Prof, you and me, we go way back, so I can talk to you about what I shouldn't be talkin' about. What we have so far is a guy in your office dead, and it looks like it was from a heart attack, but the little diggin' I've done so far tells me there're a lot of clowns down here who had it in for him. So I'll get a line on what exactly he died from, and meanwhile you...."

"Watch my back?"

"You got it."

Reagan left. Before I had time to do some big-time worrying, Bath returned from the mailroom. He'd wasted no time. He wanted to get back to throwing his fear at me.

Wiant had said to me that each of us was to be interviewed. "Who'll interview me?" now asked Bath, sitting at his desk. He tapped the index finger of his right hand against his right cheek. His left leg twitched. I was sure he'd do swell being interviewed by the cops. They'd never lay a finger on the old duffer.

"You mean how many?"

"Yes."

"I don't know," I said, feeling my anger spread over me. This was a pain in the ass, all these questions, and the problem was that I had answers.

"Two?"

"'I don't know' covers a lot of territory," I said, being more snippy, something which I didn't like a lot, but all of this was beginning to wear on me.

"Sorry. I barely knew Randle, but with him gone my chances for staying on are better and...."

"I wouldn't, if I were you, use that in your interview."

"You think not?"

"Not is what I think."

"Why?"

"Speakin' to you as a close friend, even though this is the fourth time we've ever talked, you were sent here from the main campus because you're on the chopping block."

"That's not my fault. My student reviews were unfair, I can't help it if...."

"And, once here, the plan was for you to hang on for a while and then go out into the cold, harsh world of the academic job market. But, since there is now one less of us here, you might be kept on...."

"Do you really think so?"

"...and this could mean to a suspicious detective that you had reason to want Randle to be dead."

"But surely no one could sus...."

"So, I would, if I were you, just answer the detective's questions, volunteer nothin', and hope that no one spills the beans about your job possibilities after the death of your...colleague," I said, taking relief in scaring Bath even more than he already was.

"But he wasn't murdered, it was a natural death."

"Said who?"

"Uh, well, that black security guard, I believe he told me."

"You 'believe' he told you?"

The phone rang. I got up, walked to the desk of the late Dr. Randle, and picked up the phone.

"5543."

"It's for you," I said, handing the phone to Bath.

I returned to my own desk by the window.

"Yes," said Bath.

"Yes," said Bath, who started to sweat above his upper lip. His hand shook slightly as he held the phone.

"Yes."

"I'll be right down," said Bath, who hung up the phone. He took out a handkerchief and wiped his face.

"They want me down there," he said.

I turned toward the window.

"I'd best be on my way," said Bath.

I drew on the Robusto, looking out at the old man who still sat on the toilet. He stared at me; I stared at him. We stared. I smoked, he shat.

I blew a smoke ring. Behind me, the door closed. Reagan wasn't sure Randle had died a natural death. I smoked my cigar. Reagan's ME would probably find nothing but clogged arteries in Randle. That was my hope, for the best candidate to explain the truth about Randle's death was the handsome guy blowing smoke rings.

Chapter Three

. . . .

It was lunchtime at the college. I decided to deal with my worrywarts by stuffing myself. I do that a lot, which probably accounts for my heft, although to be fair, I'm not fat, just hefty. At least that's what I tell myself and since I'm the guy doing the eating, that's all that counts.

My choices for dining were few. The tenth floor of the college was, loosely speaking, a cafeteria noted for bad food, poor service, and questionable hygiene and full of students who smoked dope, said "fuck" a lot, and played lousy music loudly. That was a place to avoid. Which meant I had to go outside, to Brooklyn in the raw, full of mean streets and bad intentions. This part of Brooklyn is undergoing gentrification, which means the thugs now have someone to clip.

I used the large glass front door to leave the college, which didn't really look like a college. The college was a ten-story, square brick building. I started to cross the Street. Stopped. Looked up. Checked to see what Mother Nature was doing now that the rain had stopped. That was a mistake and, in Brooklyn, mistakes are not forgiven.

Someone bumped into my chest. He was the one to bounce backward. That's what heft is good for.

"Watch where you're goin', old man!"

"Yeah, get out the way, you fuckin' old fuck!" said another voice.

"Fuckhead!" from still one more.

There were three of them, not small, who were suggesting I was in their space. They seemed to have formed, on a moment's notice, a bad opinion of me. Didn't they know I was a full professor with oodles of publications? Probably not.

I took a step to make sure I wasn't on the property of the Urban U.

I had choices:

A. Apologize

B. Go back inside

C. Or

I selected "or". I slammed my meaty, right forearm into the throat of the biggest one who'd spoken first. He went down and into a parked car, then down onto the slick sidewalk. He lay there, coughing, trying to find air. Before I could address my two-against-one problem, a large, black arm appeared and grabbed the crud with the offending mouth by his shirt. This was quickly followed by a shot in the chops. Foul Mouth joined his friend on the sidewalk. That left one. I sized him up. His eyes were wide open, which meant he was either on dope or scared shitless. I shifted my 250 pounds, got ready to bring my left hook into action. Too late. From my right came motion in the form of a foot, which struck the last one high up on the forehead. He also hit the pavement. Not knowing who was helping me and not wanting to appear to be a sissy, I stepped closer to the punk I'd nailed. He was still coughing, but his left hand was after something in his pocket. I saw the something. I kicked him in the face with my steel-toed right shoe. Back he went; his head whacked the concrete hard.

"Good job, Doc," said Nikki Nateal, my lab assistant.

"Thanks, and thanks for backing me up."

"No problem, Professor, we got to stick together down here," rumbled Nikki's boyfriend, J.P. Carlisle, the head honcho of the One-Percenters street gang. J.P. was about the size of Ray Lewis and had even more attitude.

I took the something from the punk's pocket; it was a switchblade.

Nikki and J.P. left me, walking away from the college, no doubt looking for more trouble.

I crossed the Street and deposited the knife in a trash can.

A tall, good-looking woman standing nearby in a tight red dress said, "You still got it, Professor."

"Thanks, Bob," I said to the woman who wasn't really a woman and went by the name of "The Teaser" in the neighborhood.

I passed a liquor store on my way to the deli on the corner. Two mostly dirty black men were sitting on the damp curb, drinking. One of them raised his bottle in a paper bag:

"Good work, Prof, got to keep these punks in line."

"Thank you," I said. I was a hit with the whores and the street drunks. Who needed the approval of Deans at the college? I was the man!

I took a seat at the end of the counter in the deli. At the other end of the counter an old, mainly dirty white man nursed a cup of coffee. I could smell the old man. I needed a cigar, or maybe a can of Lysol. He needed, in the worst way, Drakkar.

"The usual, Professor Bucceroni?" said the owner of the deli, Harry Blazakis, known in these parts as 'Fat Harry.'

"Yes."

"You want coffee, yes?" said Fat Harry, directing his considerable body toward me, carrying a coffee pot.

"Yes."

"Too bad about your office partner," said Fat Harry, pouring the coffee, then leaning on the counter to rest from the rigor of his waddling.

"Yes, too bad." I waited for the conversation to open. At Harry's bad food was served and in addition Harry probed for bits of gossip. How he used these tidbits was anyone's guess.

"Professor Randle, he was not a happy man."

"No, happy he was not."

"Will there be a funeral service?"

"Don't know."

"He had a wife?"

"Dead."

"Son?"

"Nope."

"Daughter?"

"Died three years ago."

"Will the college hold a memorial?"

"Probably not."

"What will they do?"

"Submit a short obituary to the newspaper."

Fat Harry wheezed. He didn't sound healthy. Maybe it was on account of his weighing in the vicinity of 400 pounds packed on a short frame.

"Every day he would come in here to buy his lunch and every day he would tell me how he was going to get back to the main campus. He said he had a plan, that he would, let me put it in his words, 'play their game and beat them at it.'"

"He mention what the game was?" I asked, knowing what the answer was.

"Someone was to be fired. Professor, let me ask you this, do you think he had a chance to get back?"

"No."

"Why not?"

"He was 67, he was white, and he was writing a book about a white man who shot himself."

"Hemingway?"

"Hemingway."

"So, all the work he was doing, all his research, all of it, it would have come to nothing."

"Nothing."

"And his plan, probably it, too, would have failed?"

"Probably."

"He was not a well man."

"Well, he was not."

"And you, Professor, you have no desire to go back?"

"No."

"Why?"

"Where would I dine?" I said, turning my head left, then right, to take in more of the deli.

The fat man laughed a loud, fat man's laugh.

"You are a witty man, my friend."

"My mother once told me that a boy who thinks he's a wit is usually half-right." Which was true. My mother had a way of putting things in their proper light. The only thing she couldn't get into words was the day my father got whacked.

"That was a wise saying."

"Isn't that my food?" I said, pointing to the glistening gyro platter the cook had placed ready to be picked up.

"It is, indeed."

Fat Harry retrieved the plate and set it in front of me. Nothing in it was moving, which meant one of two things, either there was nothing in the food or whatever was there was tired.

"Enjoy," said Fat Harry, who left, slowly making his way to the cash register. The fat man could barely walk. In his condition, I'd give him five years.

The old, mainly dirty white man finished his coffee. He paid his bill at the cash register. He walked past me. The old man looked closely at me. I ignored him. The old man left the deli. I turned and watched as the old man walked past the college and turned left. I knew the old man, for we were, more or less, neighbors. The old man's apartment was directly across from my office. The old man spent his late mornings, afternoons, and early and late evenings on the toilet, peeping into the women's restroom at the Urban U. while he abused himself. It was great to have such neighbors in Brooklyn. It just shows you how cozy the borough really is.

I checked my watch; I had less than thirty minutes to eat Fat Harry's food. Fast eating was sure to make a match with this grub. In my office were Tums, so I'd gulp a handful or two when I got back.

I gave some thought to what was just across the Street, which was a chemical killer who'd struck too close to home. Last time I'd been in this fix, I'd blown up one floor of the college; this time, I'd just bring down the whole place. I congratulated myself on my deep thinking.

I ate faster. I washed down the food that'd been heaped before me with hot coffee. This was not 'lite' food. Maybe I'd ask Fat Harry for a shot of Draino.

Chapter Four

· ·

I stepped outside the deli. A breeze blew down the Street. I sniffed the air. I first detected carbon monoxide, then a whiff of burning fat from Fat Harry's. Finally, I smelled urine. It was springtime in Brooklyn.

It occurred to me that Randle had died around tax time.

"Death and taxes, only two sure things in the world," had been one of my father's sayings. My father, a.k.a. "The Butcher", had left out one thing—revenge, which had resulted in his checking out of life and into the river, floating face down with the fishes. He had been chewed up so bad you couldn't really make him out in the coffin.

"Hey, man, how 'bout a dolla?" said a generally filthy man.

I now knew the origin of the urine odor.

I gave the bum a dollar. He thanked me. I your-welcomed him. And they say Brooklyn's not civilized. Here we were—two guys who weren't even neighbors and we were civil as hell.

"Hey, Prof, how you doin'?" said the black security guard with the name "Lester Norwood" on his badge. Better known as "Beef Patty", the guard stood six feet tall and weighed in the neighborhood of 400 pounds, making Beef Patty nearly a neighborhood in himself. His shirt strained to hold him in. He had a head about the size of a pumpkin and a neck which gave new meaning to the word "thick."

"I'm doin' fine, Lester."

"Goin' to teach?"

"To a meeting."

"Cops is still here."

"They are?"

"Yeah, they been goin' over everythin' and talkin' to everyone."

"They talk to you?"

"They started wit' me."

I stood in front of the elevator. I did not push the up button. I waited for Beef Patty to come to the point. This might take some time, for he was not a straight-line talker.

"Yeah, they started wit' me first."

I pressed the up button.

"Then they went down the line with all the profs."

I watched the elevator lights blink down from the tenth floor.

"They doin' the students now."

The elevator door opened.

"They talked to J.P. Carlisle and Nikki Nateal."

I did not get on the elevator. This might be important. Last year, I'd been convinced that the One-Percenters were behind some trouble. I'd been wrong.

"Jus' 'tween you and me, Prof, that J.P. he's, you know...."

"I know."

"And Nikki, she also, you know...."

"I know."

"They talked to Jimmy Fisheyes, too." Another of my wrong gueses. The Seoul Brothers were no one to fuck with, but they hadn't been the killer.

"They did?"

"Yeah, they talk to all of them."

"There was talkin' but was there listenin'?"

"That's wha' I was thinkin', Prof."

"Lester, did you tell Bath, that old guy, what happened to my office partner?"

"Never said nothin' to him, he one outta-place old dude, he like a fish outta water down here." Now we were getting someplace. Beef Patty had just unearthed a lie. Unearthing lies is important when you're solving crimes. That was one of my many mottos. When I die, my mottos will probably be collected.

"Thanks, Lester, I've got to go to class."

"Yeah, I got to get to work myself."

I had seen Beef Patty at work, which consisted mostly of him putting his feet up on his desk, reading the *Daily News* and eating Reese's Pieces by the handful, then finishing off his shift by having sex with a willing, wiggling coed on his shiny desktop. He had an odd notion of security. But then this was the Urban U., where everything's a little strange.

I left the security guard and rode the elevator.

Waiting outside my office door was Detective Pat Reagan. I was as glad to see him as a prostate exam.

"Hey, Prof, got a minute?"

I was due at a meeting in an hour.

"Five minutes, then I'm due in class," I said, slipping into lying mode.

"That'll be enough."

"Come inside."

"Someone's in there."

"Who?"

"That old guy, Bath."

I waited to hear what my former student had to ask of me. We would talk in the filthy hallway, which featured roaches of many kinds.

Chapter Five

. . . .

"This has been a long day, Prof," said Detective Reagan, leaning back against a wall.

"I bet it has."

"I been talkin' to these professors."

"They listen to you?"

"Naw, you know what professors are like, they only hear what they want to."

"Yes, I know what they are like."

"Say, Prof, let me ask you somethin'."

I stared at the detective. The thought crossed my mind that cops never ask casual questions. I switched even more into defense.

"Ask away."

"This Randle, he a good professor?"

"We're the end of the line in Brooklyn."

"How's that?"

"This is where they put profs out to pasture."

"I don't see where you're goin'."

"He was in a situation worse than dyin'."

"What could be worse than dyin'?"

"You've got a lot comin' your way."

"How's that?"

"He was no longer 35."

"Over the hill, huh?"

"'Over the hill' is right"

"So this Randle was washed up?"

"Beached."

"Why'd he get sent down here from the main campus?"

"Time passed him by. He wasn't what they wanted on the main campus."

"What'd they want?"

"Whatever it was, Randle didn't have it."

"Would any of them have anything to gain if he was out of the way?"

I said nothing. These questions were coming hot and heavy, making it difficult for me to lie. Lying isn't as easy as it seems. To lie, you need to come out with something that sounds like the truth. I wasn't right now that quick in the mind, so shutting my yap seemed the thing to do.

"Anybody comes to mind, you tell me. I've learned the hard way you never can tell what pops into someone's head as a brilliant idea. Between you and me, I hope to hell the ME turns up nothin'."

We walked back down the hall and waited for the elevator.

"Only one thing about all this that still bothers me," said Reagan.

"What's that?"

"Who called in that Randle was in trouble?"

"Who did?"

"Beats me, it's another loose end."

"And you don't like loose ends?"

"No, they drive me nuts, so I jus' keep rootin' around till I get everythin' in line."

"That it?"

"No. Say Prof, you know this Randle wasn't the first one to die down here."

"That's true."

"I checked the EMT records, there were two others...."

"T. Pennington Parker and Gerald Gaspar."

"Yeah, what was the story with them?"

"They were like Randle."

"Over the hill?"

"Yeah."

"They die in here, too?"

"Gaspar died in the men's room, Parker in the hallway."

"Of what?"

"Same as Randle. Heart attack."

"OK, Prof, got to go," said Reagan, offering his hand.

I shook the detective's hand.

"You take care of yourself, Prof."

"Thank you, Pat, I will."

Reagan left the hallway.

I remembered Reagan as a student. "The claustrophobe" had been my first nickname for him.

On the first day of class that semester, waiting at the classroom door was a short, stocky student with dark, curly hair and a square jaw.

"Need to talk to you, Prof," said the student.

"About the class?" I'd said, trying to look kindly, an attitude I always tried to project on Day One. Some profs come on from the onset as a hard-ass; bad idea, gets you nowhere.

"No, about the door."

"The door?"

"Yeah, I wanna be near it."

"And your name is?" I said, taking out my roster.

"Reagan."

"So, Mr. Reagan, why do you need to be near the door?"

"Between you and me, Prof, I dunno if this is for me."

"And near to the door, the reason?"

"If things don't go right, I wanna be able to cut out."

"Got you."

"That OK with you?"

"No problem. How about questions, you want to be not asked one?"

"Yeah, that would be good."

"Let's go in."

I walked into a class of 30 students. And I watched as Reagan moved a desk next to the door.

That was my first memory of Detective Reagan, one of my diamonds in the rough.

I decided to go home. This was no place for me. Whoever was in my office could do what he wanted. I kept little there. Most of my stuff was in the temporary lab I was housed in, temporary because I'd blown the regular lab to hell and gone in order to kill Dom.

Chapter Six

- -

Moving down the dirty hallway, taking care not to step on anyone or anything, I had a thought flash into my nimble mind. I would start at the beginning of this investigation by going to the final phase of my last attempt at being Sherlock Holmes. Then, I'd been all over the place, seeing killers at every corner, with the result that I'd nearly been poisoned and a shot had missed me by a whisker. After all was said and done, I'd asked the eyes and ears of the Urban U. what he'd noticed and he'd told me, giving me such chapter and verse that it didn't take long to scrap my other suspicions and focus on who really was the creep after me. I would go and see Beef Patty.

This was not an easy task, for one had to approach the security guard's office in the basement of the parking garage with care. If not, then a front-row seat at sex Brooklyn-style would be obtained.

In the basement, I looked to see if anyone was getting out of a car. No one. I looked behind me. No one. I listened with both ears. Nothing. I was getting to be a world-class shamus.

Having secured the area, I went toward Beef Patty's office in the corner. The door was shut, but it wasn't keeping the sounds from seeping out. Some coed was working her mouth while Beef Patty worked her over. I walked over and got into my car. Waited. Time passed. I figured they would get tired eventually.

Finally, a short Snookie look-alike emerged, fixing her hair while dangling a long cigarette from big lips. She left the parking garage.

This was my chance. Visit the big man before the next one showed up. I needed to check on what Beef Patty's diet was for him to have such stamina. Probably a lot of oysters.

I knocked.

"Yeah," rumbled a deep voice.

"It's Professor Bucceroni, can I talk to you?"

"Be right there, Prof."

Which meant he was cleaning off his desk or putting his pants back on.

The door opened. Seeing Beef Patty was always a shock because of his size. We shook hands. I have big mitts, but my hand disappeared in Patty's paw. He didn't give me any hard-ass grip, which was good. I'm strong, but this is a giant we're talkin' about.

"What I do for you, Prof?"

"You got a minute?"

"Sure, I got time, I supposed to call Malvina but that can wait. She always callin'."

Malvina Norwood nee Moore, Beef Patty's wife, was a nurse. If Malvina caught him in the act, the big man was in for a beating. Malvina was a force to be reckoned with. Candy had once speculated about what sex must be like for the two of them. I had once seen two rhinos mating; I offered that as a vision. Candy thought it was probably pretty close.

"Lester, remember when I asked you about that Latin Monarchs guy and you said you'd seen something?"

"Yeah."

"I need to ask you something else."

"OK," said Beef Patty, a wary look coming into his eye. I'd known the guard for years, but we were moving into strange territory and he was quickly on the defensive. Blacks and whites can't really talk because we don't trust one another. Too bad, but it's true. Plus, he'd done time and the questions I'd asked him last time were about a cop and he had spilled the beans on the whole drug operation at the college. This time, I'd have to be clever. Form my questions well, make Sam Spade proud of me.

"You see anything else?" Wow! What interrogation. Brilliant. No wonder it'd only taken being slapped in the face with the truth to see what was what last time.

"Like what?"

"Nikki?"

"No."

"Perez?"

"No."

I was rolling. Strategy was mine, he was like putty in my hands.

"Annie Porter?" I blurted out. Here, I was on thin ice because I was about up to where I was going.

"That lil' red-haired prof you used to go wit'?"

"Yeah, her."

"No."

I could see I was losing him.

Here I went, plunging.

"My lab assistant?"

"Dr. Candy?"

"Yes."

"Yeah, I seen them together a couple of times. They was upstairs outside your office. Nothin' wrong with that, is there, Prof?

"No," I said, but I could hear how my words had fallen flat. I continued, wanting to close this down. I needed time to digest all he'd told me. Brief as it had been, he'd shaken me up.

"Big Mac?"

"Your pal, the one who poppin' all them girls?" he said, causing me to resist blurting out that it takes one to know one. But I kept my yap shut.

"Yeah, him."

"No."

He waited for more questions. I paused. I had what I'd come for.

"Thanks, Lester."

"Say Prof, there ain't going to be more trouble, is there? I got priors, Prof, so trouble isn't good for me."

"No, Lester, no more trouble. I was just checkin' on loose ends."

"Any more crack bein' made?"

My heart went up into my teeth. Beef Patty wasn't all cock and balls, he had eyes and ears after all. That was the whole reason for last year's goings on—my lab had become crack central.

"No, that's stopped."

"That good, that crack can mess you up. I keep away from drugs. Malvina say she sees too much of it down at the hospital, says every night someone come in all fucked up."

"Malvina's a smart woman."

"Yeah, she is. You got anymore questions, I got to do my rounds."

"No thanks, Lester."

"Anytime, Prof."

The big man left the garage, leaving me behind.

A shitload of fear raced through my mind. Dom's last words echoed in my ears: "You don't think it was jus' me, do you? It was me and the knockout, she was in on it."

After I'd sent him to have an audience with the devil, I'd run into Candy. Then, I'd tried to wipe out of my mind what he'd told me. Easier said than done. Every day the words haunted me; it was like Dom was laughing at me from the grave. And now this. I'd put off asking Beef Patty because I was afraid of what he'd say. I got into my car. Sat there. Trying not to believe Candy would turn on me. But Dom still had a hold on me. Of all the people in the world I had trusted, he'd been at the very top of the list. We'd always had one another's backs. From our days in Bensonhurst until recently, we were still Mr. Inside and Mr. Outside, but Dom had forgotten all of that, flushed it down the crapper, and come after me like I was nothing.

I backed the car around. Got facing forward, used my remote. I was soon out on the street, driving fast and saying "eat it" to stop signs. I headed home.

I had some tailing to do.

Chapter Seven

So here I was, dressed in my Italian ninja outfit. All in black with a crease in my pants. No one could spot my 250 pounds for I was being clever. This is the outfit I wear when I subway-ride, looking for the creep who killed my family. Take the New Lots train, stand on the platform, see if I can get someone to take a shot at me. This is of course more nutzo activity. There's not a chance in a million that I'd run across the bastard, but if I did there'd be no hesitation. I'd break his neck like he was a chicken, then toss him into an incoming while he was still alive. I'd probably get life in the slammer for doing it, but I'd pay the price. When my wife and boy were killed, I promised them I'd find out who did it. I like to keep my promises, even when they're to the dead.

But this was different. I was in the old Plymouth with its defective heater. The night was damp, the type of weather which makes you aware of your prostate. I was across from Candy's, watching the lights in her place. I was ready for a long wait, for she was a night owl like me. Even now while I sat in the dead-quiet old car, Dom's words worked their way into my mind: "It was me and the knockout." And the problem was, that made sense. Dom had also told me he'd figured out how to use my own lectures and drugs and poisons from my own lab against me. But Dom was a cop with shaky hands. What was needed was someone who knew the chemistry, who knew how to put a deadly cocktail together and, unfortunately, Candy fit the bill. She was an excellent scientist with a good pair of hands and she knew chapter and verse about chemical weaponry. She should have been taught by a master teacher, namely clear-as-a-bell me. Furthermore, I said to myself, going deeper and deeper into my fear, she would be able to run a crack lab. That'd be duck soup for her. But why would she do it? Why would she work with Dom, push drugs at the college and on to the street, then take a shot at me to cover up what was going down? I was a big threat to the operation. Dom had seen that. The question was did he have a partner. "It was me and the knockout," he'd said, over and over, pounding it into my mind like a bad song whose lyrics can't be forgotten. Maybe all of this was just me; then again, maybe not. And if maybe not was the case, then I knew I'd better get up to speed or I'd be dead as a door nail like old Randle.

I kept my eyes on Candy's place, which was still lit up. Midnight. I hunched my shoulders against the cold. I wanted to light a cigar but that might give away who I was. Cigar smoke carries a long way. I didn't know what I'd say to her if she caught me in the act of spying. We were supposed to be close, but Dom had taught me that in this sorry-ass world there was no one to trust. It crossed my mind that if I found out Candy was Dom's partner in crime then something would have to be done about her. I pushed that thought to the back of my mind. I could do a lot of things to save myself—did that include killing Candy? Right now I had no answer for that. But with evidence in my hands that would be a different story. She would then be just another part of the downside of Brooklyn, and she would have to go. Thinking this, my mind drifted to thoughts of my old man. I remembered as a kid listening in on the phone when he was discussing his "work." Even though he spoke in mobster code, I got the point. It made no difference who the person was, facts were what counted. That was the case here. If Candy was in on it, then she would have to go and I'd be the one who'd have to do the job.

Candy's garage door opened. There was a pause while she no doubt got into her car, then out she came, moving fast. The old Plymouth turned over, and we were off.

I'm good at tailing. Dom taught me. It's actually a matter of anticipation, for you have to guess where the tail is going. Being up on the bumper is a sure way to be spotted.

We went down to 86th street, left Bay Ridge, headed into Bensonhurst. This didn't look good. Why would she be out at this hour? There were some reasons. A boyfriend? A drug deal? Cars were used to push drugs in Brooklyn. Houses were out, too easy to be busted by the cops. The way it went down was to do the deal by cell, then drive along and pass money first and then the dope got delivered. Maybe that's what she was up to.

We hit Bay Parkway and turned right, going deeper into guidoland, only to be fair there are a lot of Asians living here, too. They probably came because of the safe neighborhood. Or maybe they like pasta fagioli. Whatever the reason, the place had changed since I was a kid and it was all-Italian. Of course, you could still get branzini if you wanted.

Something black moved at the corner of my sight and I swerved, narrowly missing somebody out and about at midnight. The somebody gave me the bird, I looked at him in my rearview mirror. A mistake. I had forgotten that I was tailing. When I looked back, I was too close to Candy. I could see her looking in her mirror. To cover what I was doing, I left Bay Parkway and turned right, went down a block and turned left, picked up speed. I'd taken a chance, luck rode with me, and when I was back to the main drag, Candy was ahead of me, going east.

At Cropsey, she made a sharp right. This wasn't good. She was heading for Coney Island, which was pretty much a hellhole. At Neptune, we turned left and were in the middle of crumbuttcentral. This was the type of place to ditch a car. Just park and leave. This wasn't where cars got stripped; here they just disappeared, ending up god knows where.

Deeper and deeper, she went. Then, she did a U-turn. For a moment, I thought she was trying to shake my tail. After that the truth hit me. She was after pizza. The best in Brooklyn. Only served whole pies. No slices. Great cheese, the crust just right. An old-fashioned place which closed down for the day when they ran out of dough.

I cruised past Candy, did my own U-turn, watched as she used her cell. It wasn't long till a guy in a white apron came out and took her money and gave her a pizza. She drove away.

I didn't follow her. I didn't need to. This was off the wall what I was doing. Dom was dead; he could no longer hurt me. In life, he'd had his many chances, first with deadly drugs, then with his silenced pistol. All had failed. I'd gotten the line on him, and boom! He was history, splattered over a dirty street. Finding his pieces would've made for hard work.

Candy was OK. That I had to believe. I'd helped her when she was a drug-crazy, turned her life around, made her my lab assistant. If she wasn't OK, then no one was.

I used my cell. Dialed a Coney Island number. Got some night owl on the line. Then, I waited. The night was getting better. A west wind was coming in, blowing the dampness out to sea. The clouds were moving along. A moon shone down on Brooklyn. Half a block ahead of me was an Infiniti. Black. Not too old. Two street citizens approached it. Opened it like the door was unlocked. Drove away. Had I witnessed a crime? Should I follow the car? Pull it over, make a citizen's arrest? I thought about doing that, then opted to let Coney Island be Coney Island. That was big of me.

Someone knocked on the passenger-side window. Asked for my money. I gave it. In return, I got a hot pizza with extra cheese and lots of anchovies, which I hoped were large and hairy.

The Plymouth took me home. I'd eat a good pizza. Get a good night's sleep. Everything was good. Candy was OK.

Fuck you, Dom.

Chapter Eight

I was back at the college. The night, for once, had been peaceful. No bad dreams. It just goes to show you that spying and afterwards gorging on a large pie are conducive to sleep.

No one had phoned me. Reagan hadn't contacted me. All I had to do now was to get a line on who was killing off old professors. I'd bet good money that the two other recently deceased old professors—Parker and Gaspar—had also been snuffed.

I headed down the hall toward my office, took out my key, lowered my glasses, got ready to go in. I felt a hand on my shoulder. It was Reagan. The hallway was empty but for the two of us. I smiled at the detective. I returned the key to my pocket.

"Prof, one thing, you know your office partner...."

"Professor Bath?" I put in.

"That's him. A fuckin' nut case, pardon my French."

"He didn't do so well durin' your interrogation?"

"He sweated like a pig, he couldn't talk...."

"You mean he stammered?" I again interrupted.

"That's right, he stammered, he's one helluva stammerer."

"So was Porky Pig, who was also a stutterer," I said, showing off my considerable wit. One-liners like that are my specialty. Of course, most of them are just funny to me. But not this time.

"That's a good one, Prof. But this Bath, he's somethin' else. I'd talked much longer with him he woulda told me where Hoffa's buried," said Reagan with a laugh.

I paused; I wasn't sure what to say.

"He lied to me about how he knew what had happened to Randle," I finally said. I didn't like what I had just come out with. I was heading into deep water.

"How so?"

"I asked him who'd told him, and he said Beef Patty."

"Who?"

"The black security guard, the one who weighs about a ton."

"Oh yeah, him."

"I asked Beef Patty, and he said he'd never talked to Bath about what happened."

"Another fuckin' loose end. Anything else?"

"With Randle dead, Bath has a slim chance to keep his job."

"He don't seem to me to have it in him to do a killin, but I been in this business long enough not to overlook anybody. Let's wait until I get the report back, then maybe we'll have to talk again."

I thought of the report, about what it might contain. Sweat formed on my forehead.

Behind us, the doors of the elevator opened. I walked Reagan over.

"See you around, Prof."

"Yes, I'll watch out for you."

I returned to my office door and again took out my key. My right foot bumped into something on the floor. I looked down and saw three open cardboard boxes.

Leaning over to inspect them more closely, I noticed all of the books in the boxes were by Hemingway. Hardcover, not paperbacks. These at one time had cost some money. They were from Randle's bookshelves, which had been all Hemingway except for *The St. Martin's Handbook* he'd used for his composition classes. The *St. Martin's* was all about grammar, which our students lacked. A lot.

One box did not contain books. I reached inside the box, which was full of paper. Someone had jammed manuscripts into the box. Some of the papers had been on the floor and were soiled. I removed one of the sheets. It was part of Randle's last work, the scholarship that was to take him back to the glory of the main campus.

All of this effort would've gotten Randle exactly nada. He'd been banished to Brooklyn. Put out to pasture, where he was to take the EXIT door.

I returned the paper to the box. Randle had taught at the Urban U. for more than 30 years, and here was his legacy—his books, his writing, essentially his life stuffed into a couple boxes waiting for the janitor to add them to the college's trash. I'd been correct in what I'd told Reagan. Randle had been in hell, plowing ahead in a one-way trip to nowhere-land with his writing, giving himself ulcers with his teaching, and being tormented by a soulless Dean as a sexual predator. He was better off dead. Maybe God was interested in Hemingway. Randle could lecture to Jesus about *The Sun Also Rises*. It was then I noticed something was missing: Randle's nameplate. The college provided nameplates for each office on the considerable off-chance a student might look for an office visit. Randle had forced his students to come to his office, where he'd informed them of their errors.

Under my nameplate were two screw holes. There was no longer a nameplate for the deceased professor. Randle had been erased from academia, his life's work dumped outside the office, his identity removed for all to see. This was how the Urban U. dealt with the unwanted. It was true that having tenure was protection against getting fired, but the Urban U. had other cards to play. Randle had been sent from the main campus to the Brooklyn branch as an act of humiliation. Randle no longer had classes to teach in his area; he had no status in the department or in the college. The purpose of the transfer was to drive Randle from the profession. But Randle had not gone gently into retirement. He'd pushed on, maintaining his standards, working on his publications, going back to the main campus to attend department meetings, and all of it had been for nothing, el zippo.

Randle had been twisting in the wind, and the college's Dean had been the head twister.

Chapter Nine

• •

I opened the door and stepped into my office. Things had changed.

Gone was the filthy blue rug I did not remember seeing in the hallway. I theorized that the rug was so dirty an immediate exit had been executed. Gone also were the outdated computer and monitor. In their place were a new, clean, white rug and a brand new CPU and large monitor.

Seated at the desk was a tall, skinny blonde man. At my desk was Mac McClure.

"Hi, I'm Karl Biden," said the blonde man, standing up, holding out his right hand.

"Glad to meet you," I said, enclosing his small hand in my large one. His palm was wet.

"I'm your new office partner."

I thought about telling him my office partners kept dying on me, but I decided that wouldn't be much of a greeting.

"Yeah, Richie, you need someone to keep you company," said Mac. The reason I was housed with English professors was that I was helping Mac out. Mac had asked me if I minded having partners. I'd said no. We'd switched. Mac had my office. How he used it, I shuddered to imagine. Mac had gone the reverse route, moving from our place to the main campus, this on account of his publications. He hadn't lasted long there, getting his ass in hot water over screwing the co-eds. Back he'd come to our pleasant surroundings. He'd have one helluva time getting back to the main campus.

"You move in yourself?" I said, looking at the bookshelves full of books other than Hemingway's.

"Yes, the room was empty. I saw the boxes in the hallway. A bit cold to see that. Like a lifetime being discarded." The young prof had got that right. It should've been a warning as to what was coming his way.

"Did you know Professor Randle?"

"Somewhat. He was somewhat rigid, but if you accepted his premises there was something to be learned from him. He knew Hemingway inside and out."

"True," I said, even though I had no idea what Randle's books were about. Truth be told, I thought a lot of what English professors did in their publications was to make mountains out of molehills. Not like me. My publications were of value. Dom had found them easy reading as he used my own writings to try and do me in.

I crossed the office to the window. The old man was on the toilet, peering into the college. I lowered the blinds.

"Your neighbor," said Mac to Biden.

"Kind of gross," said Biden.

"True," I said, repeating myself, which is what I do when I don't know what to say.

To make conversation, I asked Biden what he was working on. Which I shouldn't have because if his stuff was any good he wouldn't be here. Biden was young and incompetent; he'd be here a short time and then be axed.

"Fanny Burney."

"Fanny Burney!" exclaimed Mac. Of course, I had no idea what they were talking about. The name sounded like it belonged to some type of vaudeville floozie.

"You don't like her?"

"On the contrary. I think she's better than Jane Austen."

"So do I. That's a point of my work."

"That's something of an achievement, you know, having a point in academic writing, that is," said Mac, making a joke that he probably regretted.

"I wasn't given a chance by my department Chair," Biden said.

The room went quiet. Neither Mac nor I had anything more to say.

I lit a cigar. I didn't like talking to this young man, who was on a one-way street to the unemployment line.

I thought about my words.

"This place is what you make of it. The students are here to be taught. Always do your best. Even here," I said, trying to make the best of it. What was I to do, tell the guy the truth, that nothing he did here would ever matter? That this was an outpost in the wilds of Brooklyn, which, gentrification, or not, was not Manhattan.

"What's your area?" he asked.

"Chemical weaponry."

"Richie could kill all of us if he wanted to," put in Mac.

I wished Mac would keep that to himself. The dead Randle could be traced back to me if someone sharp did some work, and Detective Pat Reagan was someone sharp. I smiled a neutral smile. Biden didn't pursue the question. He wasn't really interested in me. Mac was a hotshot in his field, which was the only reason he hadn't been shown the door. Biden would be hoping that Mac could put in a good word with an editor.

"We better get ready for the Dean's doings," said Mac, changing the subject, which was OK with me.

"What's that?" asked Biden.

"He's makin' a memorial of sorts to Randle. Nothing fancy, though. Can't have that for a prof accused of sexual harassment, even if he is dead."

I stared at Mac, who should've known all there was to know about sexual harassment. There were two reasons McClure hadn't been fired. One was that none of his victims had come forward to charge him. It had been the female faculty who'd raised an uproar. He'd been branded as a sexual predator, and his head was to roll, but charges need a charger and there was none. At the main campus, the professors had known many of the coeds who'd gone in for office sex with McClure. They had regarded it as part of their college experience. The other reason he'd avoided being axed was his publication record. "Publish or Perish" was more than a motto, for those who published and received acclaim could be rotten teachers, insult the department Chair on a daily basis, and be less than a good colleague, but all would be forgiven as long as good reviews of their critical work appeared. Mac had written several books about the nineteenth-century English novel and was now busy doing somethin' with Dickens. His exile to the downtown campus of the Urban U. was to be short-lived, the whispers being that his present crop of compliant co-eds would be allowed to graduate and move out of his grasp. I doubted this. At our place, Mac hadn't skipped a sexual beat. He was at the college for late hours in his office, which had a couch, and no one seemed to care since he was on a professor's floor and no administrator ventured forth to check on him.

I had previously tried to figure out McClure's particular addiction. Waiting every evening for him in Ho-ho-kus, where he'd moved, from Princeton no less, was a rich wife some fifteen years older than the big, blonde professor. But that didn't give me anything as a handle for his banging coeds. Mac's inability to keep it in his pants had nearly gotten him killed by the One-Percenters. Only my last-second intervention had saved his over-sexed ass.

"Ready for this weekend?" asked Mac, smiling, showing white teeth, looking like an aging Sigma Chi.

"I'm surprised you have the courage to ask," I said, glad we were now on a different topic.

"One defeat, one, and you're this cocky. Revenge, revenge I say, will be sweet, my fine feathered friend," said Mac.

We were 10K runners, good for our size, who competed on weekend runs.

"Last time was embarrassing," I said. "I thought I'd have to carry you home."

"We were in the same second, the exact same second, can't get closer than that. Besides, that was one of your namby-pamby flat courses; this weekend is the real deal: hills, a manly run."

"Namby-pamby? What kinda talk is that?"

"Macho. You'll be there by eight?"

"I will," I said, knowing this would mean an early rise. "Lots of water stops?"

"Starting to worry already, aren't you? I can feel a win coming on," said Mac.

"You fellows take this seriously," said Biden, who was tall and lean.

"We do," said Mac.

"I also run, I just started," said Biden.

"Another victim!" said Mac.

"Should we be going?" said Biden.

"You're right," I said, putting my cigar in an ashtray. Biden had said nothing about my smoking. He was in enough trouble already; picking fights with smokers would get him nowhere. Smoking is a bad habit, no one should do it, which is why I enjoy it.

"Who's in charge of this school?" said Biden as we left the office.

"The Dean handles the nuts and bolts," said Mac. "Then the Chairs drop in to keep us doin' whatever the department wants."

"So it's best to stay on the Dean's good side," said Biden, pushing the elevator's up button.

"He has no good side," said Mac.

"I second that insult," I put in.

The elevator door opened. The three of us filed onto the elevator, McClure leading the way, me bringing up the rear.

Chapter Ten

. . . .

Entering the elevator, I saw that it was occupied by one person. That person, the Dean of the college, looked first at Professor Ross McClure. He said nothing. He swung his glance to take in yours truly. He also said nothing to me. Finally, the Dean fixed his gaze on young Biden.

"Hello, Dr. Biden," said the short-ass Dean.

"Hello," said Biden, who flushed red.

"I trust that you are getting acclimated to the college."

"Yes, I am."

"You let me know if you need any help, or if matters aren't made clear," said the Dean, shifting his eyes briefly up at Mac and me.

"That Claude Raines, he could act," McClure said to me.

The elevator door closed.

Inside, silence reigned.

The elevator stopped at the eighth floor.

"Women's lingerie, haberdashery, and handguns," said McClure in a high voice not unlike the Dean's.

The beginnings of a laugh-snort came from Biden. I nudged him. The snort died away.

Two Indian girls got on. One of them was stunning, the other not so.

The stunning one smiled at big Mac.

"Hello, Noorhihira," said McClure.

"Hello, Professor," came a soft reply.

I was standing behind the Dean and to his right. I could see his shoulders stiffen at the exchange between the small dark girl and the big blonde professor.

The elevator stopped at the tenth floor.

"Tenth floor. Microwaves, Muslins, and mayhem," said McClure.

We exited the elevator.

Chapter Eleven

· ·

Entering the cafeteria, I thought of what was ahead; I would get to see a Dean in open ground. This would be a treat. He was probably scared shitless. The tenth was a long way from his office. Here was where the students were. It was like being taken by limousine to the Bronx Zoo, forced to get out, sent to the monkey cage, and being put inside to be shat upon.

"Over here," said McClure, who had found seats close to the head table.

"No, no, this is only for Randle's replacement," said the Dean.

"So there's room," said McClure, ignoring the Dean, who gave Mac a look I'd characterize as "withering." I could tell how much the Dean hated the big English professor. Mac always behaved like this around the Dean, busting his chops, not giving a rat's ass that this was his supposed boss. Maybe Mac figured that if push came to shove he could go back to Ho-ho-kus, live off the wife's money, tell all that was needed to know about Dickens.

I settled in for what was coming.

"I have convened this meeting in order to inform you of the death of one of our colleagues," began the Dean. He stood behind a gray metal desk on which he had placed a small wooden lectern. He stood on a small platform to give the appearance of height to his barely five-foot frame. It would probably not be nice if I kicked this out from underneath him. Not that I was thinking of doing that, or anything,

Seated to his right was young, green Biden, who was leaning forward, his eyes fixed, paying attention to the Dean. I was not. I was assessing the diversity of the audience.

The students sat around tables placed to face the Dean. The late Dr. Randle had started the term with three classes of 30 students each. There were now 45 students in the cafeteria seated at five large tables. I calculated the attrition rate in my former office partner's classes. I was sure it was close to a record. My classes always stayed full, this was on account of my winning ways and also because I passed everyone. Show up; breathe; pass—that was my standard.

To my far right sat J.P. Carlisle and Nicki Nateal at a table occupied solely by black students. Some of these were the One-Percenters, who were kept on the straight and narrow by J.P., who was large and vicious. I'd recently seen him in action; I was glad we were on the same side. Of course, he had standards for his followers, like no drugs and no sex with white devils like Mac.

On the far left sat a table of Asians headed by a slim, young man wearing black pegged slacks, black pointed shoes, a bright white shirt, and a narrow black tie. The young man had his jet-black hair slicked back, and he wore sunglasses. The young man was the nephew of Mr. Pang, the late proprietor of the liquor store across from the college. On the roster of Dr. Rudolf Randle, the young man was listed as James Kim, but he was better known around the Urban U. as Jimmy Fisheyes. I always called him James, figuring that "Fishy" might be an insulting nickname.

In the middle of the room were one table of Russians, one of Italians, one of Dominicans, and one of Jews. None of the groups interacted with another. They all went about their own business, which was to stick to their own tribe.

"Of course, we are all deeply troubled by the passing of Dr. Randle. We all feel pain, yet we must…." said the Dean, his voice rising and lowering as he continued. He had a high, unpleasant voice which had already started to annoy me. I could only guess what the students thought about him.

I listened to this latest example of Deanspeak.

First, there was tone: condescending.

Then, there was diction: unclear.

Finally, there was clarity: little.

The speech wore on. It concluded with a moment of silence.

"Now, we must, sadly, bear on. We must get, as it were, 'back to business.' Tonight, we will be arranging for Professor Randle's classes to continue. I will be assigning, well, in fact, not actually assigning…I amend my comments. Allow me to offer to you the choice of which professor you'd prefer to work with for the remainder of the term. You may now move to the desk of one of the two professors seated close to the dais," said the Dean, mopping his wet forehead with a very white handkerchief.

An exodus, ragged in operation, began. Forty students made their way to the desk of Mac. Five, those bringing up the rear, went toward Biden.

"Oh my, this seems unbalanced," said the Dean.

I put a cigar in my mouth. Smoking was not allowed in the cafeteria. Many of the Russians removed cigarettes. They lit up.

"Shall we return to our tables, please. I must ask you to return to your table of origin, for, I believe, another procedure needs to be…and, oh my, there can be no smoking…."

It took the Dean some time to dampen down the smoking. The Russians were not ones to follow rules. They went their own way. I didn't know if they had a gang or not. If they did, they'd give J.P. some trouble. The One-Percenters had, in my presence, referred to them as "Ivans," which I took to be insulting.

I gnawed on my cigar. This was a real treat, I wished I could smoke to celebrate. It was not often that one had the opportunity to see an administrator of the Urban U. in full frontal operation. Most Deans were concealed behind closed doors; a venture such as this was a rare occurrence, like the spotting of a spotted owl.

"Let's have a show of hands as to which professor you'd like to work with," said the Dean, who now faced students who were sitting on the tables, standing beside the tables, some putting out cigarettes on the floor, most of them talking, few listening. He was doing a swell job.

The students had heard the Dean talk before. They knew what to expect.

Forty-two students raised their hands for Mac.

"Oh," said the Dean.

Mac stood up. He'd had enough. His deep, clear voice was a clear contrast to the Dean's.

"A-L, you have Biden; M-Z, you have me. Would the M-Zs please come to my table."

Mac sat down.

The students went to their respective professors.

The Dean left the cafeteria to return to the quiet confines of his office, where only a secretary could hear him. He didn't look back. As he reached the elevator, I waved.

"Bye-bye."

Chapter Twelve

I listened to Mac and his students. Who seemed to be listening to him. This was quite a feat, getting listened to, that is. In my class I never lectured, just handed out student sheets and sat at my desk.

"What questions do you have?" said Mac.

"This last book that Professor Randle was havin' us read, it's hard," said Nikki Nateal.

Nikki and Mac had a sexual history, this much I knew, but I also knew he was now laying off (no pun intended) black girls. This was a wise move. Not too long ago, the One-Percenters had Mac in their sights, which was a bad place to be. There were a whole shitload of people who'd learned the hard way about J.P. When he talked, it was wise to listen up.

At Nikki Nateal's table now were a few students who were not black; at another table, some Italians had mingled with a couple of Asians, a few Dominicans, several Irish, and some Jews. But all of the Russians had remained together, in one ethnic clump, at a separate table. Staying together was their thing; it's probably why their ancestors did in Hitler.

I looked at the Russian table, where Natasha Natooska sat, looking sullen.

Mac talked to Nikki Nateal. "Jane Austen wasn't easy for me to read when I was your age, which was sometime during the Age of Magellan."

Laughter at the professor's joke came from two of the three tables.

"What's her point?" asked Nikki Nateal.

"Well, at least it's not a very long book," said Mac.

"She's just a rich biTCh," said one of the Jewish students.

"But does she change, improve during the course of the text?" said Mac.

"Yeah, tha's what I like about her," said Nikki Nateal. "She tryin' to help that silly fren' of hers. I'm not all the way done with the book. Does she change all around?"

"Don't let me spoil your reading," said Mac, smiling at Nikki. The black girl hesitated, then returned the smile.

"How you figure grade?" said a voice from the Russian sector.

"How I figure grade?" said Mac to Natasha Natooska.

"Yeah, how?"

"Carefully."

"No, I mean what you do with grades given by Randle."

"You mean Professor Randle?"

"Yeah, him."

"This is what I can do. We'll give a final exam. If your grade on that exam is higher than your course average was with Professor Randle, then we'll use the final exam as the final grade," said Mac, with a wide smile on his handsome, tanned face.

"That's fair," said Nikki Nateal.

"I am talking to professor," said Natasha Natooska, giving Nikki Nateal a look that would score really high on the go-to-hell meter. Ms. Natooska should beware, I thought, for Nikki had a well-earned reputation as a punch-first, knock-down street fighter. I should know; I'd seen her in action. Thanks to her fast and ferocious feet I'd not been beaten up by two street slime.

"Is that fair to you?" said Mac, smiling.

"It OK," said Natasha Natooska, not smiling.

I looked at the former student of my late office partner. She was dressed in a costume apparently modeled after a low-end streetwalker, with various body parts exposed to the world and with every item of clothing on her one size too small. Ms. Natooska also had the aroma of a bargain-basement perfume which could've dropped a mosquito at 100 meters. It was this student the Dean had listened to and on whose account he'd been preparing a sharpened stick for the now dead and buried Professor Randle, the self-same Randle he'd recently been memorializing. What a fucked-up world is academia. Here were two people—one prof, one fuck-up—and the prof was trying to do his job and what he got instead of praise was a kick in the nuts. I wondered if something should be done about Ms. Natooska.

"We will meet in this room for a regular class during club hours for the next two weeks," Mac said. "I've added an extra office hour. Also, you can e-mail me. Please give me your e-mail addresses on this sheet of paper."

The students lined up to list their e-mail addresses. The line was precise, orderly. Mac was a wonder, for here he'd gotten the underclass to behave as human beings. Mac was a Jekyll and Hyde—one minute a world-class professor, both as a scholar and a teacher, the next horny and horrible, using the coeds as his personal sex garden. At least he left his fellow female colleagues alone, which is more than can be said for me, who'd gone sniffing after Annie Porter when I should've been taking care of my family. If I'd been at home that night, I could have driven them where they needed to go so my wife wouldn't have used the subway, where death was waiting for her. Brooklyn is like that. Death is never far away.

"Thanks, Professor, for takin' over this class," said Nikki Nateal, the last student to sign.

"Glad to have you in class again," said Mac.

"See you," said the black girl.

"See you," said her professor.

The meeting was over. Several students came up and asked Mac questions. I decided to leave. I passed the tables where Biden was talking to his assigned half of his "colleague's" classes. At the ends of the front two tables sat J.P. Carlisle and Jimmy Fisheyes.

"Reading Blake is really re-reading with mirrors," Biden was saying.

Biden was sweating quite a bit while he was speaking. I listened to him talking; it didn't take long for him to lose me. What the students were thinking as they listened to this confusion was easy to guess.

I looked at J.P. and Fisheyes looking at Biden, their faces expressionless.

I got on the elevator and went "home." To my executive office where profs checked in and didn't check out. All of what I'd seen last night and done today hadn't gotten me any closer to the major question: Who killed Randle?

Chapter Thirteen

· ·

In my office, I sat at Randle's—now Biden's—desk. There had been a picture of Hemingway fishing in Key West over Randle's desk. I did not remember seeing it in the garbage in the hallway. I looked inside the large garbage can in the office. The Hemingway picture was on the bottom, next to the remains of one of Fat Harry's sandwiches.

"How you' doin', Papa?" I said to the picture. It was of Hemingway young and tanned next to a hanging upside-down huge Marlin; it was Hemingway before life had beaten him down, before the hunter had hunted himself. I had learned about Hemingway by listening to Randle. He'd explained the picture to me. The guy had made sense, which was bad. To be a successful English scholar, making sense wasn't necessarily necessary.

No one had come forward to claim the remains of Randle. That was why they'd been deposited in the hallway in a stained, unlined, plastic garbage can. What a way to go. The killer may have been kindhearted in that he/she did in the undone.

My mind drifted to thoughts of Pat Reagan and the likely progress he was making on the Randle case. Reagan was a keep-at-it kind of guy, the type who'd root and root until the answer was found. Sooner or later, that would lead him to me. At that point, I would need some answers or my hindquarters would be on the hot seat.

I opened the blinds near my desk just a tad. Across the way, the old man was not on the toilet. He was in his bedroom. He was on the phone. I could see the old man talking on the phone. The old man masturbated while he talked on the phone. It was good to have such an office. It never let me forget what Brooklyn was like.

I decided to find out who had called the college about the death of Randle.

A heart attack was the simple explanation. The detectives who'd investigated the deaths of Parker and Gaspar had been satisfied with simple explanations. But Reagan was different. Reagan believed in doing his job. All of this ran through my mind. I would've liked to have dismissed all of this high-level thinking as me being Nervous Ned, but tasting the coffee had told me a chemical killer was at work. Randle had been slipped a killing drug—in my office, no less. I was the guy Reagan would come to suspect. I ran my hand through my hair. I wished Candy were here, but she was away, visiting a friend whose father had died. For now, I was on my own in terms of high-level detective work. It occurred to me that the last time I'd played detective I'd been in the dark until it was almost too late. This time would be different. Who could've killed Randle? Bath? That was a thought. The old fellow had been uptight about being questioned. He'd also had access to Randle's coffee, but did he know about drugs?

I decided to see what Bath had on his computer. I went to Bath's desk and logged in. Which was easy. Bath could never recall his password, so he kept it on a card in his desk drawer. I looked at Bath's files.

What I found wasn't soothing.

Chapter Fourteen

· ·

Old man Bath had made a file for nearly every faculty member at the Urban U. He was a real snake in the grass. Looking at him, "kindly old man" came to mind, but his work showed him as something else. I checked out my file.

He had chapter and verse on the death of my wife and boy, and he also was up to snuff with info about Candy and me. There was also some speculation on his part, tending toward the sexual, and being way off the mark. There was nothing about Dom and about who'd blown the chem lab to bits. Nothing about the gangs. All that Bath was interested in was gathering dirt on the faculty.

I started to engage my peerless detective mind, the one which had nearly been dead wrong last time out.

A. Bath was one of the first to be sent here.

B. The others had died.

C. Which meant the old bastard got to hang onto his job.

D. Someone had put a deadly drug in Randle's coffee.

E. Bath, an English prof, had no known expertise about chemical weaponry.

F. I did not find any references to my publications on chemical weaponry in the file he'd created about me.

G. My office was clean. I kept all my publications info in the temporary lab.

I switched off the computer. In my mind, I now had a man with a motive—which was to save his sorry old ass from being fired. All I needed was to account for his coming in possession of the drug and knowing how to use it. Once I had some concrete answers, then I'd have a chitchat with Pat Reagan. For now, I'd watch myself, knowing—kinda—that I was sharing an office with a killer. This was not a pleasant feeling, for a chemical killer has a lot of targets. He could fix my coffee, dope up a cigar, put thallium in the Bengay I used for my running. The question was how would he know? The only person who had my publications on file was the Dean, and getting access to his files was like asking to spend an evening alone in Fort Knox.

Sitting in my office, I more than ever missed Candy. All of this I could've bounced off her. But she wasn't around. I'd followed her and given her a clean slate in my book, but she'd then left. I was in this again by my lonesome. What I had to do was tread water and not drown until she returned.

These thoughts rolled around my mind. The only good thing to come of the spying was that Dom's words were gone. "Me and the knockout" didn't hit me time and again. I was free of Dom; I had Candy back in my corner. All I needed to do was nail Bath as the killer and turn him over to Reagan. A new thought wiggled itself to the front of my mind. What if there wasn't enough evidence? What if Reagan said I was chasing ghosts? What then? Could I protect myself by killing someone again? There was a great piece of graffiti in the student john which summed up my feelings: TO FEEL SAFE, KILL EVERYONE. It was right there in stall number four, a place I had to visit since the faculty can was out of operation on our floor, a condition which threatened to become permanent. Those were words of wisdom. A student had hit the nail on the head. In my case, it wouldn't be EVERYONE, it would just be one old professor.

Chapter Fifteen

. . . .

The phone rang in my house. Unusual. No one except the unwanted called on my landline. Everyone who was anyone called me on my cell. I checked the number. Shit. I knew who this was. A voice from the past. And about the last person I wanted to talk to.

"Hello."

"Yes, great to hear from you."

"Me, too."

"We all miss him."

"Today?"

"OK."

"In an hour."

"Will depend on the traffic."

I went to change clothes. Wanted to look nice. Wanted to show respect. I checked the full-length mirror. Cashmere jacket. Charcoal-gray slacks. Nice crease. White shirt. A tie to draw it all together. Shiny black shoes. I had to resist the urge to wink at myself.

This would not be a pleasant visit. I was off to Bensonhurst to see the past.

Walking downstairs, I passed the rooms of my wife and boy. I didn't usually go in those rooms. Now, I did. Nothing had changed in the bedroom Carmela and I had shared. Her stuff was out, like it was waiting for her to come home. Her closet was full of her clothes. I ran my hand down one of her dresses. I felt guilt come over me; then, I felt it stop. This had to end. Mourning forever was a sign of being crazy. I'd given her all that I had in terms of asking forgiveness. The time had come to cut myself a break.

This stuff had to go. I'd get Candy to help me. The past couldn't be changed, but it could be boxed up and put away so the living could get on with life.

I looked at myself in the mirror. I'd been crying. I'd never done that before about my family. I'd felt like such a dirty bastard for leaving them alone while I was screwing Annie Porter that crying hadn't seemed right. Now, it did. I was saying good-bye to the dead. Like it or not, I was going to live.

In my garage were the Ninjamobile and my Camry. I took the Camry, backed carefully down my narrow driveway, headed toward 86th Street.

Today's journey was like my night adventure tailing Candy, heading for my old home turf. Except this time, I went past Bay Parkway, under the elevated, and turned right. I could do this route in my sleep. Memories flooded me. Bensonhurst was different, but it still had enough of its old self to make me remember.

The house I stopped at wasn't really well maintained. That was a change. This place used to be neat as a pin, outside and in. Now the yard needed some attention, and the roof had some turned-up shingles.

Walking to the door was like walking to the past. I rang the bell. Nothing. I waited. Rang again.

"Come on in, Richie," said a too-familiar voice.

I went in. Immediately, the house was different. This place always used to smell good, something would be cooking, and the residents were smokers. Now it smelled like perfume, and piss.

"Come here to me," said Immaculata Rose Mancini from her wheelchair in a corner of the living room. A table with a tea pot and a few plates of snacks had been set up next to her.

Bending over to kiss her cheek, I nearly gagged when the perfume/piss combo hit me. Not only do I have a Roman nose, it's good as a sniffer. All of my senses are that like. I've got sharp eyes, clear ears, and a nose which can detect an odor a mile away. Dom used to tease me about it. "Around you, I got to shower twice. Or you're giving me the fisheye for stinkin'." Dom had been like that, always something funny to say. He was probably a big hit in hell.

Immaculata Mancini was now fat. Really fat, to the point of being grotesque. It hadn't always been that way. There was a time when she was a hotty. I should know, for she was my first one. In the back of a car. Me knowing nothing, her knowing everything and anything. I got the job done, but I was mostly just going along for the ride while she was moving like crazy, making the old Chevy rock. Now, she wouldn't move anymore from her wheelchair. She was no longer a hotty. What she was now was a cripple.

She was wearing a white turtleneck had a big scarf wrapped around her neck and shoulders. When I leaned over, she put her hand on my shoulder, seemed to grab me, but I kind of moved back because of the smell, so she let go.

This was where she lived and where she would probably die. Her mother was dead, I guess she had a visiting nurse come in to help her with her necessities. All day and most of the night she was in this room; she spent her life watching the soaps and reading *People* magazine.

It hadn't always been like that. Time was when "Immy" was the toast of the town, guys were off the wall about her, and she didn't disappoint on a date. Dom never said anything about me banging her because we were pals. That wasn't the case with the guy who tried to rape her. Him, Dom sliced up like a Thanksgiving turkey. We'd buried the parts upstate. It was that killing which should've tipped me off that it was Dom who was after me, but I couldn't see the light until it was almost too late.

"So, Richie, you're looking good," she said.

It was for her I'd gotten dressed up. Time was, I'd have given my left ball for five minutes of chitchat with her. Now the least I could do was look nice.

She started to talk. Nonstop. All about the soaps she was watching, like I'd know the characters like she did.

Finally, she ran out of gas. She was starting to repeat herself.

"Like a cookie?" she said.

"Sure," I said, taking one.

"Good," I said, after a bite.

"Just fresh, just for you," said Immy.

"Thanks."

"Like some tea?"

"No, thanks, I'm not a tea type of guy," I said. Which was the truth. Tea and me don't agree. Now coffee, that's a different scene. I gulp down about a gallon a day.

For a moment, anger flashed in her dark eyes when I refused. I'd been a jerk. Here was a cripple trying to play hostess, and I was getting particular about tea. I should've just forced it down and smiled.

Immy went back to talking about the programs she watched on TV. Time passed by slowly. There was a cuckoo clock in the room. I started to half-listen to the tick-tocks and half listen to her. I felt myself grow sleepy.

"I bet you got to go to work," she said.

"Got to earn my pay," I said, seizing on the opportunity to get the hell out of there.

"Come here and give me a good-bye kiss," said Dom's sister, putting her arms out.

I went over to her, leaned over to give her a kiss. She again put her left hand on my shoulder instead of around my big neck. As I kissed her cheek, I kept my eyes half-open. Even with that limited vision, I saw what was coming. Immy's right hand moved in a flash toward her scarf, then came toward me. I saw what was in her hand.

I backslapped her hand, putting some steam behind my blow. Something skittered across the tile in front of the all-white fireplace.

"You fucker!" screamed Immaculata Mancini, her left hand trying to claw my face.

I stepped back. Kept my eyes on her. Went over. Picked up the stiletto which had almost taken up residence in my neck.

"I'll kill ya, ya fuck of a fuck!" she yelled, throwing the tea pot at me. Now I knew why she'd looked pissed off when I refused her offer of tea. She was like her brother, never just coming after someone in just one way.

"Ya killed Dominick, ya bastard, I know it was you! Dominick wasn't stupid, no way he'd smoke in a lab. It was you, you got him!" all of this at high decibels, pouring out. Her face was flushed a bright red, her neck was bulging, her eyes were wide and wild.

"Yeah, it was me. So the fuck what? He came after me. I went after him. He lost; I won."

"He tol' about you. You and that scar-face cunt, the two of you he said he'd have to take care of. You'd deserve what you got!"

"I got nothin', he got his," I said, quietly, knowing the effect this would have. All I could use on her were words when what I wanted to do was wring her fat neck.

This really set her off. She screamed louder, then all of her sudden, her lips flapped and no words came out.

"Help …me…Richie," she said, her words now a whisper.

"Fuck you," I said, and watched as the stroke came over her. It didn't take long. She stopped moving and slumped to the right. I waited until I was sure she was dead. I went over to her and checked for a pulse. Nothing. I looked at her. Two peas in a pod, her and Dom. Even from the grave, he was coming after me. If I'd closed my eyes for our kiss, I'd now be pig-stuck and bleeding out on her carpet instead of being here wondering what to do with a stiff.

I had two choices. Sneak out or call 911. Sneaking out in Bensonhurst isn't a great idea, for there's always an Italian mother surveying the block. I took some time to get my story straight, then punched in the number on my cell.

All of this needed some good lying. I was up to it. Lying about bastards who were trying to do me in was easy. I sat down across from the dead meat and waited for the EMTs.

Chapter Sixteen

· ·

"So, this is Ridgewood." I said, looking at the ritzy homes.

"This is it," said McClure, who was dressed all in white, including a white headband and new white New Balance running shoes. He looked like a Viking ready for war. Me? I was in my Yankee Doodle red, white, and blue outfit, which didn't make me look like a Viking ready for war. I looked more like a 40-plus, hefty, cigar-smoking Italian about ready to exert himself. People around me were giving my person the fisheye. No doubt they wanted an autograph but were too shy to ask.

"Nice. A first-class event. They even offer money," I said, staring up at Mac from the ground where I was stretching. I stopped stretching. Got up. Looked around. Most of these people were probably not meat eaters, like yours truly, and also probably not gorgers, which also I am. It wasn't that I felt fat, just huge.

"Not for us, my friend. That's for the Olympic types. Us, we'll not even have a shot at a trophy," said McClure, who also looked huge and was a gorger.

"That fast?" I said, trying to touch my toes, which I knew for a fact were down there somewhere.

"That fast. You're probably exhausted from the drive up here, aren't you?" said McClure, practicing his good gamesmanship. "Up quite early, weren't you?"

"Naw, I'm fresh as a daisy, slept behind the wheel for half of the way here. I'm ready to go," I said, enjoying this back and forth, which was a lot better than screaming at Immy Mancini until she croaked. Her dying turned out not to be such a big deal. My lying opened doors for me, and I drove my murderous self right through them. As it turned out, she had a history of blood clots, so this dying from a stroke was not really unexpected. The EMTs showed up, then a cop, I looked sorry, and they took her to some cold slab where she'd get stuffed and then sent to meet the devil and hook up with her brother. The two of them could watch and see me live, which would be the biggest slap in the face to the both of them. It had been close, though; she'd nearly got me, but nearly ain't enough in Brooklyn. So now here I was, out and about, having a good time while the two of them were getting roasted. Did I feel bad about my last words to her being "Fuck you"? Yeah, I did, I should of added "and fuck your brother, too."

"You look like a wilted black-eyed Susan to me," said Mac, bringing me back to the here and now. I wished Candy were here; I'd like to show off in front of her.

"Looks are deceiving," I said, smiling at his wit. Mac was a funny guy. I liked him. What I didn't like was him banging on a too-regular basis the coeds/kids at our place.

A young woman attired in a bright yellow running outfit was stretching out next to us. She easily touched her toes; in fact, she put her palms on the pavement. I could do that, too, except I'd have to sever a hand.

"This your first time runnin'?" she said, not smiling.

This she said on account of our bulk. Big Mac was not so called for no reason. He packed 240 pounds on his six-foot-three, and I was…more. So lean and mean, we were not.

"Yes, we're from Weight Watchers. Are there hills here?" said Mac.

"What hills?" said the young woman, still not smiling.

"Isn't this course known for its hills?" I said, taking a sidelong glance at McClure, who had gone into silence.

"So there are no hills?"

"None," said the young woman, getting up from where she'd been showing off how flexible she was. I never show off; I just touch my knees and move on.

"Take care of yourselves," she said, moving away. No doubt she'd report us to the EMTs as potential heat stroke victims.

"You lied to me."

"A harsh word, suggestive of an attack on my character," said McClure, putting his hand over his heart.

"What character?" I said, smiling.

"This information was on the registration form, you know. Flat and fast was, I believe, the term."

"I don't read handouts, here or at the college."

"So I've noticed. Don't you miss being out of the loop?"

"No. Out of the loop is my goal. Don't change the subject. You lied to me."

"True, but I did so with aplomb," said McClure.

"Don't use big words," I said.

"Five minutes to race time," came a voice from a blow horn.

Flat and fast meant the Ridgewood Run was made to order for McClure. Maybe it was good Candy was not here; wouldn't want her to see her boss humiliated.

"I'll get us a nice spot," said McClure as he led me into the crowd of runners. Several of them looked at us. I saw more than a few nudges. Which probably meant they thought we were famous or something.

"A bit crowded. Don't fall and break an ankle at the start." McClure laughed, showing bright white teeth. I laughed.

A countdown from ten began.

"Good luck, buddy," said McClure, offering a large hand.

"Good luck to you, don't trip," I said, getting in the last zinger.

A gun went off, and the entire crowd sprang into action, at first maneuvering for position and eventually settling into a steady pace. McClure pulled away from me before too long. That I could not help. Mac was simply faster; no matter how much I tried I could not keep up with him. So I didn't try.

In the previous ten races we'd run together, we'd had split wins. In our last race, we'd ended in a virtual dead heat with me a winner by a step. That was the day Candy should've been there.

A hot sun beat down on me. Sunshine was not good. It was bad enough being beefy, I'd have to watch my intake of water or I'd be having a chin-chin with the EMTs. Running and heat are a bad combo. That was what had done in Brzenk, one of my office partners that Dom had nailed while he was gunning for me. Dom had been a cunning bastard, using my own lectures on chemical weaponry to send me to the promised land. That time, it had been by adding atropine to my Gatorade; before that he'd tried brucine. Both times he'd missed, and here I was, hale and hearty, but hefty.

The race wore on. I checked my running watch. We were moving fast. Too fast. This was beyond me. I scaled back my pace. Two miles passed, then three. The hot sun worked on me to set off some real sweating. I'm like that—a heavy sweater—so I took on water whenever I could, slowing down, making sure I drank to the last drop. This was a wise move. Drink now, live to see tomorrow—not a bad motto.

Still, I had no sighting of McClure. Today did not seem to be my day. I'd be in for one hell of a ribbing from the big guy.

The young woman runner had been right. McClure's warning of hills had been merely a bluff meant to ruin my confidence. The course was very flat, moving through the streets of Ridgewood. Lining the route were the Ridgewood rich, cheering on the sweating runners. I was getting tired; I felt like telling all of them to leave the premises so I could lie down by the side of the road, go into fetal position, and whine.

At mile marker number four, I got sight of McClure's all-white racing outfit. My attitude changed. Maybe I could catch him. I increased my pace. Checked my watch. Not bad. I could run at this pace and not die. Running is all about staying aerobic, for once you're out of air the game is over.

At mile number five, I was close behind McClure and could see he was laboring, no longer up on his toes striding out but running, head down, with a short shuffle.

Two voices went off in my head. Both of them clear, showing that heat stroke was not having its way with me.

"I've got him," said one voice. I liked that voice.

"He's still got something left. Be careful," said a voice I didn't care for. But I paid attention to that voice. Mac was an experienced runner. He'd go out fast, then let up, save something in the tank for the finish. I was more of a steady pacer, but now the tortoise had caught the hare. The question was: Did I have anything left for the end game? There was only one way to find out.

I eased next to McClure.

"How you doin'?" I said, knowing full well the effect my words would have on him.

"Been…better," said McClure, struggling to get the words out.

I moved away from him.

The question of my having a lead was soon answered as I sensed someone at my right elbow. It was McClure, returned to life. The race was now really on. I felt less than confident; I'd hoped to run slowly away from him but that was not to be the case. We were now hell-bent for the end, where his speed would again assert itself.

Fifty meters from the finish McClure blew by me, running up on his toes, no longer shuffling along with his head down; I managed to stay two meters behind and to the left. I felt my lungs start to burn. My air was running out; it wouldn't take much for me to tie up and look like a running robot.

With twenty or so long meters to go, I thought I had lost but then

McClure began to tie up himself, pumping his big arms as he strained to complete the race. It took all I had to keep pace.

At ten meters, I caught McClure; at five I was ahead. I won.

The next few minutes were not pleasant as air was hard to come by.

A wet hand touched my wet shoulder. My legs were shaking, didn't feel like they were under me.

"You got me," gasped McClure. "Now I'll have to kill myself so as to maintain my honor."

"Kill me, too, while you're at it," I said, with not enough oxygen to laugh.

An EMT appeared next to me.

"You two guys OK?" she said. She was short and tanned and looked in shape. She was not breathing hard. I did not like her.

"We're fine, except for the breathing and maybe a vomit or two," I said.

She laughed. Mac laughed.

I wished Candy were here.

Chapter Seventeen

. . . .

I drove through the streets of Ho-ho-kus, noticing it was a village with classy homes. Where the name had come from I did not know, although I'd guess it had something to do with Indians. I obeyed the speed limit of 25 mph and stopped at all the stop signs. McClure drove considerably faster than 25 mph and largely ignored the stop signs. He was daring; I was chicken shit. But I had won the race.

Finally, a stoplight stopped him. A large arm waved at me. I waved back. This had turned out to be a good day. I needed a good day. First, I'd gone off the deep end thinking that Candy was Dom's partner and spending the late hours following her. Until she picked up a pizza. Then I'd gone and done my duty, only to miss a stiletto by inches. Compared to that, this day had been duck soup. I'd traded barbs, run hard, won, and now I was going to enjoy myself. Life was looking up.

My car was a silver Toyota Camry LE I'd bought online for a bargain price. McClure's means of transportation was a silver Porsche 911 GT which hadn't been bought online and cost big bucks. Still, my car got me where I needed to go. Mac had better not drive his Porsche to Brooklyn, where there were only too many ready and willing to relieve him of his toy. That was Brooklyn for you. Whatever you had seemed to some creep like what he/she/it needed.

The light changed, and McClure zoomed ahead. His Porsche would've been more comfortable on a track like the Pocono 500 rather than on the tree-lined streets of a quaint, quiet village. I followed in his wake, moving at a normal pace, taking comfort in knowing my miles per gallon were better than Mac's.

McClure accelerated, moving out of sight, but I knew where I was going. I'd been there before. That's how I'd gotten a line on who he lived with. Maybe that was why he was such a sex troller. Or maybe it was something more than that. If it was, I didn't want to know. Professors who fuck their students should be kicked out of the profession. The students may look like adults, then they open their mouths and sound like kids. Eighteen is a funny age; on the one hand is appearance and on the other is the truth that they're still kids. Too many coeds at the college were looking for a thrill, although I could not imagine what thrill was to be obtained from getting Beef Patty's beef.

Arriving at McClure's home, which was slightly smaller than a castle, I parked my car in a large driveway in front of a three-car garage which wasn't bigger than an arena.

"You drive fast," I said.

"Have to exercise this beast," said McClure, pointing to the silver Porsche.

"You have death-caused-by-high-speed-in-village insurance?" I asked.

"Yes," said McClure, smiling his white smile.

"You have an idea how fast this thing will go?"

"I've had it up to 200 once, but that was on Highway 17."

"You're kiddin.'"

"God's truth. Let's get inside and take a shower before we tighten up."

As we walked along the stone walkway, a large front door opened, and a servant appeared.

"Good afternoon, Dr. McClure," said the servant.

"Hello, Julia," said McClure to a middle-aged woman dressed in servant attire.

This was some place. Maybe if I win Lucky Lotto for a bundle I'll get a servant who'll call me Dr. Bucceroni.

We entered Mac's home, which was nice and cool. The hot day wasn't winning out in here. I walked carefully in the big house. I took care not to brush any of the vases on the tables to the floor, for they were probably worth more than a year's salary. Everything here looked expensive. There was more than one Oriental rug, about which I knew a thing or two. These rugs had set someone back a pretty penny.

"You want me to help you to the shower, or are you OK?" said McClure.

"I'm a little tired, could you scrub my back?" I said.

McClure laughed.

Out of the shower, dried, wearing an Izod and khakis, I thought I looked presentable until I saw McClure, who looked as if he were wearing clothes worth a month of a professor's pay.

"Nice duds."

"Oh, these? They're just any old thing," said McClure in a falsetto voice. "Beer?"

"Lots."

"Follow me, me boy." McClure led me through the big house to a large redwood deck which I was sure could've accommodated the faculty and students at the Urban U. and still have room for a full orchestra for entertainment. So this was how the other half lived. Nice. Made one think about committing crimes to get the bucks needed to live like this. There was something to be said about the evils of capitalism, like how to cash in for oneself.

I had just settled in when Mrs. McClure appeared. I got slowly up.

"Hello, Audrey."

"Hello." With her short gray hair and dressed in a black pants suit,

Audrey McClure looked good for a woman of 60, but she was 60 while her husband was in his 40s. It was a bit of a shock to see them together. Especially when I'd seen Mac with students gathered around him, and him giving the once over to the ones he had picked out for a romp in his office. If walls could talk, there was one helluva dirty book to write about Mac's office.

"So I hear you humiliated Ross," she said in a soft, rich-sounding voice. You could almost hear the cash as she talked.

"Sorry," I said.

"Nothing to be sorry for, defeat will make him mature," said Audrey McClure. Maybe she didn't realize the truth of those words. Then again, maybe she did.

"He cheated, took a cab, or else I would've moidered him," said McClure.

"You boys relax here, have your beers. Heinrik has the grill ready. We'll eat when you're ready," said Mac's wife.

I looked at the backyard, which was not as large as Giant Stadium, and saw another servant working at an all-brick fireplace grill. This was some life Mac had.

"That sounds good."

"I'll leave you two alone to talk shop," Audrey McClure said, and left the room. She had a nice figure. I hoped for two things—one, that Mac had something left for her when he came home and two, that he didn't stick her with some god-awful disease picked up by entering the sex network of a coed who liked to do it.

"Shop sucks," I said when she was gone.

"That it does," said McClure, who took a long drink of Harp enriched with lime. "Too bad about Rudy."

"Too bad."

"Every day he was after me to look at that book of his."

"A lost cause?"

"Totally. But he kept at it. He was really in a bad position. You see, what he wanted to do has already been done. He was just out of step and behind the time." Mac should know, for his books were always being reviewed in the *Times* as being cutting-edge, whatever the fuck that means.

"That he was."

"That young fellow, Biden, is also in bad shape. He's just up a blind alley. I could name three books that've been published which have done what he wants to do. He won't last long down there."

"That is true," I said, and the thought passed through my mind that Mac was saying more than he knew. One reason Biden might not make it is that Bath would kill him. I drank more beer. Best not to dwell on such matters now.

McClure took a long drink. I sensed he had something to say other than to comment on the academic down-and-outs who populated my office.

"Speaking of causes, I wanted to give you a heads up," said McClure, not making eye contact.

"Nikki Nateal," I said quickly, guessing where he was going.

"She's a half and half," said McClure. Which was true; one half of her was into college, the other half was still in the street, with her gang.

"So what's the point?" I asked, not really wanting to hear this. The last person who should be lecturing about proper behavior was him. I took a deep breath. Let my heat back down. What was the point of getting pissed? These were just words; they would go in one ear and out the other.

"Watch yourself," he said, still not looking at me. His voice sounded like he was having trouble getting this out.

I nearly choked on my beer. Here was a guy who was fucking every teenager in sight and it was me he was warning. Talk about balls, this guy had golden ones. And he used them.

"What should I do?"

"Watch yourself, is all. Don't ever forget what she is."

"But maybe she can change."

"Gang bangers seldom change." He was right about that. What he didn't know was I'd saved his sorry ass when J.P. and Nikki were dead on to doing a number on him. Mac and I never talked about that day. Either he was unaware or he was too aware. Whatever, he'd never asked me, and I hadn't volunteered the truth. Let sleeping dogs lie was no doubt his motto.

"Ready?" Audrey McClure stood in the yard now, next to Heinrik the servant. She was calling up to us.

"Yes," said McClure.

"Thanks," I said.

"No problem," said McClure.

I relaxed in the big chair. I watched Heinrik cook the steaks. I drank the cold Harp. I was relieved that McClure had not dropped the other shoe, which was that Candy was also a half and half. But I was convinced she'd come over to my side. That much, I was now sure of. I drank more.

I felt my mind drift toward hoping Candy would call and stopped its progress. That was the future. I cut off the future. I focused on the present, which right now consisted of good beer and fine steak in a Gatsby house.

Chapter Eighteen

. . . .

I didn't get home quite as soon as I wanted. Mac and I had put down a beer or two, or three. We were, to be polite, a bit tipsy. Actually, we were drunk.

When I said it was time to go, I was led to his office.

"Sit there," he said.

"You gonna read from one of your books?" I said, looking around at his home office, which was lined with books and had its own fireplace. This was some life Mac had. It must be some shock to leave this palace and come to our Brooklyn rat hole.

"No, I'm gonna save you some money."

I was all for that, maybe he planned to give one of his wife's spare millions to me as a gift.

Instead, he took out this small machine. He sat it on a small, wooden, highly polished table which was no doubt worth a buck or two.

"Breathe in here," said Mac, adjusting something on the machine.

I did.

"You're goin' nowhere for a while," said Mac, after he read the breathalyzer.

"Bad?"

"You'd be in the drunk tank, with people who are beneath you," he said, which meant I'd blown a bad score. This was a wise move on his part. First, I didn't want to kill someone drinking and driving, thinking I was OK when I really wasn't. Second, I didn't need to lose my license and some big bucks for driving drunk. Third, I liked it here. Hobbing and nobbing with the ultra-wealthy was OK in my book. I could get used to this.

"Thanks," I said.

"No problem."

"Where'd you get that machine?"

He told me. I wrote down the info. Only had to check my spelling three times and ask him to repeat all of it twice. Oh yeah, I was ready for the road. No problem. Gee, Officer, I only had a couple, are you sure that I'm drink? I mean drunk?

We passed the time playing pool. He trounced me. We tossed sticks to his dogs. They brought them to Mac, ignoring me. We took a walk. My legs were really happy with me about doing that. I had to stop with cramps about every fourth step. Mac just walked along. He said I was slipping. He had a point.

Finally, he tested me again.

"OK?"

"Hate to say it but you're, all things considered, normal."

"I resemble that remark."

Goodbyes were said. Backing out of the large and long driveway, I saw Mac at the door with his arm around the Mrs. They looked like an ad for country living, except for the fact that come Monday he'd be back in his office at the Urban U., pants down, servicing one of his more susceptible students.

I drove slowly through Ho-ho-kus, kept my sharp eyes peeled for any cop who was after a scalp. Mac had tested me and I'd checked out, but I was taking no chances. I needed a ticket like I needed a hole in the head.

Down Highway 17 I went along with about a million other people.

I didn't know the suburbs were this crowded. Whatever happened to open fields and forests? Wasn't New Jersey supposed to be the Garden State? All the way down, I saw no patches of tomatoes or rows of cucumbers.

The turnpike heading south was also full, three rows across, no doubt with saphead tourists who'd just blown a considerable wad in the Big Apple. I crept, driving at well below any reasonable speed limit. I passed the turn for the Lincoln Tunnel, still heading south, but the traffic thinned just a bit.

Finally, I passed Newark International and got off at exit 13. Again, more traffic. These were people heading back to Brooklyn after a day spent in the wilds of New Jersey. I crossed the Goethals Bridge, which, to my mind, hadn't been well planned. The turnpike was three lanes, but the bridge had only two. It would take nothing for one accident to screw things up. Speaking of which, ahead of me, to my right, a Lincoln Town Car rear-ended a small red Mazda. At the time we were inching along so I don't know what the hell the guy was thinking. Out of the Lincoln came this short, fat guy bawling his mouth off. He stopped working his mouth when he encountered the occupants of the Mazda, three large, but not fat, black fellows. They seemed to take offence at what the fat man had said. As I moved slowly away, I could see the fat man getting his head banged into the hood of his big car. Just goes to show road rage is a bad idea unless you're armed.

Ahead was the Staten Island Expressway. When Mac was giving me the best route to his place, he'd called it the Fuckingstatenislandexpressway, all one word. Being on it now, I got his point. From the two lanes of the Goethals, I'd gone back to three lanes, but that fact didn't change the reality that it was all bumper to bumper. More inching. More honking. More potential road rage. I looked to see if the three large, but not fat, black men were back in line. Didn't see them.

I did see one Asian woman who wanted into my lane. I wasn't in the mood. I gave her nothing. She honked and flipped me the bird. I gave her a thumb-wave. She ran into the car in front of her while she was digesting the meaning of my gesture. I kept on, convinced that I was the nicest guy out here. Which I no doubt was.

Finally, we were at the Verrazano, named after another brilliant Italian, in the mold of yours truly, although probably not nearly as nice. The traffic was really bad here. Brooklynites returning home to their nests and pissed off at anyone in their way. As I moved at glacier speed, I look ahead at Brooklyn. The day was coming to an end. All day, it had been sunny in New Jersey, but now, going home, ahead of me, clouds were rolling in, and the darkness was coming on. I pushed to the back of my mind what was waiting for me. That was for tomorrow. Manana. Then, I would go back to being a detective. As for now, I was another poor slob trying to get back into a borough that advertised itself as being "How Sweet It Is."

Chapter Nineteen

. . . .

I was in a field, not of high grass, but nicely mowed, just the way the outdoors should be—green but manageable. I was behind two people in wheelchairs. The grass was hot under my feet, even through my shoes. I started to push the two, using one hand on each of their chairs. They were hard to push. It took all of my strength to get them going. We moved slowly, not making much headway. The grass got hotter. I strained to keep them going. My arms burned like I was doing a workout. Ahead, I saw the end of the field and beyond it just the gray sky. I walked faster. One of the people turned and talked to me.

"Where we goin', Richie?" said Dom.

"Yeah, where you takin' us," said the other person, Immaculata Mancini but like she used to be, young and slim, not fat and crippled. Dom was his old self, too, his hair no longer thinning on top, his body young and trim, like when he was Mr. Outside.

"To the end," I said.

"End of what?" said Dom, his voice rising, fear coming into it. I liked to hear the fear.

"You'll see," I said, pulling Immy, who'd tried to get up, back into her seat. I walked faster on the grass, which was now burning my feet even though I had on my specially made Italian wing tips.

The three of us came to the end of the field. I went around them and looked down. This was the spot. This was where I wanted them to be.

I got behind Immy's chair, moved it to the edge. As she went over, she cursed me.

I went over to the remaining wheelchair.

"Hey Richie, don't do this, this is me, this is Dom, OK?" he said, pleading with me.

"I know who the fuck it is, you don' have to tell me," I said and pushed him off after his sister.

I waited to hear a splash. Heard nothing. Then heard a lot.

"Help me, Richie!" screamed Immy.

"Help us," yelled Dom.

Both of their voices were weak, not much oomph to them.

I went to the edge. Looked down. I saw the two of them, lying broken. They'd missed the water and hit the jagged rocks. There was a lot of blood around them. I moved closer to the cliffs, took it out, pissed an arching stream down at the dying brother and sister.

A phone rang somewhere.

I came half-awake in a dead-dark room. The window air conditioner blew cool air over my face. The air calmed me down. I fell back asleep. Now, I started to dream about my family. I could see my wife and son dead, torn up by the New Lots train, lying not quite under white sheets in a stark-white morgue. One white arm was flopped out toward the floor. I recognized the ring on the finger. There were people in the room who could see them naked and dead, they tugged at me to come closer. I didn't want to look. I pulled back while they tugged harder.

The phone rang on.

I came full awake. A sheet was half-strangling me. I ripped it away from my throat. I gasped for air.

I turned on the reading light next to my small bed. I put on my computer glasses. I answered the phone.

"Hello," said Candy. "You dead, the phone's been ringin' forever."

"I was sleepin'," I said, wondering if I was still dreaming. I pinched myself. I was awake.

"It's ten o'clock."

"I ran a race with Mac today...."

"And I bet you won and now you're in bed at ten o'clock," she said, laughing.

"I'm old. It's not nice to laugh at the old, you'll be called an ageist."

She laughed harder.

It was great to talk with her. She was right there in my ear. She was back, and she was OK. She wasn't Dom's partner, she was my...I couldn't come up with a term as to what I thought she was.

"Anything new at the shop?"

"You gonna be up for a while?" I said.

"Yes."

"I'll come over."

I rolled out of bed. These were some dreams I'd had. I know something about dreaming. There's a prof at the Urban U. named Aaron Brightman who's also a psychiatrist, he filled me in about dreams. That they originate from life, which I already knew but that the important thing about them is who's running the show. It's the dreamer. He sets the stage, directs the whole thing, arranges people, makes them say what they say. That I hadn't known. These dreams proved one thing: I wasn't satisfied with killing the Mancinis once; I wanted to do it twice. The other dream was my avoidance. I didn't want to let my family be dead. That would have to change. Candy could help me do that.

Chapter Twenty

. . . .

Candy was curled up on her white couch, sipping a glass of white wine. I was nursing a large drink of J.D. I'd brought her up to speed on my suspicions. This was like old times. Me shooting off my mouth and her straightening me out. I need straightening out at times, which is on account of me being a little loony.

"So you think that old duffer Bath is killing off his colleagues to keep his job," she said.

"Parker and Gaspar were before his time. I think he got the idea that old profs can die of natural causes, so he took out Randle with a drug which suggests a heart attack."

"It's traceable."

"How close will the ME look?"

"I'll find out tomorrow; I know the new ME."

"Be...."

"Careful, I know. We don't want to show our hand before we count the cards."

That's why I was glad she was back. We were on the same wavelength. Plus, she was always about two steps ahead of me. Which meant either she was sharp or I was slow.

"At least we won't have a cop to worry about," I said.

"We didn't worry about Dom, his bein' the killer was a total surprise," said Candy.

"That's true," I said, sagely, taking a drink of my J.D. I hadn't seen Dom as the one who was after me. It was only at the last moment that I'd gotten a line on him, and that had come from Beef Patty, no less. This time would be different; this time I'd keep my mind clear and let the suspicions flow, no matter who the suspect was. Last time, I'd refused to look at where I should've been looking, with the result that I'd nearly ended up a stiff.

"So tomorrow will be a busy day," she said.

"That it will," I said, standing up, feeling the stiffness in my legs.

"Let's do this right this time," said Candy.

"Will try," I said as I made my way carefully to the door.

"Want to stay here?" said Candy, no doubt noticing how less-than-steady on my pins I was.

"I can make it home," I said, resisting the invite to curl up on her couch.

"I've got something to tell you," she said.

I hoped to hell she wasn't going to tell me she had a boyfriend.

"What?" I said.

"I changed my name."

I walked back into the living room and sat down.

"You did what?"

"Changed my name," she said, her blue-gray eyes looking into me.

"To what?"

"Lorraine."

"Lorraine?"

"Lorraine."

This was something of a shock. One, why would she do that, and two why pick such a god-awful name? The only Lorraine I'd ever known was one Miss Lorraine Puchizello, who'd given new meaning to the word ugly. She'd had straggly-assed hair, bad skin, a big hook nose, a creature forehead, and elephant ears. To make matters worse, her mother knew my mother, so there were times I'd have to take Lorraine out. The other thing about her was that she was large and made for some trouble when you tried to twirl her on a dance floor. The guys used to rib me pretty good about her. There was one guy in particular, Sloppy Simonetti, who really busted my chops. At a dance, I was doing my best to steer Lorraine around the floor when I heard him say, pretty loudly, that there were two beasts out tonight. I stopped dancing with Lorraine and walked over to Sloppy. He wasn't exactly small, but I up and heaved him into a wall. He hit hard and slid down, like a half-squashed bug. The room got real quiet. Then Dom walked over to me.

"Richie, good job. Now go back to dancin'. Only let me give you a little advice, don't whisper in her ear, you could use your tongue in there."

I'd hesitated, then laughed. All of the gang had joined in. That was my memory of a Lorraine.

"Well, if that's what you want, I…."

"Just kiddin'. I changed my last name."

"To Schwartz?"

"Touché," she said. "No, to Dyer."

"Not much of a change," I said.

"It's enough if someone is looking for you."

I got the point. There'd been two bastards who'd worked Candy over and ironed her face, leaving it scarred for life. One of them had gone to meet his maker. Candy had seen to that. She'd never gone into detail, but I could guess the silenced pistol in her purse had come into action. That left one. Candy wanted to make sure she wasn't in someone's computer list.

"You'll have to make some changes at the college."

"I'll do that on Monday. I'll see the Dean. He likes me," she said, emphasizing the last two words.

"That means you belong to a very, I mean very, select group."

She laughed.

I got up and made my way to the door again.

"One last thing," said Candy.

"Yeah," I said. We were face to face. Her eyes were locked on mine. She was smiling.

"I'm checked out now, aren't I?" she said.

My heart took off, beating about a million times a minute.

"You knew?"

"I knew," she said, still smiling, her teeth white against her golden tan.

"How?"

"When you rear-ended me on Bay Parkway, that was a dead giveaway."

"Sorry."

"Nothin' to be sorry about. I could've been what you were thinkin'."

"But you're not."

"No, I'm not."

Candy moved close to me, I could smell her great-smelling perfume. She kissed me on the cheek. I didn't know what to do, so I gently patted her shoulder.

I left her place. Tomorrow would be the beginning of it all. Candy was back. Alone, I was a questionable detective; with Candy, I'd get the goods on Bath. Then what? I put off that thought and walked home.

As I walked, I thought about what a piss-poor tail job I'd done. Candy had known. That's probably why she'd been away, to take some time to think about whether she wanted to still work with me.

I walked faster. I moved my right hand to my cheek and touched where she'd kissed me.

Chapter Twenty-One

● ●

"Hey Prof, how you doin'?" said Beef Patty, whose uniform strained to hold in his enormous stomach. The Urban U. should buy him a more flowing garment, like a tent. Of course, then they'd have to watch it with PETA for mistreating an elephant.

"I'm doing fine, Lester, how about you?" I said. Which was true. I was fine, especially now that Candy was back.

"Not so good."

"Why's that?"

"We got trouble down here."

"We do?"

"Yeah, someone set off the gangs."

"Oh, boy."

"Yeah, the One-Percenters, the Seoul Brothers, the Monarchs, they all on the warpath."

"They are?"

"Yeah, somebody sent one of them e-mails and the gangs got ahold of it."

"They did?" I was beginning to sound like a dope with all of these short-ass questions.

"Someone was e-mailin' to their friend and called Nikki Nateal a nigger and Jimmy Fisheyes a gook and Morales a spic."

"How did they find out what was said about them in someone else's e-mail?"

"This e-mail stuff, I don' know much 'bout it, but my wife Malvina… you 'member Malvina, right?" said Beef Patty.

Malvina was not considerably smaller than Beef Patty and was known as "Heavy Duty." On account of her tonnage.

"Of course I remember her." Which was true. I taught, at times, a science course for nurses, and she'd taken it. A hard worker. And now she was on the night shift at Brooklyn Hospital, which was no piece a cake job. She'd been there when Walt Brzenk had died. That had been some night. One of my colleagues had been killed from a doping and as it turned out, the dope had been meant for me. I could remember seeing Brzenk, who was a tall, skinny redhead, dead in the hospital. I could remember how I felt. I clamped down on my memory. This recall would get me nowhere.

"Well, she work on the side for the Webmaster down at the main campus. She say who sent the e-mail they fucked up and sent it to the whole class. Malvina say that easy to do. Malvina think the person who sent it is askin' for it."

"I think Malvina is doin' some correct thinking."

"Yeah, she one smart woman, thas why I married her. You know who sent the e-mail?"

"No," I said, lying. If Beef Patty wanted to collar someone, he was damn close to a suspect. I'd viewed my action as score one for Randle. The old guy hadn't deserved a kick in the jollies for doing his job. He was one of the few at the Urban U. who'd tried to maintain standards. Most just blew off their teaching by handing out passing grades and focused their time on how to get the hell out of here. Not Randle. He may have been a bit of a cuckoo on Hemingway, but his head was in the right place as far as doing his job. Thusly, I had done something about his passing.

"That lil' tight-assed Russian gal." I noticed what Beef Patty noticed about the troublemaker. He never skipped a beat. Maybe I should organize a coed scoring contest and pit Mac against Beef Patty. Tape the proceedings. Send it to Youtube. See if it would go viral. "Natasha Natooska?"

"That her name. She gonna get it, Prof, these gangs they no one to fuck wit'." That was true. Anyone hearing the words gang and college together would think they were no big deal. That wasn't true. These kids/young men had a mission, and anyone who got in the way was in for trouble. And that anyone would now be the aforementioned "tight-assed Russian gal."

"Anything else, Lester?"

"Thas it."

"Lester, did you get the call about Professor Randle?" I said, starting my detective work for the day. I'd talked to Candy, and she had made this suggestion. I was now heeding her suggestion. I was good at heeding.

"Yeah, tha' was me."

"What'd the voice sound like?" I said, boring in.

"What I tol' the cop was that it was one of them high, white folk's voices."

"Man, woman?" I continued.

"Couldn't really tell."

"Old or young?" I said, probably overdoing my interrogation.

"Probably old, but I guessin'. Why you want to know?" he said, looking at me carefully. I'd now have to watch it or I'd lose him. He would go on the defensive and give me no more than yes and no, which wouldn't really help a lot. Blacks and whites are like that, wary of one another. Probably with good reason.

"Cop asked me all these questions about what happened and who called," I said. "How was I supposed to know, I wasn't there, know what I mean?"

"I hear ya, Prof, these cops they always got questions," he said. True words from the big man. I knew all about cops and their questions. I was worried about the probing ones which would come from Detective Reagan.

He was another guy who had standards and did his job. Sooner or later, he'd find out what killed Randle and then he'd come looking for the source. The choices were few, and I would be high on the suspect list. Being high on such a list was not a good thing.

"I got to go, Lester. Duty calls."

"Yeah, me too, I got to patrol the halls jus' in case some shit starts. I sure hope it don't."

I agreed with Beef Patty, for being in the middle of a gang fight was a sure way to a short life. The gangs at the college weren't Bloods and Crips, but they could still do damage.

I assessed what I'd learned, which was nothing. I'd better be careful or I'd get fired from my detective work. Candy would hire someone new to do the fieldwork.

Beef Patty disappeared into an elevator. The parking garage was now quiet. There were no sounds of sexual combat coming from the office of Mr. Lester Norwood. I looked around. None of the cars was really fancy. As wisely absent was the Porsche which belonged to the other prime sexual warrior of the Urban U. Both had better watch themselves. If Malvina found out what Beef Patty was up to, she would raise some serious bumps on the large head of the big man. I'd seen her in action at the hospital; she was not to be trifled with, especially over sex outside marriage. Which she would take seriously, even if her man did not. Why Beef Patty took this risk, I didn't have a clue. Of course, now he had a reputation, and the coeds came after him. No doubt doing it on a dare from their friends. I just hoped the Dean did not get wind of the escapades going on in the garage below him. As for Mac, he was walking a tightrope. To this point, he'd escaped being charged because none of his romantic interludes had come forward and told the Dean what was going on in the office of an English professor. Then, the Dean would make a case, and Mac's ass would be in hot water that he probably could not escape. Knowing that possibility existed was no doubt one of the many turn-ons for Mac. He had the thrill of conquering coeds and the extra benefit of knowing he was teetering on the edge of the Dean's power. The Dean and he were locked in a mutual hate relationship. It was just that when push came to shove, as it could over a professor, tenured or not, having sex with students, the Dean would hold all the cards. All of this was my high-level, really deep speculation, but I'd bet a bad cup of coffee from Fat Harry's that I was right. I'd seen where Mac lived. He had it made, and all he needed to do was keep it in his pants. Why he didn't said a lot about who he really was. The problem was I liked him; it was just that he could never be a real friend because of what he did during his office hours.

I left the parking garage.

Chapter Twenty-Two

. . . .

I walked down the dirty hallway, taking care where I stepped. Last week, there'd been a splash of vomit that would've soiled my expensive wing tips. The janitorial crew was seldom seen at the upper floors of the Urban U. One reason was the lawlessness of these floors. It was one thing to clean up after the student/slobs; it was another to be stabbed by one of them for staring too long. The students were something to stare at— the boys wearing low-riding jeans which exposed their underwear, the girls in stretch pants which exposed nearly everything. In addition, there were metal piercings of various face parts, brightly colored spiky hair, and attitude, lots of attitude. At least the janitors could just leave them alone and sweep the floor and make sure the Dean's surroundings were neat and tidy. I had to close the door and be alone with 35 troublemakers who had little interest in their studies. The only reason they were here was that society had no place for them other than the army or jail. Their attitudes made work in the service area, where a winning smile and an agreeable manner were essential, problematic. I, of course, was just the guy to teach them. I was like one of those guys at the Lincoln Tunnel who takes your dough and doesn't know you from Adam. I didn't take attendance. Didn't lecture. Didn't grade down for stupidity. What I did was tend a potentially vicious herd and keep them moving. I still wore my suits, though. Why I did that I don't know. Maybe I wanted to be ready for the undertaker if one of my charges got the bright idea to pig-stick a professor. I wouldn't call myself a complete burn-out, but I was toasted.

Approaching my office, I could see that no light was on. That was good. That way, I would not have to chit and chat with two losers. It was hard to be around Biden and Bath without slamming them with the truth, which was that their days here were numbered. On my way, I passed the student restroom, which was on the mostly otherwise dark floor. There was not a working faculty restroom. I remembered Randle complaining about that fact.

"It's bad enough that I have to be in the same classroom with them. Now I have to piss with them," he'd said.

"Better to just piss on them, huh?" I had said, being witty.

Randle had not laughed. Probably because he thought I was right. In the student can were dope-smokers, most of grass of a questionable quality, who at times made the air thick enough to give you a buzz when you were taking a leak. The smoke did help to cover the odor of shit. The only good thing about the john was the graffiti, some of which was directed at me— BURY THE BASTERD BUCERONI—with only two mizpellings.

Inside my office, I encountered young Professor Biden, sitting in the dark. This was not good. Sitting in the dark was a sign of mental disturbance. I was not in the mood to ferret out what was disturbing him. Although I could guess. It was one thing to be old, over the hill, and on the way out of a job. It was another to be shit-canned when young. I remembered lending my ear to Walt Brzenk's whinings. I hadn't liked that then; I wouldn't like it now.

Today was Tuesday. Biden was a Monday/Wednesday man. Something important must be occurring for a professor at the Urban U. to be at his job more than twice a week. I felt like reporting Biden to the union. We would not want such practices to become common.

"Biden, people will say we're in love," I said, starting off with humor. That was me, a joke a minute, a real funnyman.

Biden nodded but did not speak.

I walked to my desk. By Biden's desk, on the floor, was a green workout bag.

"You work out?"

"Remember I said I've just commenced running. It's, I never, but…." answered Biden, who went on with his explanation. It took him some time. He must not have a girlfriend to listen to his wordy words.

I glanced out the window at the old white man who was sitting on the toilet. I wondered what type of voice the old man had—high or low. That was the one tidbit I'd wormed out of Beef Patty. Maybe I was now staring at the guy who'd called in the death of Randle. That was comforting to know. If I died in my office, I could rest assured that the aging masturbator next door would contact the cops.

Biden continued to talk about running. He actually knew a thing or two. Me, I just put on my sneakers and ran. This guy had chapter and verse on shoes, clothes, diet, stretching—you name it, he knew it.

I glanced out the window again. The old man had moved to his bedroom. It was early, but I felt assured that the operators at 1-800-Call-n-Wank were on the job. The world of the Internet was great. It provided for all of one's needs. No matter how fucked up they were.

The phone rang. I got up from my desk. I picked up the phone. I recognized the voice of the caller. It was not a voice I wanted to hear.

"It's for you, it's someone disreputable," I said, talking loud enough for the caller to hear, then handing the phone to my colleague.

"Yes," said Biden into the phone.

"Yes," said Biden, getting red in the face.

"Yes, I can come there right now."

Biden hung up the phone. His hand was shaking.

"That was for me," said Biden.

"Really?" I said, immediately being not proud of myself for being a wiseass. Pick on someone your own size had been a lesson I'd learned from my old man. This guy had enough troubles; he didn't need me exercising my wit on him.

"Yes, I'm wanted downstairs."

"You are?" I said, still in wiseass mode.

"Yes, I have to go there now."

I opened my desk drawer and removed a Don Tomas Corona from a leather case.

"I probably won't be back before you start teaching."

"OK."

"Good-bye."

"Good-bye," I said, cutting the cigar, then starting to gnaw on it.

Biden left the office.

I noted Biden had not told me the purpose of his meeting. I had recognized the voice of the caller as that of Dr. Stewart Bodner, the Chair of the English department at the main campus. Bodner was someone I didn't like. I had known Bodner from my days in the Chemistry department. We'd served on committees together. Not hitting it off was a mild way to describe our relationship. He was to my mind a four-square jerk. And he was someone who had a reputation for giving junior faculty under his thumb a hard time. He and our Dean would hit it off. Two peas in a pod.

I took out my master key. I looked out the window. The old white man was still in his bedroom. He was using a white towel to clean up the results of his efforts. What a place this was. I was glad I'd busted my ass to get a Ph.D. so I could be a prof and get to see such sights.

I opened Biden's desk drawer. I started to examine the contents. This I did to keep my knowledge base up to date. Curiosity was one of my character traits. So was a criminal streak, as witnessed by this bit of breaking and entering.

Chapter Twenty-Three

. . . .

I read through the messages that Biden had picked up that very day. I didn't use rubber gloves while I was doing this, which meant if the Dean fingerprinted me, I'd be in hot water. I just wanted to know what there was to be known. No harm in that. Which is what criminals always think.

One was from the Dean, who wanted to 'consult' with him. That would be a cheery meeting. Consultation would be a laying on by the Dean of his power in an attempt to scare the shit out of Biden. It wouldn't take much to do that. This was one nervous guy. There was another message from Bodner, informing Bath he would be "on" the Brooklyn campus for a "visitation" and would call Biden. This sounded like an angel would be descending, which was kinda true, only Bodner was a fallen angel, more like a demon, really. I wondered if I had messages in my mailbox and decided to retrieve my mail. What I had told Mac was true. I don't check my mail very often. Candy gets on my ass about that. What was to check? If the Dean truly wanted something, he'd e-mail me. Hard to avoid an e-mail.

I thought of Randle, whose life was still on display in the hallway; the janitors had not yet made their way up here. I would bet myself a bad lunch from Fat Harry's that the Dean had been given orders from the main campus to nail Randle for anything from being a sexual predator to leaving pee-stains on his pants. Scenarios like Randle's were played out in every college in the country with old professors passed by time and trends, nasty students making academic careers out of getting over, and not-very-bright Deans, VPs, and Provosts with agendas for the faculty. This was the underbelly of academia. Every organization had its bad side, and college administrators were, to my mind, largely scumchickens who couldn't cut it in the classroom or with publications, so they latched onto being an administrator. The Dean was a good example. Plus, he kept on Winston Wiant, who was a perfect companion for him. I knew for a fact that Wiant had the goods on all of the faculty and it probably hadn't taken him long to bring his boss up to speed with dirt about Randle, everything from what did and did not get published to sexual habits and even personal hygiene. A real sweetheart, Wiant, the Dean's right-hand man.

A thought forced itself to the front of my mind. Randle had been killed. And maybe another professor was the killer. That was what I needed to keep my mind on. The motive was job security. Biden was now in Randle's seat. Before I started my world-class investigation, should I warn Biden? I paused. This was a hard matter to bring up with a colleague. How could I tell Biden not to eat or drink anything because a chemical killer was on the loose? My eyes focused on Biden's running bag. Inside was a water bottle. Bath could easily load up the bottle with a drug, pass off the death as a Jim Fixx occurrence. I decided to put a hold on my warning to Biden until I talked to Candy. Which was largely the way I dealt with important matters—think deeply, then talk to Candy, then do what she says to do. I believe that shifting responsibility is not a character flaw but a sign of my breadth of knowledge.

Chapter Twenty-Four

. . . .

The phone rang. I hesitated about answering it. Only bad things happen when you answer an office phone. A student wants to know something that's been explained about ten times in class. Or a higher-up wants to give someone a hard time. Randle was always being called. It'd been part of the campaign against him.

I answered the phone.

Shit.

The Dean wanted to see me.

"You do?" I said. "Right now?"

The answer was in the affirmative.

"I'll be there later," I replied.

There'd been some trouble down at the college. The trouble had something to do with the One-Percenters, the Seoul Brothers, the Latin Monarchs, and Nastasha Natooska. This was old news. I knew the cause of all of this trouble. Right now, if I wanted, I could give him a good slap on the noggin.

I set out to talk to an administrator.

Chapter Twenty-Five

• •

"Professor, Natasha Natooska is now in the class of Professor McClure, is that not correct?" said the short, un-slim, still unsmiling Dean. This guy was a piece of work. Maybe I should give him a good tickling just to lighten him up. Then again, maybe not.

His office still smelled musty, which I was beginning to suspect came from him. The only good point was that Wiant wasn't there. I'd asked why. I'd been told Dr. Wiant was ill. How would anyone be able to tell? He was already a pasty-face, so unless he had a case of jaundice, he would just look like his normal self, which was looking like hell warmed over. Which was an expression my mother had used, the meaning of which I could not, even after she'd passed, ever determine.

"Kinda," I said, smiling

"Excuse me?" said the Dean.

"She's elusive. Professor McClure said it's hard to teach a movin' target." Which was true. Mac said her attendance record had set a new mark. And that when she did show up she expected him to fill her in about what she'd missed. She, too, was a piece of work.

"But she is on his roster, is she not?"

I looked at the Dean, who was wearing a gray suit. I had seen photos of Louis Farrakhan, who also wore suits. The Dean's suit was nicer than the suits of Louis Farrakhan, but I did not believe the Dean himself was nicer than Louis Farrakhan.

"Nice suit," I said, smiling at the Dean. I again sat in the small green plastic chair so the two of us were nearly at eye level. This meant the Dean's none-too-small behind was sitting on a pillow. I knew I was sitting on the Dean's hot seat, the one he used to bring faculty into line. Here, Dr. Rudolf Randle had sat and been forced to listen as the Dean added to his humiliation. His reward for maintaining some semblance of standards had been to be confronted by a cheating student who, not satisfied with being told the truth, had run for aid from a higher-up. The Dean had been only too willing to listen to Ms. Natooska as she wagged her evil, semi-literate tongue about her literature professor and his unfair ways. Seeing an opening, the Dean had no doubt put the idea of being sexually harassed into the student's so-called mind. Biden would also be placed here and have the shit scared out of him. What a sweetheart this Dean was.

"This meeting is not about my personal attire," said the Dean, still grinless.

"Then I won't say anything about your shoes," I said, taking a Corona from a leather case. I used my fancy-schmancy Davidoff cigar cutter to cut the cigar. I turned and flicked the slice into the Dean's garbage can. It hit dead center.

"Yes!" I exclaimed, raising both arms above my head.

I began to gnaw on the cigar.

The Dean cold-stared at me, but I was hard to stare down because of my sunglasses.

"Let us keep to the agenda," he said, his tone even.

"OK."

"Do you know what has happened to Ms. Natooska?" said the Dean.

"She won the school prize for the best job of plagiarism?" I said, smiling a winning smile at my supervisor.

"This is a serious matter."

"Plagiarism is a serious matter. It's in the Urban U. handbook, page 34, paragraph six, line..."

"Professor, please, she's been mutilated!"

"Well, that's a little harsh as a punishment for plagiarism."

"This has nothing to do with plagiarism!"

"Oh."

"Over the weekend, she was kidnapped as she got off a bus near her home, taken somewhere, and there... she had...'things' done to her."

"Unspeakable things?"

"Well, yes," said the Dean, looking uncomfortable. Administrators do not like discussion. Their idea of dialogue is their talking and professors listening. Give and take is not in their handbook for talking to faculty. We're supposed to sit here and be dumped on and like it.

"Then I'd better leave if we cannot speak of what was done to her," I said, starting to get up.

"No, no, I'll tell you, but this is in the very strictest confidence."

"My lips are very strictly sealed."

"She had something tattooed to her forehead," said the Dean.

"Something?"

The Dean took a deep breath. "She had a black swastika tattooed to her forehead. She had her tongue pierced and a swastika emblem attached. She also had her nose broken. Can you think of a reason why something like this would happen to her?"

I had a very good idea. I could fill the Dean in on who had set the gangs off. That I could do, but then I'd be led away in handcuffs.

"Mr. Norwood told me...."

"Who?" said the Dean.

"Lester."

"I don't know anyone of...."

"Beef Patty."

"Oh, him."

"Well, Mr. 'Patty' told me our Ms. Natooska had insulted blacks, Koreans and Dominicans in one e-mail. It was an effort worthy of the attention of Guinness."

"What shall be done?" asked the Dean.

"Was she kidnapped from here?" I said.

"No," said the Dean, looking uneasy from being questioned.

"We have a tattoo parlor here?"

"No."

"What's all this have to do with us?"

"She used her school e-mail address to insult some of our students. I fear retaliation," said the Dean.

"By whom?"

"You know very well by whom! You know all about the One-Percenters, the Seoul Brothers, and the Latin Monarchs and how every action causes a reaction," said the Dean, his high voice rising.

"Next thing you'll be tellin' me that the Mafia exists."

"This is no time for your infantile jokes," said the Dean.

"My jokes are not infantile; they're adolescent."

"Whatever they are, they're inappropriate. We need to take action."

"No, we don't," I said.

"Why not?"

"What's today's date?"

The Dean gave me the date, grudgingly.

"Next week is spring vacation. The college closes down for ten days. By the time it re-opens, all of this will be old news. A mutilation will be replaced by somethin' worse."

"Do you really think so?"

"I speak with unforked tongue."

"Maybe you're right," said the Dean.

"This meeting over?"

"Yes, I believe it is."

I stood up. I looked down at the Dean.

"Thank you for coming in," he said, not rising.

"Why question me and not Professor McClure?" I asked.

"He is not reliable," the Dean said, the words coming out quickly. If there was anyone he hated more than me, it was Mac, who never missed a chance to zing the Dean with a good one.

"And I am?"

"It's a matter of degree."

"Oh."

"This meeting is now concluded," said the Dean, looking down at his desk at some papers. I did not truly believe the papers were of significant importance. I suspected he wanted me to leave the premises.

I went to the door, opened it, left it standing open. I walked away from the safe haven of the Dean's office, back into the Wild West. The Dean had told me what I wanted to know. Randle was partially revenged. The "tight-assed little Russian gal" had gotten the attentions of the gangs. I was walking, so it was hard to pat myself on the back. I'd wait until I was alone in my office.

Chapter Twenty-Six

• •

I headed toward the elevator. Then I recalled my mailbox mission. I turned to the left. This was still a cared-for area. So, looked at from afar, one would conclude that the Dean and the U.S. Mail got attention. As for the rest of the school, it could just decay.

Standing in the mailroom doorway was McClure, who looked like an ad for *GQ*. Added to his expensive clothes were a golden tan and brushed-back, thick blonde hair. I reminded myself to check with McClure about what it was that he ate. Maybe he and Beef Patty shared dietary tips, this done to give them stamina to do what they shouldn't be doing. One point was interesting. Mac had been told that black coeds were strictly hands-off, this done by the One-Percenters, while Beef Patty was allowed to be an equal-opportunity sex machine. In fact, he had more white girls than black.

"I left a message in your mailbox," interrupted Dr. Stewart Bodner. I hadn't seen him; he was behind Mac.

The short, skinny English department Chair was wearing a very black suit, a very white shirt, a very narrow, very black tie, all of which led to a very thin face whose coloring tended toward the very pasty. He didn't look good. He looked like Winston Wiant, which was looking like the dead. Maybe he and Wiant were related.

"The Undertaker is a has-been," said McClure to Bodner. Mac had his serious face on.

"What?" said Bodner, looking wary. He was all too aware of how Mac liked to rag him.

Behind the chair was a short, curvaceous woman with red hair streaked with gray, wearing an Annie Hall outfit. She smiled at me and McClure, showing bright white teeth.

"Oh, I'm sorry," McClure continued, "I thought you were the Undertaker's manager. You're the expectorate image of Paul Bearer."

"You're not funny, you know," said Bodner, his voice dripping icicles. If a voice could kill, Mac would be a dead man.

"Hey, you're not tall, but do I insult you? I bet you don't even know who The Rock is," said McClure.

"Do I care?" said the department Chair.

"His book went to number two on the *New York Times* bestseller list. Last time I checked, your epic tome *Cross-Cultural Queer Theory and the Toilet of Aphra Behn* never rose with a bullet. In fact, it never rose at all, it sank like a dead duck, went under with nary a quack," said McClure.

The woman behind the department Chair covered her full red lips to stop from laughing.

"I left you a message, which...."

"Well, why didn't you just say so, instead of coming down here dressed like Paul Bearer and gettin' us all discombobulated?" said McClure.

"You are tiresome," said Bodner.

"I'm tiresome? Here you're supposed to be a hip twenty-first century guy and we all know that hip twenty-first century guys use e-mail for messages. Even half-hip twentieth-century guys use voice-mail. But here you, you leave a message in a mailbox, strictly Age of Magellan. Why didn't you put your message in a bottle and float it down the Gowanus?"

McClure had nothing to fear from his department Chair. Bodner had passively listened to the assault on McClure from the female faction of the department and gone along with the big blonde man's banishment. McClure knew his ticket back to the main campus lay higher up the administrative food chain. It would be a Provost who would decide that McClure's stature as a scholar outweighed his sexual "tastes." Colleges had their own sense of values, and an impressive publication record covered a great number of sins and made forgiveness possible. I thought this policy was for the birds. Who really cares about some book that only other scholars read? There was a job to be done, and it was called teaching. Only, to be fair, I had recently fallen down in that area. Since Dom's demise, I couldn't seem to get myself to really teach. Now, all I did was shepherd.

Bodner tried to talk to me. He found that hard going.

"The message informs you that you've been named the replacement for Dr. Randle on the Appointments Committee and…."

"Demand a recount!" said McClure, laughing loudly.

"…next week is the first…."

"Have the results come in from upstate? What about the hanging chards? Are they hung?" said Mac.

Trying not to laugh wasn't easy.

"…meeting. I'll e-mail you the precise time." Bodner finished and looked up at Mac, a cold hatred in his dead, dark eyes.

Bodner walked away. The woman stayed behind.

"Are you going to be in your office?" Annie Porter said to me.

"Yes."

"I'll see you in a bit."

"He does look like Paul Bearer, you know," put in McClure.

"I know," said Annie Porter, who smiled at him. She then walked away, following her Chair, who was already out of sight.

I entered the mailroom, which was like a strange land. I moved a blue plastic trash can close to my cluttered mailbox. I "read" my mail, quickly depositing all of it in the trash can. I had been seen doing this once by a professor about to retire. I'd given my reasons. Next time I saw him, he was beaming broadly as he ash-canned his mail.

"So that's how you treat the college's essential correspondence," said McClure, who came over and stood next to me.

"I took a speed-dumping course in grad school."

"Must've aced it," said McClure.

"I was top of the class. Incidentally, that was a good job you did back there with Bodner. That's one vote less you'll have on your side in the English department."

"He wouldn't vote for me to come back even if I black-painted his suits myself. Besides, I'm learning to like it here."

"You have no English major students to hang on your every word," I said.

"That's true, but I'm immersed in my writing." He went on for a while about what he was doing. Most of it—like 99 percent of it—was Greek to me.

"What will it take for you to get back to the main campus, if you so desire?" I asked.

"Intervention by a Provost or VP. Bodner is pure, 100-percent chicken shit. He couldn't get me back on his own if he did try."

"So I will have the pleasure of your company again next year?" I said, which was OK with me. I liked being with Mac, even if I had to divide my mind between liking him and disliking his sexcapades.

"That you will and, in two weeks, I'll be your guest for the Flatbush 5."

"Let me tell you about the hills."

McClure's laugh was loud in the small mailroom.

He left, and I went on practicing avoidance by discarding what the college had sent me. On the one hand this was immature, on the other hand it was childish, but whatever it was it worked, for if someone wanted me they used e-mail or called. Who knows what I got free of with this practice? Most college missives would be better placed in the men's can on a roll. At least that's my humble view. Take it for what it's worth.

Chapter Twenty-Seven

. . . .

I decided to check my attire. I entered the student restroom on my floor, which had two kinds of roaches. Lucky for me, at this point in the day there were no students lighting up, and nothing scurried as I walked in. It was the type of place that reminded me of a ditty: "There were spirochetes on the toilet seats." Those words of wisdom were from the john on the student cafeteria floor and probably had the ring of truth to them.

I walked over to the sink which had been washed sometime, but I was not sure when. Or with what or by whom. The restroom smelled of urine. One toilet was full of unflushed feces. I made a point of holding it until I could go to Fat Harry's, whose restroom was not clean but was at least not filthy. There's a lot to be learned about civilization by going to a john. At our place, here was the real deal, what we really were. Which was a shit hole.

I washed my hands. I rubbed my fingers over my teeth. I used water to slick back my black hair, which was thinning on top. I gave myself the once-over. I didn't really look like a guy who'd kill his best friend and his crippled sister, but looks can be deceiving. And I hoped I was deceptive as hell. I didn't want one of those midnight knocks at the door from New York's finest who had a thing or two to go over with me. That would be the end of me. At some point, I'd have to face the music for what I'd done.

I just hoped Jesus would give me four or five minutes to explain why I'd turned into a killer. I'm sure I could win him over, smooth talker that I am.

Opening the door to my office, I noticed that Randle's life effects had been removed. That was a first. Trash removal was not usually done promptly at the Urban U. Randle himself could've been lying in the hall and the janitors would've ignored him, there being nothing in the union contract about getting rid of a corpse, even if it was a professor's. The only floor which approached cleanliness was that of the Dean. Which was good because I was beginning to have doubts about his own personal habits. The musty smell could just be rising from his person and filling the room.

Someone knocked at the door.

"Hello, Annie."

"Hello, this is my end-of-term visit," said Annie Porter, opening the door and then standing there.

"Come in," I said.

The short woman walked toward me. I could smell the shampoo she'd used on her red hair. She stood next to Bath's desk. Annie Porter was once more Professor Porter. Her stint as Assistant Dean had ended with her being shot in the ass, twice, by the wife of the former Dean. Annie had held onto her job as a professor. She'd been an art historian at our place but apparently that wasn't her real background, for she'd wrangled the job of English Composition Director. I didn't want to know how.

Annie Porter sat down at Bath's desk.

"So, you'll be giving the troops a pep talk?" I said, trying to get the conversation started. She wanted something or she wouldn't be here. It'd take a while but I would wait her out.

"I'll try," said Annie Porter, looking at the bare wall over my bare desk. She said nothing about that. Which was good. I still had enough sense of what a real prof should do to be just a bit more than unhappy with being found out that I wasn't pulling my weight.

"I got your e-mail about doing all of this by computer," I said, giving us something to talk about other than why R.V. Bucceroni was getting close to "Neglect of Duty" as a professor.

"What did you think of it?"

"Not much. I deleted it with haste," I said.

"Why? Each end of term, X number of essays have to be graded in a hurry, which results in a mad dash to get the grades out."

"And your computer program will avoid the rush?"

"Yes. By grading hundreds of essays in a nanosecond, maybe two. Like this," said Annie Porter, snapping her fingers. She was always like that. Confident. Knowing what she wanted. Which at one time was me. She hadn't cared that I was married. She set about to make us a couple and to cut Carmela out. Sad to say, I went along for the ride.

"And the faculty at the main campus, their gung is ho?"

"Of course."

"Could it be just possible because they don't want to get their literary critical mitts dirty by teaching composition?"

"Yes, but the idea still seems sound to me."

"Is it, now?"

"Oh, I recognize that tone," said Annie Porter, smiling at me. Her pink tongue seemed to stick in the gap between her front teeth. There had been a time when I had enjoyed seeing Annie Porter smile like that. I had seen too much of that smile. Annie Porter and I had been doing more than smiling at one another when my family had been slammed out of existence. I fought off the memory. I focused on the present. Which was easier said than done. Annie was there in front of me like she had been before. It was hard to separate the past from the present. I read somewhere that if you can't deal logically with time then you're well on the way to the funny farm. I wondered if that was where I was headed. Also, I had a sneaking suspicion there wasn't a whole lot funny about a nuthouse.

"Educate me," I said, trying to focus on what she was saying...and stalling a bit to get back to the here and now.

"Grading essays is a programmable task. It's a waste of time to have faculty doing the job. The machine never gets tired. It's never biased," said Annie Porter, who sounded like she knew a thing or two.

"Not quite. I did some research. What happened was that during testing of the computer, human graders were used as a measuring stick. The computer had fed into it grammar and the length of paragraphs, and it knew when a writer was on topic. But the kicker was that the human graders were bullied into dumbing down." All of this was true. I'd spent some time getting the goods on this computer stuff. Even got on the phone with an old colleague who now worked for ETS. They were the ones with a real grading program. I thought theirs was crap also, but I didn't tell him that. To Annie, I would say what I believed.

"Well, not quite, the computer grades holistically, it doesn't get hung up on...."

"Coherence."

"You know what I mean," said Annie Porter.

"Yes. What this means is that the only real job an English professor does is now being totally fobbed off. On the main campus, over 75 percent of the comp classes are taught by trainees, which the department calls 'adjunct lecturers,' but you and I know these are underpaid grad students who know next to nothing about teaching writing or math or basic science," I said, getting into the argument.

"Some of them are fine tea...."

"No, they're not. They're MFAs or Ph.D. candidates who do this to pay the bills so they can become literary theorists or wow the crowd at a poetry slam. This computer crap is classic avoidance by professors from teachin' what they regard as 'bonehead English.'"

"But isn't that what you consider it to be? This is an interdisciplinary school, where even chemists are required to have writing assignments. Why not make the job easier?"

"Unlike Yale, we have to teach what comes through the door. The least we can do is to offer a human being as a professor, not a computer,"

I said, feeling guilty that I was not putting my money where my mouth was. I was talking a good fight with Annie, but it was mostly just to make contact with her. I didn't really have what it took anymore to be a real teacher. To do that, you have to like the students. It was as simple as that. It was what Mac was doing. When he wasn't screwing them, he was doing a bang-up, no pun intended, job of educating the sweaty masses. Me, I just saw them as someone who might kill me if I turned my back on them.

"Can we agree to disagree?"

"I hate talk like that. How about instead you admit you're wrong and I'm right and you give me five dollars as evidence of my rightness?" I said, a bit unhappy that this part of our conversation was coming to an end.

I leaned back in my chair. I could feel she had something else on her mind.

"Too bad about Rudy," said Annie Porter.

"The Notre Dame guy? He turned out OK, didn't he?" I said, switching into my wiseass defense.

"You know who I mean," said Annie Porter, not smiling.

"Oh, that Rudy."

"Wasn't he your colleague?"

"We didn't hit it off."

"Why?"

"He couldn't accept where he was and why he was here. I tried to give him some perspective so he could stop grinding his guts over the students. For some reason, we just didn't get on."

"Still, it's sad that he died. And died down here."

"Yeah, sad," I said. She didn't know the half of it. Randle hadn't died, he'd been pushed out of life, and I had better stop wasting my time debating with her about her own area and get back to solving crimes.

"I wanted to talk to you about Jim," she said, finally getting to the point.

Jim was Jim McDougal, her current boyfriend, a good guy I'd known for years.

"Randle…Rudy didn't like Jim," I said.

"I know, that's what I want to talk about. Rudy'd talked to some people in the department. The plan was to move Jim down here. All of this high-level maneuvering was, in Rudy's mind, to be his ticket back to the main campus," said Annie Porter.

"I knew about that plan."

"How?"

"Who cares 'how'? Besides that, Randle was just whistlin' in the dark. No one at the main campus wanted him back. Telling him that resulted in our not gettin' along," I said, feeling my temperature rise.

"Bodner is such a weasel."

"Please, I've known some weasels who're much nicer."

"What about the charges against Rudy?"

"Trumped up."

"So you think those charges were phoney?"

"What I think is that the Dean also wants to get his short, little suit-wearing self back to the main campus and that Ms. Nastooska, our harassee, came in complainin' about Randle and the Dean put a bee in her bonnet."

"Really?"

"Really. It's all there, in black and white, in chapter two of the administrator's guidebook—How to Screw the Faculty."

"I don't want Jim to come down here," said Annie, her voice dropping. She stared at me with her light green eyes.

"Because it's the end of the line?" I said.

I could see Annie Porter's eyes moisten. I didn't like to see that. At one time, she'd had a high opinion of me, or at least given me that impression. Not the sex thing but of me as a professor. Now, I wasn't what I was. I had Dom to thank for that. Of, course Dom was now residing in hell so I guess I won that little battle.

"Yes. The end of the line," she said.

"Anything I can do to help?"

"Try to get Biden another year."

"That won't be easy." And it wouldn't. Biden was a four-square loser. She was asking for the world.

"I know it won't."

"If Biden is here for one more year, that's one more year for Jim at the main campus."

"But what will stop Bodner from sending him down here next year?"

"There's an election next year."

"You runnin'?"

"No, I like being Director of Freshman English, but Jill Carmody, you remember her, don't you? She's going to run. She's more reasonable."

Annie Porter paused. "I'm asking for your help. I don't like doing this."

"You and Jim, you two happy?"

"For who we are and when we are, we're good for one another."

I hate talk like that. What the fuck did that mean? Sounded like a greeting card that comes in a ten-dollar card with ten-cent sentiments.

"I'll do my best," I said, not knowing quite how to respond to her explanation of her and Jim.

"I'm sure you will," said Annie Porter. She stood up and walked quickly toward me, who did not get up. She kissed me on the cheek and left the room. I sat at my desk. I could smell that Annie Porter had been in the office. I could feel where she had kissed me. I touched the spot. Jim McDougal was a good guy. Jim McDougal was a good teacher. Jim McDougal wrote articles that actually said something about literature. Mac told me they were no good. He'd showed me one of them. I could understand it, that's probably why it was no good.

I opened the blinds to the office window. The old white man was in his bedroom. He was working on a camera. Jim McDougal lived with Annie Porter. I had been with Annie Porter in the wrong time and in the wrong place. Doing the wrong thing. Three wrongs don't make a right. Truer words were never spake, as my father used to say. He was always murdering the king's English just to get my mother's goat. He teased her pretty good. He was a real half and half, my father. Half-killer, half-good father. I was now a killer, so what was I good at? I gave some thought to the old man across the street and what he might have seen. Maybe I'd pay him a visit.

I checked my watch. It was that time. I gathered my teaching tools, which consisted of one piece of chalk and a stack of study questions. I'd sit there at my desk, plodding through the questions while the students looked every which way but at me. There'd be talking while I was talking, more than a few texters. A lot would come late to class. Some would sleep. What the fuck did I care?

I got up, I walked to the door, I hit the lights. I went to go do what the City paid me for. Kinda.

Chapter Twenty-Eight

. . . .

As I waited for the elevator, my mind drifted to thoughts of Annie Porter. My memory engaged. Guilt bore in. Sometimes I hate my mind. That's the trouble with having one, sometimes it can take you over and push you around in terms of time. Here I was, with a shitload of problems in the present and my mind was doing a rehash. Until I got what I did with Annie under control, I was going to have trouble functioning.

The hallway I was in smelled to high heaven. Dope, sweat, god knows what filled my large nose. I thought about holding my breath until I was outside.

The elevator door opened. Detective Pat Reagan got off. He was just about the last person on earth that I wanted to see. I wasn't really ready for a line of questioning which would require quick and convincing lying on my part. Reagan always acted like he was my friend but that was just a good cop/bad cop scenario. The bottom line was that Randle had been murdered and that there was a good chance the murder weapon could be traced to the prince of the Urban U., namely me. I'd have to be on my guard or he'd nail me for an inconsistency.

"Got a minute, Prof?" This was the way he always began our "sessions": polite, friendly, like it was the two of us against the world of crime.

"Sure," I said, trying to sound normal, which is usually when you sound guilty as hell. I wiped out the past, got a line on the present, where I was coming into the line of fire. I was an easy target. A good 250 pounds of guilty Italian.

"Nobody's around. We can talk here, can't we?" said the detective who smiled at me, showing crooked but white teeth.

"Yes, we can."

"So, anyway, I got a report from the ME. There was somethin' in this Randle which shouldn't've been there." This was not good news.

"There was?" I said, keeping my voice calm while my heart took off.

"Yeah, I got it written down, it's got a funny name. Here it is, it's an alkahoid, I think that's how you say it." He'd taken out a pair of glasses, put them on, removed a small piece of paper from his jacket pocket. From that he had read. Slowly.

"Alkaloid," I said, knowing that I was in for it now.

"Oh," said the detective.

There was a pause. Maybe he was waiting for me to volunteer something. If that was the case, then he was out of luck. I was strictly on the defensive and would answer what I was asked.

"There's somethin' goin' on down here," said Reagan.

"Maybe not. Maybe someone used it for certain health problems," I said, deciding on the spot not to give Reagan my theory about Bath. Which was probably a mistake, me not being the world's greatest on-the-spot thinker and doer. I was taking a chance, but I could feel trouble tightening its grip on me. Sometimes, I feel like I'm a lightning rod.

"Like?" This was an open-ended question. I'd have to be careful or I'd stumble and throw the spotlight on me and what I knew.

"Randle once told me he used scopolamine to avoid being seasick. Maybe that's it," I said, offering a plausible explanation which wasn't bad for a shoot-from-the-hip response.

"That takes a load off my mind. I'll run that by the ME. Say the name again."

I did. "One less loose end?" I said, hoping I was right and that I'd given myself an out.

"Yeah, you heard about this Natooska broad?"

"Yes." Here was another area that wasn't so good for me. It'd been little me who'd set the gangs out to take care of her. Was that a crime? Probably.

"Whatta you think?"

"She asked for it?" I'd better be careful with answers like that. No matter what she really was, in the eyes of the law, she was now a victim.

"More than that. Someone's tryin' to shut someone up without killin' her." I could not see where he was going with that.

"I think it may have been payback time."

"For what?"

"The Dean told me about some e-mail she wrote that managed to insult mostly everyone down here and that got routed to the wrong addresses," I said, switching my lying machine into high. This would take some skill for the ground ahead was full of land mines which could blow my lie apart.

"More fuckin' loose ends. Maybe someone let the gangs do the dirty work for them."

"Maybe."

"Hey, I got to go. Let's keep all this stuff to just you and me. My captain, he don't like long drawn-out cases, he likes them bing-bang-boom and onto the next one. Most of this is me playin' around with loose ends. You think this is gonna set off the gangs?" he said, looking closely at me.

"No," I said, going back to short-and-sweet mode. This was the best plan of attack/defense I could think of right now.

"Why?"

"It's almost spring vacation. Everyone will go separate ways," I said, trying to steer him off course. I liked Reagan, but he was a cop and he was now talking to the guilty party.

"Hope you're right. I gotta see this Russian girl's father, he's bustin' my balls."

"You might point out to him that his daughter's foul mouth e-mail doesn't give her, and him, a leg to stand on," I said, hoping this sounded reasonable.

"You're probably right, Prof."

"I hope so."

"OK, I gotta run. I hope I can make this Russian see the light."

"I'm sure you can."

"You keep in touch, you talk only to me, OK? Nothin' else to nobody."

"Got you."

We shook hands. The detective got on an elevator going down. I took the stairs. I made my way slowly down to the first floor. The stairway smelled like hashish. Some student had got a hold of the real stuff. I felt like breathing in deeply and giving myself a buzz, but that would be a bad idea. I needed to keep my faculties, limited though they were, as sharp as possible.

I thought about the lie I had fed Reagan.

Scopolamine had been named after Giovanni Scopoli, a hard-working Italian, one who no doubt did not kill his best friend, cause the murder of a cripple, set off gangs to rough up a "tight-assed Russian girl" and lie about what he knew. Maybe that's why he was a success.

Chapter Twenty-Nine

· ·

I had decided to work out. Candy hadn't come in. Odd. She hadn't called. Also odd. I wasn't a big fan of "odd." I like to keep my ducks in a row, not that Candy Dyer was a duck or anything.

Before I stepped away from my place of work, I looked both ways, this to give me a head's up about any bad-mouthing bullies. I was ready for them. I was in a mood to let out a little aggression. This time, I wouldn't need J.P. and Nikki to back me up or even the odds, I'd take out the street punks myself. This I said to boost my ego. The fact is that punching out a punk is taking a considerable chance. Down he might go from my powerful Batman assault but instead of saying "uncle" he'd probably take out a pistol and blow a hole into my hefty 250.

A lot was racing in my mind. I'd not told Reagan my suspicions; I'd given an out for Randle's death. Next time we talked, the cop would remember that. I would have to get on task with what I'd said earlier. He no doubt kept notes and was reading from a script which probably had for a title: Bucceroni!

I needed to talk to Candy, but her cell was off. She was always one to put my worrying into perspective, give it a context, show me where I was right and where I was wrong. Although, to be fair, last time out she did not see Dom coming, either.

I put my hand in the left pocket of my pants. My thick fingers closed on an adjustable wrench. I wondered if the professors at Harvard carried adjustable wrenches as weapons.

Behind me was movement. I got a good hold of the wrench.

I turned quickly, ready to take on whoever was there.

"Hello, Lester."

"Hi Prof, can't talk…got to go upstairs," said the big man, wheezing out the words. His dark blue uniform shirt was sweated dark at the armpits.

"Trouble?"

"Sounds like it. J.P. straightin' out some black kid upstairs." That was not an unusual occurrence. J.P. laid down the law about a lot of things and, unlike the law, he delivered justice on the spot. It was usually about drugs, but he'd also warned off the black girls about getting it on with Mac. Both of these were good ideas, it's just that his methods of enforcement were a tad violent.

"You have to go?"

"The Dean he called me. I don' want to get on his bad side," said Beef Patty.

"Only side he has."

"That true," said Beef Patty, laughing. I actually liked the big man. He had his bad side, as did Mac, but he was one of the few around the place that could be trusted. He was the guy who'd finally put me on the straight path about Dom.

"Good luck."

The big black security guard left the lobby, moving toward the elevators.

I left the college, crossed the Street. No street citizens seeking donations accosted me. No street walkers offered their services. No punks threatened my person. I passed Fat Harry's corner deli, which was busier than usual with students who had apparently avoided the college's cafeteria food to take a dietary chance on the large man's greasy platters. The other possibility was that word had gone out that the One-Percenters were in operation. No one at the college who was in his or her right mind crossed J.P. Carlisle and his gang. Once J.P. was on the warpath, the best place to be was elsewhere. The city should hire J.P. when they were gentrifying, he'd take out the drug-peddlers real quick.

I began my journey. I didn't get far.

Standing at the corner were five young men, all Asian, all of them wearing black slacks, white shirts, narrow black ties, and black wing tips, which I suspected as being steel-reinforced and meant to do damage to the unprotected privates of an incoming enemy. All of them were smoking. These were the Seoul Brothers, rival to the One-Percenters, and the two gangs were heading for a final showdown. I hoped I wasn't in the middle when that went down.

I felt the need for a smoke, myself.

"Hello, Professor," said the leader of the pack.

"Hello, Jim, you men out on the town?"

"Yes, we are 'out on the town'," said Jimmy Fisheyes, who laughed. It was not a particularly happy laugh. It was like he was listening to a professor who thought he was funny.

"Say, Professor, might I speak with you?" said Jimmy Fisheyes. The other four moved away, giving me and my student some street space. They did so on the basis of a nod from their leader. They were well trained.

"Sure."

"You have some ability to gain respect from others," said Jimmy Fisheyes.

"I do?" I said, playing coy. That's me, Dr. Coy.

"That is what I know from my experience and from what I have heard."

"From whom?"

"Does it matter where I was told this?" said Jimmy Fisheyes, sounding a bit nettled that his point was being obscured.

"No, it doesn't," I said, hoping I hadn't pissed him off.

"How do you manage to gain respect without making people dislike you?" said Jimmy Fisheyes as he blew smoke my way.

"Be fair, be true to a set of principles," I said, sounding a bit like John Wayne and wondering why I was having this conversation.

"Professor, I was in the service, the army, and there I learned a great deal. I was a sergeant," he said. That was no doubt where he'd learned his discipline, plus a few tips on how to kill people.

"What was it like to be your age and to have such power?" I said, aware of how stilted my speech was becoming.

"It was a job. It had its good points and its bad."

"And the bad were?"

"Grunts who were careless."

"They could get you killed, right?"

"Right."

"It is hard to control others."

"You can't 'control' them, you have to get them to do what they can do."

"I will remember that."

The conversation waned. I had nothing to say to this young man, and I hoped he wouldn't get threatening and make me kill him. That might get me a letter in my personnel file.

"A nice night," I said, checking my watch.

Jimmy Fisheyes ignored the hint.

"Yes. My uncle, he said he knows you."

"Yes, we've talked. He's a fine man."

I had met Mr. Soo, the new owner of the liquor store on the Street across from the college, at Fat Harry's.

"Professor, I would like you to meet someone," Fat Harry had said.

"Yes?" I'd said, looking at the short, balding Asian who was standing next to the very large, Greek owner of the corner deli. Fat Harry had a moist forearm resting on the shoulder of the short, non-sweating Korean.

"This is Mr. Soo, Jimmy's uncle. He will soon be reopening the store next door."

"As a gun shop?" I said, striking a light note, using humor as an opener.

"No, no, not that," said Mr. Soo.

"There's a lot of demand for guns in Brooklyn, you could make a fortune," I said.

"I will reopen the liquor store."

"There's also a lot of demand for that, of course some of the demand isn't completely human."

"I not understand."

"He means that some of your customers will be bums," said Fat Harry.

"What 'bums'?" asked Mr. Soo.

"Drunks, men who do not work, low-lifes, bad people, Brooklynites," I put in.

"I take care of them," said Mr. Soo, pulling up his Hawaiian shirt, exposing the butt of a considerable pistol. This guy was ready, he had that right. I wonder how much of Broolkyn is like that. Last week, some Haitian came into a chicken grill down the street from Harry's, pulled a gun, demanded money from the customers. He got shot five times by four different guns. The "customers" were also carriers of weapons.

Fat Harry rubbed a fat hand over his fleshy face.

"You will be a success in Brooklyn," I said.

"I work hard all the time," said Mr. Soo.

I looked closely at Mr. Soo, wondering if he would go in for pornography as had his predecessor. His name had been Dim Pang, and he'd ended up on the roof of his own building, sliced up and red dead. That should've been the tip-off that it was Dom doing all of the killing but I didn't read the clue.

"Phirripines?" said Mr. Soo, pointing at my right arm.

"What?" said Fat Harry.

"Phirripines," said Mr. Soo, touching me on my tattoo.

"No, Bay Ridge. Third Avenue. It was done by a guy named Bennie 'Bam-Bam' Bongolan, the bam-bam on account of his being a boxer at one time. You been to the Phillipines?" I said.

"Four year I work there. In Manila, you know Manila?"

"No, never been there...."

"The professor was not in the army," put in Fat Harry.

"I was in army," added Mr. Soo. "I like army, my nephew was in army."

I drank my coffee. I knew what Mr. Soo's nephew was now into.

"My brother, he do work like that," said Mr.Soo, running a finger around the tattoo.

"Did or do?"

"He still do it, I have card. Here. You take."

I took the card from Mr. Soo. The brother of the liquor store owner had set up shop in Brooklyn. A Korean tattoo artist trained in the Philippines. He had a great future ahead of him.

"I wish you and your brother well."

"Thank you," said Mr. Soo.

"My uncle, he used to 'raise hell' in the Philippines," said Jimmy Fisheyes.

"Well, that's better than hangin' out, talking to friends about the books you should be reading," I said, regretting the words as soon as they escaped my mouth.

Jimmy Fisheyes did not laugh. My quick wit had forced me into an error. This kid, like J.P., had a high opinion of himself, took himself dead seriously. Any insult would not be taken kindly.

"This is not all we do."

"It isn't?"

"No, it isn't," said Jimmy Fisheyes, who stared at me with his black eyes.

My left hand closed on the adjustable wrench in my pocket. He was close enough that I could clip him. What I would then do about the other four I did not know. Maybe I'd scream for help, which was a four letter word which got you nothing in Brooklyn.

It would be bad publicity for the college if I killed one of the students, but given a choice, me or Fisheyes, I would sacrifice public relations. I had my standards.

When I had first come to the downtown campus, I'd regarded the gangs as clowns, as a sort of road-show *West Side Story.* I had learned to change that first impression. Jimmy Fisheyes and J.P. Carlisle were not jokes but were to be reckoned with.

"That's good."

"We take, as you say, 'no shit from anyone.'"

"That is also good."

"We not a joke. The Seoul Brothers, we the real thing," said Jimmy Fisheyes, continuing, talking faster, his voice getting higher.

The slightly ridiculous formality of Jimmy F's use of language had been erased. What was left was anger in the form of scrambled language. There would have to be a focal point of the anger, a target, and I fit that bill.

"So, Jim, how are your studies going?" I said, cleverly changing the subject. That was me, a clever one.

"Not well. Professor Biden, he is a very young man to be a professor."

"Is he?"

"Yes. I found you to be a good professor. I wish I was in Dr. McClure's group."

"It was an arbitrary division of the classes that was made."

"I know, but would you ask Dr. McClure if I can be in his class?" said Jimmy Fisheyes.

"Will do, Jim. I always enjoyed having you in class."

Jimmy Fisheyes and I shook hands. I used my right hand. I walked off into the streets of Brooklyn. Jimmy Fisheyes rejoined the other members of the Seoul Brothers on the corner.

I kept my left hand on the wrench while I walked.

Chapter Thirty

• •

I headed toward the Brooklyn Bridge, which was a pretty good hike from the Urban U. The street traffic slowly changed from crummy to snazzy. Brooklyn used to be an outpost, a punch line in a joke. It still could get you, though; all you needed to do was read the newspapers. When it came to crime, Brooklyn headed the list. Last week, some guy was at a McDonald's, ordering himself a burger. Three other guys came in, saw the burger orderer, shot him once before he could wrap his tongue around what beef there was in his burger. He ran out the side door and made it to the street, where they came at him again. Five shots, three hits, so he goes down and rolls away from them. No cops were around; they probably didn't like the food. A month later, just out of the hospital, the guy returned, but not for a Big Mac. He put a hand in his pocket, pretended he had a gun, and screamed at the server that Mickey D's hadn't protected him. The server saw he had no gun, told him to blow, the guy made for the front door where an off-duty didn't see he was pulling a robbery armed with fingers and shot him in the head. This time, he died. You can't make this stuff up.

Times had changed for the better, but the borough still had its moments.

As I walked along, I thought I would have to go to the main campus to sit on the council of a review committee chaired by Bodner. The committee would be a tribunal, a kangaroo court. Biden had little chance of surviving. He was like Randle, an academic, unwanted, hung out to dry. I quit thinking about Biden. I'd promised Annie Porter to help. How the hell I'd manage that I hadn't a clue.

I arrived at my destination, which was where I worked out.

Soon I was up the stairs and inside the "Spa." At one time, this had been a grunt and groan weight-banging place named Lou's for largely large men like me. I did some heavy lifting then, pushed a lot of iron around, making myself bigger than nature had made me, moving me close to 300 pounds. Things were different now. I ran, which kept my weight down to a svelte 250 pounds of blue twisted steel.

A trainer walked over to me. The trainer's name was Brad. Brad was taller than me; he was also younger and had all of his hair. Having a trainer was part of the Spa's appeal, for a trainer was included in the price. At Lou's, no one had a trainer, the lifters had been on their own. We'd needed no trainers.

"What're you doing tonight?" said Brad, smiling, showing even, white teeth which complemented his fair outlook.

"You mean, am I goin' out on the town?" I replied, being witty as hell.

"No, what are you going to do in here?"

"Get fit as a fiddle?"

"Which part of your 'fiddle' are you going to work on?

"Biceps, triceps, kneecaps."

"Stretch first. Thirty minutes on the bike. Then see me."

"Yes, sir," I said, snapping out a crisp salute.

Brad smiled slightly, then walked away with a spring in his step.

Springlessly, I walked to the stretch machine. I settled in. I cranked my legs apart to an angle of 60 degrees. This I held for 30 seconds. Then, I opened up to 65 degrees. I leaned forward and grabbed the horizontal handle on the stretch machine. I looked around the exercise room as I stretched. All I could see were tight buns, cut biceps, and six-pack stomachs.

I decided I hated the young. It would be a good idea to round them up, then take them to a secluded place and hit them in their ganobbins with large, knotty sticks. Which would reduce them to mush.

At the Airdyne, I punched in a 30-minute program. All around me were Stairmasters, rowing machines, treadmills, free runners and the like, and on all of them were young men and women who made more money in a morning than I did in a year. I pedaled the Airdyne ten miles in 26 minutes and 40 seconds. I was proud of myself.

"I pedaled ten miles in 26 minutes and 39 seconds," I said to my trainer. Lying. Showing that I was a force to be reckoned with. Someone he should be happy to work with. A trainer's delight.

"Good for you," said Brad, who I suspected of being able to pedal much farther than ten miles in 26 minutes and 39 seconds. This guy was really fit. Probably lived in the gym.

"Here's my chart," I said.

"You're doing well," said Brad.

"Thank you."

"Have you given any thought to what I said about your smoking?"

"You mean your tellin' me I'm killing myself?" I said, giving what he'd said some thought. Cigars weren't good for me, but I liked them. Therefore, I ignored the warning on the label which predicted dire consequences if I lit up. I treated that warning the same way I handled the mail at the college. I was a man of danger, living on the edge.

"I don't think I was that harsh."

"Well, you were very harsh. My feelings were hurt."

"Are you quitting?"

"No."

"Why?"

"Life sucks."

"Well, OK, but why smoke?"

"What am I savin' myself for? Those happy days when I'm 75 and have to ask for help to empty my Depends?" Which was true. Life was short, go for it. That was my motto. I had other mottos but most of them used a lot of four-letter words.

"But smoking is…."

"You ever smoke a Bolivar Royal Corona?" I put in.

"No."

"A Partagas Series D No. 4?" Which was illegal but which I got from my Russian students. I no doubt could've requested an AK47 and they would have delivered that, too.

"I don't smoke."

"Well then, this conversation is goin' nowhere."

"What about your diet?" said Brad.

"It's fine."

"Cutting down on red meat?"

"Ever go to Peter Lugar's and eat red meat till your lips are blue?" Which I did, when I could afford to spend $50 for a porterhouse. I did like the place, though. It had great, snarly waiters. One time, I was there with Annie Porter. I was eating my second roll when my waiter comes over, taps me on the shoulder. "Don't eat the bread, ya look like an amateur" was his comment. Annie had laughed. I'd tipped him heavily for saying that.

"Not really," said Brad, looking like he was tiring of my comments.

"Well, I'm not really cuttin' down. Stuffin' myself would be more what I do." Which was true. Eating was what I did in my spare time and was another good reason for being a runner. Run, Eat, Eat, Run—that was my life.

"You won't get the results you want unless you monitor your diet. How about your drinking?" he said.

"Jack Daniels, you like that? Or maybe Jameson's Reserve?" Which were my favorite drinks. The Reserve had changed my mind about Irish whiskey, for it was smooth and went down real easy. That actually wasn't so good, since I tended to over-indulge. Hard to believe. But it was true. I drank too much. Made me forget. A lot to be said for something that can make you forget.

"Maybe before dinner."

"What about instead of dinner, or lunch, or with hash browns and eggs?"

"Shouldn't you start your workout?" said Brad, showing more signs of tiring of the conversation. And here I thought I was a hit. I guess not.

"OK."

I sat in the tricep machine. I'd switched to this from free weights on Brad's suggestion. I lifted the weight only with my triceps. I did not grimace or snarl. I did not bob my head. I did not twist my back to lift the weight. I was a good boy. I wondered if I were being photographed.

"Good form, Professor," said Brad, who was helping a young blonde woman. I felt like asking Brad and the young blonde woman to leave the premises. I was not sure I wanted to associate with those who did not smoke, eat red meat, and get seriously drunk. Who were such people and why did they think they were better than me? Even though I knew the answer to that question, I remained quietly indignant.

"Switch to biceps," said Brad, who wiped off the tricep machine before the young blonde woman sat down. I had wiped it down myself but he was probably looking for a tip. She looked like she had money. One of those.

I did a biceps set.

"You're very strong," said the young blonde woman, who now stood by the side of the bicep machine. Brad left to help another Spa member. The young blonde was a real looker, although she wasn't quite in Candy's league. Of course, to my mind, Candy was in a league all of her own.

"I smoke, I eat red meat, I drink Jack Daniels," I said, looking stern.

The young blonde laughed. It was a young blonde's laugh. I thought I'd seen her before, which is what men quite often think when they see young blondes.

"I'm more sinister than Brad."

"Brad's gay," said the blonde.

"Well, that accounts for his not bein' very sinister."

"You're not gay, are you?"

"It would double my chances for a date on Saturday night," I said, borrowing from Woody Allen.

"Are you looking for a date on Saturday night?" she asked.

"No."

"What do you do on a Saturday night?"

"Wait for Sunday morning." Which was, sad to say, true. My weekends were long. That was why I'd been happy to spend time with Mac in Ridgewood/Ho-ho-kus. Running races filled time. I had time to fill.

"Brad said that you're a professor."

"He did?"

"Yes."

"Brad's gossipy, isn't he?"

"Are you sure you're not gay?"

"No, but I was jolly once."

"You're funny," said the blonde, laughing. She had bright white, even teeth which had probably cost a father a small fortune and full red lips which had probably given the self-same father many a sleepless night. I was sure I had seen her before.

"No, I'm just very sinister."

"I don't think so."

"Neither does Brad."

"I've seen you here before."

"I don't know if I like bein' ogled when I come to work out. This is a private Spa, you know. I should be safe in here."

"Are you sure about that?"

"Well, no."

"You're actually very funny. Older men are so much more interesting than men my age."

"That's me, old but interesting."

"See, Brad was right; you are a professor."

"Brad's a know-it-all."

"Where do you teach?"

"The Urban U. Our motto is 'We pass anyone.'" Which was a saying which fit me to a T. I didn't use the F for anybody. Randle had and all he got himself was an ulcer. Why bother? Pass them on: Next.

"I know someone who teaches there."

"You do?" I said, wondering who I knew who could know someone this good looking. Mac's name flashed into my mind. I looked at her. Too old. This was a woman, not a kid. I was about to ask her who she knew when I was interrupted.

"You done with your bicep set, Professor?" said Brad.

"Yes."

"It was nice to meet you," said the blonde, extending her hand.

"It was nice to meet you," I said, feeling her hand small and smooth inside my large mitt.

She was something, but who was I? That was the question. A pass at her might just earn me the frosty backhand. That I did not need.

I concluded my workout and left the exercise room. I'd stretched. I'd pedaled for 26 minutes and 40 seconds. I'd worked biceps and triceps to exhaustion. I'd talked to a young blonde woman. I would now shower and walk back into the night streets of Brooklyn and, if I made it to the college relatively intact and of somewhat sound mind, I would call Candy and hopefully talk to her. It had been a while. I don't do so well when I don't hear from her.

This had been a not half-bad day, except for the fact I'd screwed up with the cop and I'd...I shot down this train of thought. The only way to take life was in small bits. Move from step to step. I'd come here to give myself a break. So, if I was smart, that's what I would do.

Chapter Thirty-One

. . . .

I looked up into the Spa from the crowded street. I could see the young blonde working out. She was still by herself. She still looked good. It had been nice talking to her. It would be better yet to talk to Candy. Those were the moments when I was really alive. Phones are great, you had who you wanted all to yourself. Right there close, just like you were with them. But not so close that they could tell you to take a hike. Confidence with women, after my fling with Annie Porter, was not my strong suit. It might take me a while to locate a strong suit. I no longer truly taught. Publications were on the shelf. I avoided committee work like the plague. My only half-friend was a sex addict, and I'd become a killer. Not much there to hang a hat on.

I headed away from the Spa. The streets were still curb to curb. The bars were full, the restaurants packed, the coffeehouses busy. No recession appeared to be here. These were the survivors, the ones who used the little people to get ahead.

There were many couples in these places. In particular, I saw one couple, the man older, the woman in her prime, looking at one another as they talked. She was probably his niece. I was not that much older than Candy. I was not yet ancient, but a warning thought said I was of an age to watch myself for foolishness. Whatever my plans for Candy and me, I didn't want to expose myself as an idiot who'd gone where he shouldn't.

A lot rolled through my mind. Like the plans of others, especially those of Annie Porter and her boyfriend. Professors were always like that. Annie had a role mapped out for Biden that had nothing to do with his well-being and everything to do with her own wants and desires. She had a reputation for doing what it took to get ahead. I had a tape, stolen from the bedroom of the last Dean, Fenner the fuckup, which showed her in action. Now she had a new career and a new love interest. I had a pretty good idea what she'd used to get where she now was. Thinking about her in this way was not pleasant, for sooner or later this train of thought would lead to why she'd shown an interest in me, fucked my lights out, told me I was the best ever, etc. Enough of that.

I felt reality creep into my mind. I'd worked out, I'd been a wiseass, but now I was heading into a world which could, on a whim, erase me.

Crossing the Plaza, I returned my hand to the pocket of my pants and grasped the adjustable wrench. I did not expect to encounter many chit-chatty young blondes as I approached the Urban. U. What lay ahead was ungentrified, ready and raw Brooklyn.

Before me was darkness, below me was pavement covered with items I could smell. I was careful with my footing. It was 9 p.m. The down and out were up and about. And here I was, a professor who still thought he was a tough guy. In Brooklyn, believing you're tough is a sure way to get your face punched in. My old man always told that on the next block there was always someone who could clean my clock. This he'd done when he saw me running with Dom and Mendy "The Cup" Levy. We had a whole gang, did it all from minor to major crimes, and we especially liked to get in the face of anyone coming our way. However, I had listened to my old man, started to cool it with the gang stuff, set my sights on something else. That, as it turned out, was being a professor. Not many from my background had being a Ph.D. for a goal; that was for nerds, eggheads, book-reading pussies. I kept my mouth shut and began to hit the books. From that point on, I started to leave the streets behind. Which was what I wished I could do right now.

Coming my way were six figures, three large, three small. The six were using most of the sidewalk. I didn't believe they were up to any good. This would take some doing on my part to get back to the college in one large unscathed piece.

I drew in a breath, held it, let the air out slowly. I was still warm from working out. The six would come up to me spread out. Six against one was not as bad as three against one. Six was too many; they would get in one another's way. I removed the wrench from my pants pocket. The adjustable part of the steel wrench jutted out from my far-left knuckle. The six, whoever they were, would probably have as their first motive robbery. After that, they might go in for some fun. I didn't give a fuck what they wanted, I would take care of business.

I would have just one motive. Which was to get past them and run. Street punks don't usually run 10Ks. If I could get through them, I could get away. First, I would kill the one in the middle. I would break the nose of the one in the middle north and south and drive the bone into the brain. I would clear a path. I would run down the path I had made.

"Hello, Professor, goin' back to your office?" asked J.P. Carlisle with his deep voice.

Up close, I could see that one of the six, the one in the middle, the one I was set to kill, was J.P. Carlisle. Next to him was Nikki Nateal. There were two more big black young men and two more small black young women. This was a big "oops."

"Yes," I said, returning my left hand to my pants pocket. I'd been lucky. Now, I wouldn't have to kill anyone. All I would have to do was listen and nod.

"We didn't listen to the lecture 'bout the exit exam," said Nikki Nateal, who smiled at me. Some time ago it had come through the grapevine that an art historian had tried his charms on her. They'd been in his office after hours on the excuse that Nikki needed to examine his private collection of etchings. After a while, the art historian had snaked his plump white arm around Ms. Nateal's small black waist. She'd used the side of her hand and driven the man's privates up toward bone. This info had come my way from Beef Patty:

"Yeah, Nikki took care of him, it gonna be a while before that man use his Johnson."

I now smiled a sexually neutral smile at Ms. Nateal.

"Was that wise?" I said.

"We don' think much of some of the profs," said Nikki.

She had a point there. We agreed. There were very few of my colleagues who I thought were worth spit. Our faculty of burn-outs and fuck-ups didn't command much respect.

"Yeah, we don' need their 'tude," said one of the young large black men that I had seen at the Urban U. but not had in my classes. I smiled at him, too. Who would hit a smiler?

"He means we know their opinion of us," said J.P.

"How you doin' with my office partner, Biden?" I asked.

"That man sweat a lot when he talk," said one of the other small black women.

They all laughed; I laughed. We were a jolly bunch.

"Does he, between sweats, say anything of value?"

"No." The six formed a chorus.

"Professor, you hear what happen to that Russian?" asked Nikki Nateal.

"Yes," I said, wondering if they knew what I'd done. Sometimes, the gangs knew more than the cops and knew it sooner.

"The cop, he think it was us?"

"The cop was one of my students. He's just doin' his job. He doesn't know who did it."

"He will keep on the case?" said J.P.

"The Russians retaliate, he'll have to do something. If they do nothin', this will all blow over."

"You think we did it?" asked Nikki.

"No," I said, feeling sweat form on my forehead. Best to be careful doing that, I didn't want to appear to be like Biden. These kids could smell fear a mile away, and they'd hone in on it like sharks after chum.

"Who do you think did it?" said J.P., who took the lead in the group. J.P. and I had a history, I just hoped for my health and well being that he remembered it.

"Jimmy Fisheyes," I said, fingering someone who wasn't there to defend himself. Clever on my part, like that other wily Italian. Machiavelli, that was his name. Mac used him in his writings and once had me read something. The guy sounded like he knew a thing or two.

"That what we think," said one of the other big black men. Didn't J.P. have any puny comrades? This guy had muscles in his ears. I wouldn't like to have to tangle with him. He had youth and vim and vigor on his side, while I had only old age and treachery.

"The Ivans better let it drop with Jimmy Fisheyes," said one of the other small black women. This one I'd also not had in class, which is no doubt the reason she was a street crazy. All it took to take the street out of a Brooklyn female was a semester with Dr. R.V. Bucceroni, molder of young minds and builder of character, extraordinaire.

"That's what I told the cop to tell the Russians," I said, trying to worm my way into their good graces. What I wanted was to get the hell away from there, and I could do or say anything to that end. Go with the flow—that was me.

"They will listen?" said J.P. This guy never missed a beat, and now he had me dancing to his tune.

"They don' listen, they get more than they can handle from the Seoul Brothers," said Nikki Nateal. This was why Mac was right. In our lab, Nikki was quiet, dead, was treated as if she was a part of our team. She had half there. This was her other half. On the street. Ready to cave in someone's head at a moment's notice. Which side would win out? That was the $64,000 question.

"The Ivans, they not the only ones who better do some listenin'," said one of the large black men. His tone had a threatening air about it which showed he meant business. Whoever got in the way of this guy was in for a rough time. I was going to make sure that the Whoever wasn't me.

J.P. coughed. The other black man said no more. This was going well. Violence was all around me. J.P. could whistle, and I'd be dead meat. Of course, why would he do that, me being his kindly professor and all?

I looked at my watch. This was supposed to be a hint. I hoped they noticed.

"We'll see you after vacation, Professor," said J.P. Carlisle.

"I'll look forward to seeing you."

J.P. Carlisle and I shook hands. I used my right hand to shake hands with my former student. J.P.'s hand was large and rough. Neither one of us went in for the hard-shake nonsense.

The One-Percenters went west. I went east. I had no more than two blocks to go. Two blocks on the night streets of Brooklyn. I hoped I did not encounter any more of my students. It would be unfortunate if I made a mistake and drove the business end of an adjustable wrench into a nose bone and killed him, or her, or it.

It would be difficult to gloss over such an incident during my Annual Evaluation Conference. Of course, I could just say that I was killing holistically.

Chapter Thirty-Two

· ·

Approaching the college, I encountered no more students that I would have to consider killing. That was good. I was a bit pooped from the workout and only had strength to kill two or three. Hey, even Batman has his down periods.

Ahead of me, coming out of the liquor store owned by Mr. Soo, tattoo enthusiast and gun owner, was an old, dirty white man. The old, dirty white man gripped what appeared to be a large brown envelope. I had a sneaking suspicion that I knew what was inside. This old bastard wasn't apparently using his pictures for self-stimulation, he wanted to test the market for photos of black girls using the can. In Brooklyn, he might make a fortune.

The old, dirty white man passed by; I smelled him. He was easy to smell. My Roman nose didn't have to exert itself to pick up on him. He smelled like what he was photographing.

I came up on Fat Harry's Deli. Fat Harry himself stood in the doorway, looking past me at the old, dirty white—and smelly—man.

"Late hours, Professor?" asked Fat Harry.

"Yes."

"A large, regular coffee?"

"Yes."

"To go?"

"No, for here." I needed to sit down. Collect my nerves. This had been an evening with two too-close encounters with the gangs. With me, a little of the Seoul Brothers and the One-Percenters went a long way. It was bad enough that I had to teach them in a closed room, with no gun or machete in hand. Now I was having evening chitchats with them in the street, which was their theatre of operation.

Fat Harry aimed his bulk at the counter of his deli. He went behind the counter to pour a large, regular coffee. I wondered if Fat Harry had ever heard of Weight Watchers. This guy was really fat, an ideal candidate to drop dead with his face in a cup of his lousy, although hot, coffee. Beef Patty was fat but big; Fat Harry was just fat. He looked like he'd never exercised a moment in his life, unless you counted stretching out his arms to put a spanakopita in his mouth.

I took my usual seat at the end of the counter. No one could sit to my right. No one could sit behind me. Someone could sit beside me or on my left. I had closed off two out of three avenues for ambush. In Brooklyn, at night, there were no better odds. Well, if I could surround myself with a Marine division that might help. It was in this place that I'd sat with Dom, me still thinking he was my pal and protecting me. This was the last time I saw him before I killed him. He'd been in a piss-poor mood; at the time I thought he was just burnt out when in reality he was angry because I wasn't dead.

"That old man, I had to ask him to leave," said Harry, who was back in front of his counter to talk to me. He wanted no one to hear us. His breath was really something, like he'd been chewing on garlic. I smiled at him.

"Why?" I said, putting myself in for a long conversation.

"I am a tolerant man, Professor, but I have my limits." I knew all about Harry's limits, which didn't include not using the rooms above the deli to shoot shunt shots of coeds. This was what he and Pang, the relative of Mr. Soo, had been into. "So did Dirty Harry."

"Yes. That is true. I enjoy those movies. The two of us, we have often discussed the philosophy of those movies."

"Yes, we have," I said, knowing this was just Fat Harry's opener and he had something to tell me which was of importance to him. Why am I always the guy who gets his ears bent? I'm going to have to work on being surly and impolite.

"Do you know why I had to ask the old man to leave?"

"No," I said, although I could guess.

"He was trying to sell his pictures to my customers."

"Mr. Soo not like Mr. Pang?"

"No."

"Why not?"

"Mr. Soo received a visit from the One-Percenters."

"Really?"

"Yes."

"Jimmy Fisheyes was not aware of their visit."

"He wasn't?"

"No. And it is good he was not aware."

"Around here a little lack of awareness goes a long way," I said, and that was the truth. Contrary to popular belief, in Brooklyn, the less you know about what's going down behind closed doors the better. Then you can just blissfully walk through the borough.

"Mr. Soo was told by the One-Percenters that he must not buy pictures of the black co-eds using the bathroom over at the college," said the fat man, with sweat forming on his fat neck.

"Kind of anti-capitalist, aren't they?"

"Yes, they attach a moral aspect to commerce."

"And, apparently, a racial aspect." Which was true. J.P. laid down the law for what blacks could and could not do; he didn't give a rat's ass about anyone else. Which is the way most of us are. We just want to get on with what's good for us. The rest of the world can go to hell.

"Yes."

"Mr. Soo listen to them?"

"I think so."

"For his sake he had better so."

"Professor, the One-Percenters do not yet know that the old man is the source of the pictures."

"Mr. Soo clam up?"

"Yes, but J.P., he said he would return. He said he wanted the name."

"J.P.'s persistent."

"Mr. Soo called me a few minutes ago. He told me about the visit. He asked me what to do."

I said nothing. This was getting into an area which involved me offering an opinion. My view would be to do whatever the hell J.P. wanted done. If not, one could be separated from his jewels.

"Professor, I know the old man's name."

"Do you?"

"Yes, his name is Claymore Catawba."

"A local boy, no doubt. Born and raised right around here."

"No, he is from out West."

"Out West?"

"Ohio."

"Well, since he's from Ohio, he must be a cowboy."

"Whatever he is, he is not welcome here."

"You won't serve him?"

"I will serve him only if he does not try to sell his pictures of the black co-eds using the bathroom to my customers."

I digested Fat Harry's claim to rectitude. I believed in cause and effect.

The fat deli owner's staking out of the moral high ground might have something to do with the One-Percenters' quite recent visit to the Korean liquor peddler. The two stores were next to one another. First it would be Mr. Soo, then Fat Harry. J.P. would come calling.

"Do your customers want to buy the pictures?"

"Unfortunately, yes."

"You're not an anti-capitalist, are you?"

"I am a family man, Professor. I have two daughters. Look, please."

Fat Harry removed his wallet. He took out a picture. He held out in a fat, hairy, sweating hand a picture of two young fat women who looked like the moustache type. Too bad female wrestling was on the wane or these two could've made a bundle.

"Very nice. Do you have a picture of your wife?"

"Yes. Look, please."

Fat Harry laid the picture of his two fat daughters on the counter. He removed another picture from his wallet. I looked at a picture of a short fat woman standing in a kitchen. Sitting by her side was a small skinny dog. The family of Fat Harry probably licked their platters clean and left few table scraps for their little Arfer. This did look like a nice family, though. At any rate, it was more than I had. Maybe I should buy a dog.

"Very nice."

"This Catawba, he took an apartment next to the college so he could take pictures. You know this?"

"Yes."

"Is there anything to be done?"

"Did the old man in fact take pictures of Nikki Nateal and her friends?"

"Yes, he did."

"Did J.P. see the pictures?"

"He learned of their existence through an e-mail sent to one of the

One-Percenters, the cute little black girl." I should know all about this since I was the one who'd done it. I was teaming up with J.P., black and white together, ebony and ivory, making MLK's dream come true. Sort of. I wanted the old man to be removed. Pictures he took could be of me. I didn't want to be in someone's photo album.

Harry's reference to Nikki as "cute" meant disaster for the fat man. Nikki Nateal was about as cute as a fer-de-lance. If Fat Harry went down that sexual avenue, he too would have to experience injury to his essentials. Half and halfs are dangerous for they come at you when it's least expected. Harry could think he was flirting with a student when, in reality, he was making a pass at J.P.'s right-hand woman.

"On this e-mail was also a reference to Mr. Soo," said Fat Harry.

"So, J.P. is 'doing something?'"

"Yes, he is. You think I should tell J.P. the old man's name?"

"No."

"Why?"

"J.P. might kill you just as a warm-up before he kills Mr. Soo."

Water ran down Fat Harry's greasy, fat face.

"You think Jimmy Fisheyes will do something?" asked Fat Harry.

"Yes."

"What do you think he will do?"

"If the One-Percenters muscle Mr. Soo, the Seoul Brothers will retaliate. He'll try to take on J.P."

More water ran down Fat Harry's greasy fat face. This guy was a world-class sweater.

"Such a state of affairs will not be good for business."

"That's the problem with capitalism. There's always the unexpected."

"Harry, some coffee, por favor," called a voice from the other end of the counter.

I moved my head to the left toward the owner of the voice. I smiled at the speaker.

"Que pasa, Professor?" said Jose Morales, the new president of the Latin Monarchs. The last president had been squeezed to death by a drug given by Dom Mancini.

"Nada, y tu?"

"Excuse me, Professor," said Fat Harry.

President Morales and Fat Harry went into the kitchen. I could see them talking. I could not hear them talking. I did not have to hear them talking. The Latin Monarchs provided drugs for the students of the Urban U. This was the gang Dom Mancini, my old buddy, had forced his way into. So Fat Harry dealt drugs, but he did not allow pornography to be sold in his deli. I was glad Fat Harry had scruples.

Señor Morales left the deli. As he did so, he waved; I returned the wave.

"Professor, do you think a word about this matter to your friend Detective Reagan would be a wise move?" said Fat Harry.

"No."

"Why not?"

"Once you ask a cop into your house, he's gonna want to look at your whole house, every room, every closet, every desk, everywhere."

It was obvious that such scrutiny did not appeal to the deli owner.

"What should I do?"

I made a twisting motion over my closed lips as if to lock them.

Fat Harry looked intently to see if this was another joke.

"I would like another large, regular coffee," I said.

"To go?"

"Yes."

"You have work to do?"

"Yes."

"Your job, it is more difficult than it would seem to be."

"Yes, I do a lot of work."

"And you enjoy your work?" asked Fat Harry.

"It pays the bills."

Fat Harry made his way, slowly, from the counter to his coffee machine.

Upon his return, I reached for my wallet.

"No, no, this is on me, Professor, enjoy," said Fat Harry, handing me the coffee, then extending his hand. I get a lot of free coffee. It's because I'm such a good listener. Also, I'm an advice giver. Ann Landers was nothing compared to me.

"Thank you."

I shook hands with Fat Harry. My hand had not been wet until I had shaken his.

I stepped outside the deli.

I dried my hand on my pants. I looked left and right. I had only to cross the Street to be back in the cozy confines of the Urban U.

Chapter Thirty-Three

● ●

I made it across the Street without making human contact. I was questioned once by a shabby, skinny fellow about a financial matter and I did make eye contact with a young man whose pupil size suggested a recent chemical experiment. There're a shitload of drugs in Brooklyn and most of it was getting inside those who were the last ones who should be high. I got a peep of this by teaching at the Urban U., where far too many of the students turned on during the day and night. Of all the groups who didn't need their brains scrambled with "designer drugs," the Urban U. students headed the list. Most of them were on the low side of intelligence, or at least that's the way they appeared to me, so overworking their brains with drugs was less than a good idea. I had students in my classes who'd make it through about half a period and then have to go take a toot. When they came back, they were ready for a good nap, not a lesson on the basics of science. I said nothing to them. It's their life, let them fuck it up if they want. J.P., he felt different. A pusher comes selling in the hallways, he's going to get a large, angry black man in his face. I'd seen J.P. in action. No one to fuck with. Anyone who wanted to start another war on drugs, I could fix them up with a class-A warrior. J.P. had a mission. It's good to have a mission. Maybe one day, I'll have one.

I walked past the street-high slimeball; I did not consider such contacts to be human.

Inside the building, in a uniform which seemed at least two sizes too small, sitting in a chair which appeared to be inadequate to its task, next to the elevator, was Beef Patty. He looked tired. Maybe even worn down. Which was understandable. Banging two or three coeds a day would be a workload for any man.

"Still at work, Prof?" said the big black man.

"Yes, Lester, I am."

"I off in an hour."

"Good for you."

"I goin' to pick up Malvina. We goin' out."

"Tell her I said hello."

"I do that. Say Prof, you know J.P., he ask me about who been sellin' pussy pictures."

"And you told him?"

"I don' really know so that what I tol' J.P."

"He believe you?"

"You know J.P. He wan' hear what he wan' hear, know what I mean?" That was true. J.P. had a way of cutting to the chase, which was usually to smack someone in the head. J.P. might, however, have some trouble with Beef Patty; J.P. was in terrific shape, and the security guard was fat. But he was also massive; he looked like someone whose pumpkin head you could doink with a crowbar, and he'd just smile and then take you apart. I'd fought guys the size of Beef Patty back when I was a street runner; I was always careful with them and wore them down, then put them away. I could really sock, but I also knew a thing or two about fighting. One of which was to wear down King Kong before you went in for the kill.

"Yes," I said.

"That ol' man, he better watch hisself."

"Yes, he should. Things get straightened out upstairs?"

"Yeah, J.P. done with what he had to do by the time I get there."

"Done with what?"

"Some black kid actin' like what J.P. considered to be no good so J.P. smack him around a little bit. No big deal. Bust the kid's nose, that all. J.P., he do a lot of that." That was true. J.P. was the god of the upper stories at the Urban U. And he was a vengeful deity.

"Nothing that involved you?"

"Nothin'. You got the remote for the garage door, right?"

"Right."

"You leave, Professor, you jus' drive away. You punch in the code from your car. Don' you get outta your car." Beef Patty was giving me good advice. Waiting in the street out of one's car was asking for it. Ask and ye shall receive was a truism in Brooklyn.

"I won't."

The elevators arrived. A flood of students exited. They headed right for me. I backed into the halls. These kids had no respect for professors. They'd bump into you like you were a nobody.

I rode the elevator up to the second floor. This was the home of the Urban U.'s small library. This was usually not a busy floor. In the twenty-first century, libraries had lost their function for students. Asked to research almost any topic, they went first to Google rather than to a stack of old books. The only people who spent time in the library were the professors. McClure used the library as a second office. There, he employed JSTOR to find whatever articles the library did not have. I'll give it to Mac for still doing his duty. He took his teaching seriously, and he poured out articles and just last year another of his critically acclaimed books. Mac was a big deal as an academic. Of course, he spent the rest of his time fucking who he shouldn't, but then no one is perfect. I was now a minimalist teacher, a non-publisher, and a no-show at committee meetings. I did not, however, spend my extra time doing coeds who were willing and, no doubt, very able.

Off the elevator, I stepped into a deserted hallway. Walking toward the library, I saw no students, no professors, and no janitors. I looked at the floors. I speculated about the layers of grime I was walking on. The floor had a crunchy feel to it.

The library door opened. A tall man and a short woman came out of the library.

"Hello, Annie. Hello, Jim."

The two professors looked startled. These were not professors who taught at the Brooklyn branch of the Urban U. These were professors from the main campus. They were strangers in a strange land, sent here to help the Brooklyn students prepare for the Urban U.'s English exit exam. That exam was what was left of standards for the students. Randle had drilled his students to pass the exam. He'd taken it upon himself to get them a chance at passing. That was his job. He'd been doing the right thing to the end of his life.

"Oh, hello," said Annie Porter, smiling a bit tentatively.

"Hello," said Jim McDougal, not smiling at all. I smiled a broad smile at the two of them.

"You two done?" I asked.

"Yes, the librarian left," said Jim McDougal.

"That's because she wanted to get home alive. She's funny that way."

"Why are you here?" said Annie Porter.

I looked at Jim McDougal, who was tall with a neatly trimmed beard that went with his properly barbered blonde hair. Jim McDougal was dressed like a professor. Jim McDougal and Annie Porter looked good together.

"What's the best route to the Heights from here?" asked Annie Porter, starting a second question before I could answer the first.

"Helicopter."

"I know a way," said Jim McDougal, taking Annie Porter's hand.

"We're going to a party at Jill Carmody's," said Annie Porter.

"Or an armored vehicle."

"It's not that bad," said Jim McDougal.

"Yes, it is."

"Annie, could you give us a minute?" said McDougal.

"I'll be on the first floor," said Annie Porter.

Annie Porter headed toward the elevators. She punched the down button. She waved to us. Jim McDougal waved back. She got on the elevator. The door closed. Jim McDougal and I were alone in the dim, dirty hallway.

"You want me to walk you home, that why you sent her away?" I said.

"No, that's not...."

"Because I can walk you home, no problem. I'll take the point, we'll use hand signals. Do you have any flares on you?"

Jim McDougal took a deep breath. He apparently had something to ask me or else he wouldn't put up with my attempt at being funny.

"Annie told me that she told you about my...."

"Oh boy, two 'tolds' in one sentence...."

"Listen! This is serious. We need to talk about this," said Jim McDougal. Who seemed to have had enough of my wiseass demeanor. I didn't really blame him.

I lit a cigar. I leaned back against a dirty wall which blended, seamlessly, with the dirty floor and the dirty ceiling. I got ready to listen. Later on, I'd send my clothes to the cleaners and give my neck and back a double scrubbing.

"The situation at the main campus is very fluid...."

"So that's why your Chair is known as Pee Pee Bodner."

Jim McDougal smiled. "That's a good one."

"What do you want?"

"Annie and I live together. We're good together. I know about you two. She's still not completely over you."

I drew again on my cigar. I blew smoke McDougal's way.

Annie was lying to her new lover. What she wasn't over was her ass-shooting by an irate wife. As for me, I had been no more than a fling. She'd been willing to fuck a turd of a Dean to get what she wanted. What did she want from this guy? Or was it love? I hoped for her sake it was the latter.

"If I'm sent down here, I won't make it; I need your help. I don't like to ask you…."

"But you're doin' it for the sake of Annie?"

"Yes, I am."

"That's nice," I said, catching myself. It was not his fault that I had no love life and he did; the fault was mine. I'd never looked after Carmela had been killed. I spent my time feeling sorry for myself. I wouldn't recommend that to anyone. Except if you're hell bent to go off the deep end.

"The committee will be stacked against Biden, but…."

"But you believe my golden tongue and my winning ways will carry the day."

"Annie said you know a lot about the committee members."

"You mean Lipschitz and Zoltar?"

"Yes."

"You mean Annie believes I may know something about them from the past that I can use?" So, this was it. Annie knew all about me. She knew my past. This was an attempt to use what connections I still had.

"Yes. I'm not proud. I want to stay where I am, not come down here," said McDougal, glancing around at the surroundings.

"OK."

"That means you'll help me," said Jim McDougal.

"Kinda."

"I'll take that as a 'yes.'" He could take it any fucking way he wanted. I felt myself get pissed. So this is what I was good for. Being a force in some campus politics. What a world was the academic world.

"There is one thing," I said.

"What's that?"

"Take a cab to the Heights."

"You takin' the elevator?" asked Jim McDougal.

"No, I'll use the stairs."

Jim McDougal punched the down button. The elevator lights blinked from 2 to 1.

I returned to the library.

I locked the library door behind me. I left the lights off.

I picked up the phone directory from the librarian's desk. I used a pen flashlight to find the number I wanted. I used the librarian's portable phone, walking with it to the window. From this place, two floors down from my own office, I had to look up to see the old man's apartment. I punched in a number. The phone rang three times.

"Yeah?" said an old man's voice, high pitched to the extent it could be taken for a woman's voice.

"Mosquito Net Condoms?"

"What?"

"Leaky Rubbers, Inc.?"

"What the hell ya want!"

"Dented Dicky Wrappers?"

"Fuck you," said the old man, who hung up.

I could see the lights coming from the old man's bedroom and bathroom. I had been in the apartment building when the college had considered buying the building and using it for student dormitories. I had been on the committee which had investigated the building. At that time, the building had been just redone. I had a master key. I had retained the master key after the Urban U. had backed out as a buyer, their reason being that the streets were not hospitable to student, or human, life. They did have a point there. At first, the college stood out for being bright and clean, but the Urban U. had adapted to its surroundings. We were now just as shitty as everything else.

I returned the portable phone to the librarian's desk. The old man was a photographer. The old man took pictures which would not be easy to develop. The old man probably had a darkroom. The old man took a lot of pictures of what went on at the Urban U. The old man could, if he had wanted to, take pictures of my office. He could have pictures of the day Randle died, maybe of Bath doing his dirty work. This was a chance to get some answers. I was back on the case, so the criminal/killer had better watch his ass.

I left the library, used the back stairs to descend to the parking garage.

The end of the week was the first day of vacation.

I had an incoming message. From Candy. She was sick. Didn't want me to get it. Damn, I was on my own as a detective. The criminals were in for it now. I would have to draw upon my considerable experience, use my superior intelligence to nail whoever was doing the chemical killings down here. This time, I had better be sharp, get the facts, look at them without blinders, and come to a definite final conclusion. Then, I'd talk to Candy and see if my theory held water or was just hot-air crapola.

Chapter Thirty-Four

· ·

Candy was soon well. The young are like that. Resilient. I hate the young. I get sick these days I'm down for a week. Now, a skeptic might say that a diet heavy on red meat and lots of whiskey plus cigar smoking might be a reason for my slow recuperations. Maybe that's the case.

I used the phone for this, being totally chicken-shit to try it in person. I called from my place. Didn't use my cell. Stood in my foyer. Circled the old black telephone on a wooden table for what seemed forever. Then I speed-dialed.

I called Candy. We got quickly through the hello, how-are-yous, then the phoney reason I'd given for phoning her, something about the lab, something which could have waited.

"I thought if you were free we'd celebrate your return to health with a dinner," I said, speaking quickly, trying to sound casual. And no doubt doing less than a good job.

"Dutch?" she said.

"No, no, my treat," I said, waiting for the hammer to fall. I was wearing light-colored slacks, a light white linen jacket over a white Izod. I had on brown sandals. I was whiteness itself. Quite a change from my black, doom-and-gloom suits. They were good quality but best suited for viewings and funerals.

"I'd love to. Where shall we go?" said Candy.

Whee!

"A surprise," I said.

"I like surprises."

The knot in my stomach went away. My heart rate backed down, my palms began to dry. I'd passed step number one without getting the frosty mitt of rejection. I'd been afraid that there would be a pause and she would say: "Is this a good idea?" But she had not.

"Pick me up when?"

I gave her a time.

"I'll be here."

She hung up. I stood there with the phone in my hand. This was my first step out of this house. It'd been too long being in the dark. The light was for me.

Chapter Thirty-Five

. . . .

W e—Drs. Candice Dyer and Richard (a.k.a. Richie) Bucceroni—sat, all spiffed up, at a reasonably quiet corner table in The Street Grill in Park Slope. I'd looked for some time for a spot to take her to that wasn't obviously romantic, but I didn't want to go to a place that played ear-splitting music and was jammed with the young and ferociously upwardly mobile.

"What a great choice this is," she said, smiling at me, her teeth pearl white against her full, pink lips, not that I was checking her out or anything.

"I read about it online."

"What do they have for food?" said Candy, who was wearing a black dress of the type I would call slinky. We formed a considerable contrast, me in all white. The midnight crowd at South Beach would've loved me.

In the dark of the restaurant, I could see just flashes of her scar. Such was not the case with a large drunk at the bar.

He wobbled our way. I saw him arrive out of the corner of my eye.

"Wha' happen' to your face, sweetie? Ya look like fuckin' 'ell," he slurred. The words "uh oh" came into my mind. I took in a deep breath; I'd have to interrupt my date to punch this guy's face in. Maybe not.

Rising quickly, Candy drove the point of a steel-toed shoe into the drunk's balls. He screamed, dropping straight to his knees, cupping his privates. His bald head was close to me, so I slammed it into the marble tabletop. Something ticked against the salt shaker. The dirty-mouth drunk hit the tile floor hard.

A wide-eyed waiter appeared, uttering "sorrys", followed by a maitre de who was also sorry. They dragged off the drunk, who really had something to be sorry about.

The Street Grill, in Park Slope, was now very quiet.

A busboy showed up.

"Remove that from the table, por favor," I said, pointing at a bloody bicuspid. He did so and then left, the red tooth in a white napkin.

"This is a nice place," said Candy, slowly winking one of her pale blue-gray eyes at me.

"Glad you like it," I replied, wondering how I could now segue into romance.

Chapter Thirty-Six

· ·

"Seafood seems to be the order of the day," I said casually, scanning a menu I'd already been through several times online.

Candy was drinking white wine, me J.D. on the rocks. I was being careful not to get sloshed.

"Here's to your health," I said, holding up my glass.

"Well, I'm not sure I was sick enough to deserve this," said Candy.

"OK then, how about 'here's to me' or maybe 'success to crime'."

We clinked glasses.

"Shall we order?" I said, motioning for the waiter. He was there quickly, probably worried we'd shoot him if he was late. I gave him a winning smile to show I was not going to pound him into the floor.

After the waiter left, Candy asked, "So what do I need to know about Bath?"

"Let's don't talk about all of that."

"What shall we talk about?"

There was a pause.

I had to focus in order to speak. There was a sense of unreality about this entire scene. The last time I'd gone to a restaurant with a good-looking woman it had been with Annie Porter on the rainy night my family had been killed. That had followed an afternoon of ugly bumping that was now painful to recall. This was different. This was the start of a new life. This was Candy—and me.

"Us," I said.

Candy looked at me. She ran a slim finger around the rim of her glass.

"That sounds good."

A man my age passed by the window to The Street Grill. The man looked in the restaurant. For once, I was not the man in the street viewing the happiness of others. For once, I was the man with someone. I wished I could see me/us.

"Well, you see...."

"You like me."

"That's it," I said, feeling foolish that I couldn't get the words out, glad that Candy had filled in the blank spot.

"I like you too, Rich."

"So, we're in 'like'," I said, instantly regretting sounding like a wiseass. This was not the time to be a jokester. I do that too much, most of the time to keep from blowing my top. There was no danger here. What there was here was a chance for a life.

"It's more than that for me, Rich," said Candy.

"Me, too," I got out. I reached slowly across the table, giving her plenty of time to leave, call for help, or stab me. I slowly took her hand. It felt good to touch a woman again.

"How about 'success to us'?"

"Perfect," said Candy.

The food arrived, and the conversation changed to comments about the nature of the Grill's fare. The food was excellent. I gave myself an imaginary pat on the back. I'd done a good job in selecting a place for a first date. And that is what this was turning out to be.

Too soon, the dinner came to an end.

The maitre de smiled us out the door, no doubt glad we'd only damaged one patron and hadn't killed any of his staff.

Chapter Thirty-Seven

· ·

"Anything to declare?" said the customs agent at the Buffalo-Canadian border crossing.

"No," I said.

"On business?"

"No, I'm going to open up my cabin."

"Where?"

"The Island."

"Nice country."

"Yes, it is."

"The fishin's not what it used to be."

"No, it's not."

"For the whole summer?"

"No, just long enough to open up."

"Ten days long enough?"

"Yes."

"Here you go." He handed me a ten-day permit.

"Thanks."

I drove my silver Camry into Canada. I'd asked Candy to come, but she was behind on her work. That was OK. Our date had turned out just right. It'd been followed by others. We were now a couple. I'd have someone to return to. For once, I wouldn't be alone in my dead-dark house.

I'd been driving into Canada for many years. I'd first visited Canada when I was a little kid, when my parents found a place for the summer where my hay fever wouldn't have at me. I could recall my father's dealings with the customs officials.

"Don't look suspicious," he'd always said, which was something he himself should've taken to heart. My father looked like what he was, which was a wise guy, and like his nickname, which was "The Butcher." He also had a voice which was mostly a deep rumble. It was a voice that probably scared the hell out of everybody but his family.

"The boy's six years old, how suspicious could he look?" said my mother, laughing.

"Don't say anythin', let me do the talkin'," said my father.

"You goin' to tell them about my rifle?" I asked.

"No."

"What about your rifle?"

"No."

"And Mommy's pistol?"

"No."

"We'll be lucky if we all don't end up in jail," said my mother, laughing again.

"Here we go," said my father.

"Anything to declare?" asked the customs official.

"No."

"You here on business?"

"No, we're goin' to our cabin."

"For how long?"

My father told him.

"Here you go," said the customs official, handing my father his permit.

"That was easy," said my father, driving away.

"Are those flashing lights behind us?" said my mother.

"Where?" I asked, turning around.

"She's kiddin'," said my father, whose job was about murder and mayhem but who, at home, was something else.

"Are you just kiddin', Mommy?"

"Yes," she said.

Wherever we crossed, it was always the same. My father worried about the contraband and the weapons they had hidden and my mother teased him about it. The trip to Canada was itself an event. It was a good time for the family, for my father was away from his deadly day job.

Now, I drove on, alone, deeper into Canada.

Since it was not summer, I would have to drive around the North Channel to get to the Island. I would be unable to drive to Owen Sound and then over to Tobermory, where a ferry would take me to the Eastern end of the island, because the Che-che-maun wasn't yet in service. The Che-che-maun was not an improvement on the classier old ferry, which had been named the Norisle. The new ferry simply moved tourists from here to there like cattle with no thought of class.

I stopped for gas in Parry Sound. At an Esso station on the outskirts of the town, I looked at the welcoming sign put up by the Chamber of Commerce. It declared Parry Sound the hometown of a hockey player who was now no doubt an unknown except to the devout. Fame was fleeting in professional sports. Yesterday's adored hero was today's nobody. "Glory Days" was Springsteen's tune for the condition.

"Great player, eh?" said the station attendant, pointing to the sign.

"Didn't he play for the Rangers?" I said.

The station attendant gave me a look that could be categorized as withering.

"No, he only played for the Bruins."

"That the team from Buffalo?"

"That'll be ten bucks," said the attendant.

"Here you go. That's ten bucks, American," I said, forcing the attendant to calculate the exchange. I could recall my father's attitude toward the exchange.

"Why'd you make him figure in the exchange rate?" I had asked, sitting behind the wheel. My father was in the passenger seat.

"You remember last year when it was the other way?"

"No."

"They charged me."

"So?"

"So nothin'. Before that, all through the past, when the exchange was to our favor, I never asked them for it. Then one year it changed, and, bada boom, they're askin' me."

"So, the Canadians don't like us?"

"They like our money."

"But what about us?"

"No, us they don't like," said my father.

"Here you go," said the attendant, handing me the change.

I counted it, slowly.

"Is it correct?" asked the attendant.

"Yes, it is."

"You were jokin' about the hockey team, weren't you?" he said, looking worried. I should cut the guy a break. It was bad enough that his job was being a service "attendant"; he didn't need me busting his chops about a local boy who'd made it in the big time.

"The best hockey joke I ever heard was: 'Jesus saves! But Ratelle knocks in the rebound.'"

"The GAG line?"

"Wasn't there a guy named Esposito used to play somewhere in the States? With someone named Sanderson and an enforcer Wayne…." I said, repeating names I knew about from reading but not from seeing. I know a lot of stuff like that. One way I could impress my father and his gangster friends was by reciting the names of all the boxing champions, in every weight class, from day one to yesterday. I was no more than eight or ten, and he'd call me in and asked me a question, like who was welterweight champ of the world in 1937, and I'd know. "He's a smart kid, takes after me, a chip off the old block," he'd say to his pals.

"I know you were jokin'," said the attendant.

I got into the car. The sun was out, but the day was cold. I was heading north. It would be even colder on the Island, the largest freshwater island in the world. As a fact that item shrank in importance the more it was thought about, so best not to.

It was much later in the day when I turned off the King's highway and headed for Espanola. My father had gotten lost once in Espanola. My father, like most men but even more so, had hated asking for directions. It had been so late at night that no gas stations were open. What had been open was Louie's Chop Suey.

"We need to get to the Island. Can you help me?" said my father.

"You go Go'Be?" asked Louie.

"We're goin' to the island."

"Goin' Go'Be?"

"How about we order somethin'?"

In the background, my mother snorted a laugh.

"What you want?"

"Chow Mein. Fried Rice. Egg rolls."

"Fo tree?"

"Yeah, I think so."

Louis left to fill the order.

"What the hell did he say?" asked my father.

"He wanted to know if you are going to Gore Bay," I said.

"I missed that."

"What about the order?" asked my mother.

"We'll take it with us."

"Chow Mein for breakfast? Yummy," said my mother.

"Give it a try," said my father.

I drove through the Le Cloche Mountains. At one time, the drive through the Le Cloche Mountains had been 40 miles or so of rough and winding road.

My father had not liked the drive through the Le Cloche Mountains.

My father had owned, at that time, a Buick Roadmaster which was pulling a homemade plywood trailer. Such a connection made for difficult road handling.

"Hope that water pump holds up," said my father.

"Yes, wouldn't want the nutcases to have at us," said my mother.

"Don't scare the boy."

"What nutcases?" I said.

"Your father believes there's a nuthouse up in these mountains."

"That true, Daddy?"

"That's what I was told."

"Who told you?"

"The guy who runs the gift shop out on the highway."

"How did he know?"

"He's a nutcase," said the mother.

"That true, Daddy?"

"Your mother's just kiddin' me."

"You kiddin' Daddy, Mommy?"

"Is that a nutcase ahead on the highway?" said my mother.

"Don't tease the boy."

"Is it a nutcase, Mommy?"

"No."

"What is it?" I asked.

"A bear."

"What kind of bear?"

"A nutcase bear; they're the worst," said my mother.

My father had laughed. I had laughed. It was good to remember that laughter.

I drove toward the island. I would have to hurry to make the cabin by nightfall. I crossed onto the island from the mainland at Little Current.

I checked my watch. I should make it.

I had Highway 540 mostly to myself. During the summer, the road would be filled with tourists, but this was not a tourist month on the Island.

I passed through and around towns I had known as long as I could remember. Mindemoya. Kagawong. Ice Lake. Gore Bay.

Crossing the bridge at Indian Point, I had Lake Huron on both sides of the car. The bridge had split the big lake. The other lake was called Lake Wolsey. My father and I had fished for pike on Lake Wolsey. That had been long ago. We had caught many big fish on the big lake. Those had been good times.

The traffic, such as it had been, now thinned even more.

I stopped in Silverwater to gas up.

"Hello, Richie, here to open up, eh?"

"Yes," I said.

"Good to see you again," said the gas man.

"Good to see you," I said, and shook hands with a man I'd known through many decades. The man's parents and, before that, his grandparents had run the general store, gas station, the laundromat, and even served, on a rotating basis, as the postmaster.

"The black flies are bad."

"But only if you're outside."

"That's right," said the man, laughing.

"They're OK, aren't they?" I had asked about the owners of the general store in Silverwater where my father and I had just bought fishing licenses.

"They're OK."

"You don't sound like you mean it."

"If you got money, everyone treats you right."

"And if you don't have money?"

"Don't you ever be without money," said my father, putting a big hand on my arm to get my attention. He did that when he had something important to say.

I slowed the car as I came down the hill to the lake.

I passed cabins now owned by new people. Most of the people who had bought cabins in the past were now, like my parents, in the ground.

But the lake had not changed. I saw the lake as I had seen it every year of my remembering life. I saw the sun setting, the white caps, the tall spruce on the far shore. I liked to see the lake. It was much better than seeing Brooklyn, even a gentrified, snooty-assed Brooklyn.

I turned right after I came down the hill and traveled along the Lake Road. The road curved left as it passed the bay on the east end of the lake.

I came upon a long row of Blue Spruce. I stopped at a point where there was a chain between two of the trees. I got out of the car and worked the combination lock. I drove into a cleared yard with one sleeping cabin and one storage cabin. Between the cabins was a large, stone fireplace no longer connected to a cabin. Ahead, nearly in the bush, I could see the main cabin which I had moved, some years ago, from its original spot near the road.

I parked, walked toward the cabin. I had brought no luggage. All I needed was in the cabin. I breathed in the clean air. The only sound was the wind moving the bush. There were no other cabins within a mile.

I was far away from my troubles in Brooklyn.

And, tonight, I would dream of holding Candy, which was a great improvement on the nightmares I was used to.

Chapter Thirty-Eight

● ●

Back "home" at the Urban U., I encountered someone I didn't much like. And the feeling was no doubt mutual.

"Hello," said the someone.

I looked down at the non-smiling Dean.

"Oh, Professor, you would have to be pleased to actually know that you seem to have been correct with respect of your previous observation," said the Dean.

I wondered if the Dean had always talked that way or if he had been struck with a club at an early age into talking like he did. I wished I had a club now. I would force him to amend his comments—that is, if he could speak through broken teeth.

"Many times, my being correct, to the relative knowledge, seemingly, is not always, with respect to, this point of time, without mention," I said.

"Excuse me?"

"Thanks."

"Yes, well, it turns out that the so-called 'gang problem' here has come to nothing," said the Dean.

"That's nice."

"Yes, and the young woman was able to have her, you know, 'marking', removed successfully." He was talking about the tight-assed Russian. I probably should've felt some guilt about what I had set up for her. But I didn't.

"Our hunky sounds dory."

"Pardon?"

"Everything is, like, I mean, you know, OK. Right?"

"Yes, right, and I hope we can end the semester without incident," he said, a bit stiffly, like he was tired of talking to me. The feeling was mutual. This guy was a prick, a four-square fuckhead, those no doubt the qualities that propelled him to dean-hood.

"That is too my hope."

"Are you going up to your office?" asked the Dean as we left the lobby and moved toward the elevators which would carry us into the working parts of the Urban U.

"Nope."

"Where are you going?"

"To Never-Never Land," I said, walking away from the Dean toward the large glass doors that opened onto the Street.

My keen senses, which had been recently informing me of the odors of spruce, the sound of waves slapping against a cedar boat, and the sight of the sun rising over a deep blue lake, now made me aware of Brooklyn. I could now smell the defrosted vomit in the doorway, I could see the spent condoms and the unfrozen dog droppings on the curb, and I could hear the blasting of rap-crap coming from cars and from handhelds.

"You ain't in Kansas anymore," I said.

"You talkin' to me?" said a tall, young white man wearing a white muscle shirt, smoking, standing in front of the liquor store owned by Mr. Soo.

"DeNiro did it better," I said.

"Yeah, he did. How you doin', Professor?"

"I'm fine, Gino, you workin'?"

"Yeah, but this old gook, he's a ball buster."

"How so?"

"Every time he's got to count and recount the delivery."

"He's got some nerve to think you'd rip him off," I said, laughing.

The young man, who was named Gino "Moo-Moo" Mucchiato, laughed.

"Yeah, what's his fuckin' problem."

"Yeah."

"Remember our class?"

"Hard to forget."

"We was OK, though, weren't we?"

"You were more than OK."

"You still hangin' on?"

"Yes."

"This not right," said Mr. Soo, coming over to us with a list in his hand.

"What the fuck's your fuckin' problem!" said Moo-Moo.

I left Mr. Soo and my former student Moo-Moo to deal with their cultural differences.

I walked into Fat Harry's. I sat at the counter.

A short Indian came over to me.

"Wha' ya wan'?" said the Indian, mumbling his words.

"I wan' coffee," I said.

"Regular?"

"Regular."

"Anythin' else?"

"A cup with no thumbprints."

The Indian did not laugh. Instead, he went to get the coffee.

Fat Harry came in from the kitchen.

"Professor, welcome back from your vacation. You've met Aditya, I see."

"Yes, I have." He was the replacement for the previous Indian kid. God knows what'd happened to him.

"Nice clothes, very bright," said Fat Harry, touching the sleeve of my shirt.

"Thank you."

"Aditya's my new helper."

"That's nice, he'll fit in nicely around here."

Aditya put the coffee in front of me. He spilled the coffee as he set it down. Aditya brought out a rag which, in another time and place and life, had no doubt been partially clean. He wiped up the coffee.

"Sorry," said Aditya, now wiping his nose with the rag.

"No problem."

Up close, I got a good look at the Indian's pupils. Aditya was a doper who sold dope for the Latin Monarchs; this I had learned from listening in on student conversations.

Aditya went into the kitchen.

"Professor, you are just returned. I take it you have not heard about Mr. Claymore Catawba."

"No, I have not."

"He's in the hospital."

"Really."

"Yes. J.P. was somehow informed that Catawba was the one taking the pictures of the black co-eds in the bathroom. He and the One-Percenters paid a visit to Catawba," said Fat Harry.

I knew how that had happened. I could lay my hands on the informant.

"And this chitchat occasion resulted in?"

"He was taken to the emergency room first. It was the One-Percenters who drove him there. They dumped him out of the car. The doctors had to work fast to save his, his, ah...."

"Dick?"

"Yes."

Springtime in Brooklyn promised to be interesting. That's what I love about this place. Never a dull moment thanks to laughter, jokes, pranks, and a penis removal or two.

"So, I now have no problem with the One-Percenters," said Fat Harry.

"All is well."

"Yes, all is well. Enjoy, Professor, enjoy," said Fat Harry, who was looking past the professor at two black girls who'd entered the deli.

"Aditya, customers," said Fat Harry.

The Indian appeared from the kitchen. The two black girls sat in a booth. Aditya waited on them. I looked at the glass case where Fat Harry kept his pastries. The glass reflected the black girls and Aditya. I saw one of the black girls give Aditya money. She gave him more money than was the usual for the purchase of the fine cuisine of the deli.

I hoped for his sake that Fat Harry had no plans to produce any more children.

Chapter Thirty-Nine

• •

I left the deli, carrying the coffee in my left hand. I wondered what diseases the Indian kid had and what my chances were of getting one of them. Then again, I had worked up a pretty good immune system over the years. Students would come up to me, sneeze, cough, shake my hand and I just took it all in. By now, nothing fazed me. Even snotty coffee from a dead-on doper.

I walked down the Street, turned left, went over to the apartment building next to the college. Up to the fifth floor I went, moving quickly, acting like I belonged there. The walls were dirty, the floors filthy, the air in need of an airing. It was not a place for true humans to exist, which was no doubt the reason for the reasonable rent.

Looking left and right, seeing no one, I used the master key I'd retained from the time the college had been a potential buyer of the building. Inside the old man's apartment, which still smelled of the dirty old man, I looked for the camera, looked hard, finally found it. This would be my only opportunity. The old man would recover from his dick wound and leave for the Wild West of Ohio where he could exercise his vice without a J.P. coming after him. Creeps like him never give up their creephood, so he'd be back in the bathroom-peeping business in no time.

On my way out with my coffee and the camera, my luck ran out. I could hear someone getting off the elevator. I ducked back into the old man's apartment and hid just inside the door of the old man's bedroom. The door to the apartment opened. Someone came in. Guessing it was the old man and assuming he'd head straight for his favorite room—the bathroom—I waited a minute until he did just that, then quietly left.

Outside, no one was in the hall. Down in the elevator, still no one. I returned to the college. I'd been lucky. That was all right. Being lucky was better than being caught any day. I'd taken a chance, but I wanted to see what pictures had been taken.

Inside the Urban U., I did not see Lester "Beef Patty" Norwood. Another security guard was on duty. This guard was small and Irish and glum and didn't talk a lot. The guard was my age. It was my assumption that the guard had not done well in school.

"Lester off today?"

"Who?"

"Lester, Lester Norwood, a big man, twice your size, and dusky."

"Ya mean Beef Patty?"

"Yes, is Mr. 'Patty' off today?"

"No, he ain't 'off,' he's goin' to nights."

"So, you're the man."

"Yeah, thas' me."

"Have a good day."

"Yeah, right," said the guard, who sat in a chair next to the elevator, where he'd spend eight hours a day watching students get on and off the elevators and where, at times, he'd remove the street flotsam which, occasionally, washed up outside the entrance to the Urban U. This was what he got for being a fuck-up. He was a dead man sitting with a dead-end job.

I took the empty elevator to my floor.

Walking down the dirty hallway, passing the dirty walls, not looking up at the dirty ceiling, I noted the light was on in my office. This was not good. I debated about going in. Decided to.

"Hello," said Biden, who was seated at his neat desk.

"Hi," I said, moving past Biden to my own desk next to the window.

"I need to talk to you ...about my career," said Biden, coming immediately to the point.

"You do?" I looked out the office window. Someone was in the apartment. It looked like they were moving out the old man's belongings. I had been very lucky.

"And?" I said, sitting down at my desk.

"You're on the committee...."

"Yes, I am."

"I, I need this job."

"OK."

"I have nothing else lined up. I believe, with some hard work, I can return to the main campus and then...."

Biden went on for some time creating castles in the sky. This is what losers do, work their mouth, exercise what they call a brain, all to the point of convincing themselves they've got a shot at something when really their odds are next to nothing. I didn't like listening to this young soon-to-be-axed professor.

"You could help me, you know. You may have more clout on that committee than you realize," said Biden, coming to the end of his self-promotional spiel.

"Look, this will be unpleasant for you to hear, but the committee is stacked against you, it's a 3-2 slam dunk...."

"No, it's not...." interrupted Biden, his voice rising.

"You're wrong. Bodner's the Chair, which means even though he's a jerk, he's important in this instance. He sent you here because he wants you out. He'll not vote to retain you. Sidney Lipschitz is a well-known flunky who was promoted to full prof by virtue of Bodner making weasel-deals with the other department Chairs to support a record that a gerbil could've beaten. Then there's the old woman from Classics, Zelda Zoltar, who hates men. She would vote to have you neutered, with her doing the procedure, then fired. That leaves the very shapely, very leggy, very blonde, very, very Ms. Carmody, who'll vote to give you another year. Randle was the other committee member. He would've, sorry to say, also voted against you because he thought destroying your career would get him back into Bodner's good graces. All that's happened is that you've gone from four-to-one against you to three-to-two," I said, summing up Biden's academic potential in a somewhat brutal fashion. Still, it was what he needed to hear. Maybe some of it would get through to him.

"No, no, you're wrong, something's happened to change the whole dynamic of the committee," said the tall young professor who was, for once, direct in his speech. "Zelda Zoltar is ill, breast cancer. She's been replaced."

I said nothing.

"Jill Carmody forced a vote at a meeting of the faculty…."

"When?"

"Yesterday. Monday. She got the faculty to put onto the committee Mary Mastoris."

I snorted a laugh, which set off a bout of coughing. I knew of Dr. Mastoris.

"Mary Mastoris is a moron. I reviewed her class when she was up for tenure. She's an absolutely god-awful teacher…."

"I care nothing about that. She will vote for me. That is all I care about."

I noticed Biden was not sweating and that he was, for once, understandable. This was Biden's last shot at this job. The job market was tight. The downtown campus of the Urban U., sad sack that it was, was one of only three shows in the big town. The other two were an Ivy League institution which seldom, like never, gave tenure, and the last one a popular, very expensive university which employed a lot of adjuncts and visiting profs. Biden had no chance, none at all, to get taken on by them, except if they needed a janitor.

"So I'm the tie-breaker."

"That's correct."

"Will you support me?" said Biden, after I was mute. What was I supposed to say?

"If I answer that question, you would have a legal case, you know."

"How's that?"

"The committee has not convened. I have not reviewed your record. I have not participated in the discussion."

"You never impressed me as one who cared about the rules," he said, issuing a zinger which was actually true.

"I see no reason to vote against you."

"So you're for me," said Biden, still not smiling.

Biden stood up, came over to me, offered his hand.

We shook hands.

"I'll never forget this," said Biden, his voice breaking. "You see, I, I have no other real possibilities. If, if I lose this, this job I'll have nowhere to go. You see, my father is emeritus at Williams, he's never had much of a view of my own.... My father was, you see, a professor of note. I don't know how he'd take my, my being...."

Biden began to cry.

"Being fired?" I put in.

"Yes, yes. I just don't know, what, what I'd do," said Biden, his words being gobbled up by his sobbing.

The crying made a loud sound in the small room.

I waited.

"I have to go now," said Biden, wiping his eyes.

I took out a Churchill.

Biden left the room.

I lit the cigar. Sherlock Holmes had divided the solving of his cases into one-pipe, two-pipe, and three-pipe problems. Einstein had smoked up a storm when he was trying to figure out if we were coming or going in the universe. Two thoughts collided in my mind. One was of Biden, the other was of Bath. Was the old professor planning to do in Biden and ruin his plan?

The smoke from the Churchill filled the room.

I didn't know how to get pictures from a camera, but I knew someone who did.

Chapter Forty

. . . .

I stood out like a blonde in Bushwick. I was alone on Coney Island Avenue, feeling naked without a head cap, carrying a shopping bag that housed the camera I'd lifted from the old man's apartment. This was where I could get done what was needed.

My beachcomber outfit drew further attention to myself. I thought for a moment about the cause of my new appearance in the world. Candy was both alluring and disturbing. I had deep-sixed sex along with my wife. Now, a day spent without Candy was a day I'd prefer not to spend. Was that good? The answer "Who cares?" forced itself to the front of my mind.

I stopped at a real estate office at Avenue O and Coney Island Avenue.

"Hey, Professor, a long time, too long since I've seen you," said a short, mostly bald man.

"Hello, Mendy."

The man was Mendy Levy, known in younger days as "Mendy the Cup" because the goyim liked to rough him up so he always wore a steel athletic supporter.

"How long has it been that I've seen you?" asked Mendy, looking wary. The last time I'd called on Mendy it'd been for breaking into some of his rentals so I could get a line on a killer. He'd not been happy about it, but he'd helped me. We went back a long ways. At one point, he and I had been nearly as tight as me with Dom. Mendy was a stand-up guy, someone you could trust. I was a little burned with regard to trust, but now I had no choice.

"Too long."

"Same old, same old? Right?"

"Right."

I needed Mendy to do something. I hesitated. Once someone was asked a favor, then that person had some power over you. I had to trust Mendy to ask him.

"Listen, Mendy, I need a favor. It's not housebreaking."

"So, ask," said Mendy.

"There are pictures that need to be developed."

"That's the favor?"

"These are not those type of pictures."

"Richie, let's go out for a coffee. Mina, I'll be back," Mendy said to a young woman stacking shelves.

Mendy Levy and I walked to a corner coffee shop, took a table off to the side. I ordered two coffees. When they arrived, he poured a shot of Jameson's in each one. I took a long drink. It tasted good.

"So, what's with the pictures?" asked Mendy.

"Some old guy in the office building next to the college was taking shots of black women in the can. I'm not interested in them. He may've taken pictures of my office."

"You in some kind of trouble?"

"If I wanted to answer questions, would I be here?"

"What do you want me to do?" he said, talking quickly, recognizing my temperature on the rise. I had always had a rep for a short fuse and he didn't want to set me off.

"Scrap the shunt pictures. Give me any pictures of my office."

"Will do."

"No more questions?" I said, willing to tell him only what I had to. That was the extent of my trust.

"What's to question? This that you are asking, this is nothing," said Mendy the Cup.

"You'll do the work yourself?"

"Just me. Not to worry. I'll get them back to you."

I gave Mendy the bag with the camera. We shook hands. I went on my way.

Chapter Forty-One

· ·

Upon returning to my office, I encountered Detective Pat Reagan, who was waiting by the door. I needed to see him like I needed a knee in the nuts.

"You look like a surfer," said Reagan.

"How many surfers you ever seen?"

"Only in pictures. But you look like one."

We entered the office, took seats. Me by the window.

"Oh yeah, one thing, off the point, guess what fight I jus' broke up?"

"Moo-Moo and the legal dope dealer?" I said.

"Who?"

"Mr. Soo."

"How'd you know?"

"Lucky guess."

"Yeah, well, guess who was on the losin' end?"

"Not our boy Moo-Moo?"

"No one else. You know, Prof, I tol' Moo-Moo after I got the little chink off him that I think we're slippin.'"

"We are slipping. Mr. Soo is 65 years old."

"Well he didn't look like no old guy. He was givin' Moo-moo a time of it."

I lit a cigar. I blew the smoke away from Reagan just in case he was interested in staying alive.

"Those things will kill you, Prof."

"But at least I'll know what killed me."

"You got a minute?" I hate questions like that from cops, for they aren't really questions. He could force me to answer anything he wanted to ask under the sun. And I'd have to answer. While he wasn't looking, I switched on my lying apparatus, one that I'd gotten real expert with recently.

"Just about."

"You know you were right about this place."

"I was?"

"Yeah, it all blew over about that Russian broad, you know, the one who got her head tattooed."

"That's good."

"Yeah, but what happened to the old guy next door ain't so good."

I drew on my cigar.

"You know about him, don' you?"

"He sold shunt shots of the black girls in the bathroom. Fat Harry told me he'd been asked by J.P. if he knew the photographer. Harry told J.P. he didn't know. Today, Fat Harry told me the old guy, Claymore Catawba is his name, had his dick cut off sometime last week. That's all I know." Which was a brief summary of the case, all of it on the money and lacking only the detail about who set the whole thing in motion.

There was a pause in the conversation.

"This is just like what happened to that skinhead who roughed up that black professor. You think J.P. did that?"

"I don't know."

"Would you tell me if you did know?"

I smiled at the detective but said zip. J.P. was a nut ball in a lot of ways, but he also had a point about what he was doing. I'd just handed him the Russian girl and the sleaze ball to make some of his points, so I was not about to turn him in now.

"Between the two of us, I don' give a rat's ass what J.P. does to a fuckin' piece of shit like that Catawba, it's just that I got to do my job."

"Will Mr. Catawba be leavin' town?"

"He left today. His place is cleaned out."

"Now what?"

"Now, my captain says we got bigger fish to fry, but he also says we can't have no vigilantes," he said, looking at me. I didn't like the look.

"You got anything you can take to the D.A. about J.P.?"

"Nothin' that'll stick."

"Sounds like this case will have to remain open until definitive evidence appears."

Pat Reagan looked at me. For a moment, we both said nothing.

"Who do you suppose tipped J.P.?"

"Who said he was tipped?"

"How'd he know it was this Catawba guy?"

"Maybe one of the girls looked up and saw him snappin' pictures."

"Oh, yeah."

I looked at my watch.

"You got to teach?"

"Yes."

Reagan walked over and shook hands. I went with him into the hallway. We walked together to the elevators.

"OK Prof, keep on watchin' your back," Reagan said as he got into the elevator.

"I will do that," I said. The elevator doors shut.

I wondered how long it would be before I had the pictures from Mendy Levy.

Chapter Forty-Two

. . . .

I went to my lab—the temporary one, this on account of my blowing up the last one with a crum-bum of a killer in it.

Inside was someone. She was soon in my arms. Candy kissed me. I kissed her. We kissed.

Behind me, the door opened.

"'Bout time you two got together," said Nikki Nateal, heading for the lab itself.

"That's certainly so," said Candy.

She stopped kissing me and went to work.

What was I to do?

"I'll go get the mail," I said.

"You do that, sweetie," said Candy, calling from the other room.

"Yeah, 'sweetie'," echoed Nikki.

On the way to the mailroom, I made a rest stop at the usually filthy restroom. This was the faculty john which had recently reopened. That's all, just reopened. Not cleaned.

What happened next is what you get for being curious. One of my traits that I'm real proud of. If you ask me, the curious in the world should be shot.

Leaving the urinal, trying not to breathe the shit-flavored air, I noticed something red outside one of the stalls, not much red, more like a thin trail. Me being me, I stopped in front of the stall. The door was barely open. I pushed it. It came only partly open; it was bumping into a man's shoe. I saw him; he wasn't going to complain about my coming into his space.

It was Professor Bath, wearing a white linen suit, sandals, dressed for the warm weather. The heat had attracted flies; they were on him, especially his white shirt, which was stained red. I nudged him to see if he was OK. He wasn't. Bath fell over to the side of the stall, and it was then that I saw what'd been done to the old, white-haired professor of English. His throat was slit clear across, some of the gouges deep, as if a knife had been worked in. My mind went into high gear. So much for my theory about Bath's being a chemical killer. He was now a bloody stiff, and here I was, first on the scene. Hooray for nosey me. I had taken care not to get any blood on me, so that some eager-beaver cop didn't show interest in good old, kindly Doc Bucceroni, hard to believe, as a prime suspect.

Choices I now had:

A. Go back to my lab and wait until someone else found him.

B. Call the security guard and call Pat Reagan.

I chose B.

It wasn't long before the restroom was swarming with cops and EMTs. I answered a boatload of questions, then told the cops where I was going to be, and returned to the relative safety of my lab. I was beginning to wonder if there was any place safe at the Urban U. If you can't use the john without getting slit open, then where resides safety?

"So tell me, I already have the general picture," said Candy as soon as I was inside with the door closed.

Bad news travels fast at the Urban U.

"She here?" I asked, looking past her for Nikki.

"Doing searches."

"The long and the short is that Bath was in a stall, pants down, throat slit. Whoever did it had some hand strength, the knife was worked in," I said, then added a few more details. Candy said nothing; she was taking it all in.

"So much for your theory about him," she said.

"Yeah, wrong again."

"So, who?"

"Haven't a clue."

"Biden?"

"He'd benefit from Bath being dead, but I just had a heart-to-heart with him, told him I'd help him stay on."

"That true?"

"Kinda."

"Cops seem OK with you?"

"They told me Pat Reagan's on his way."

"Let's hope this isn't the start of something involving us," said Candy, reaching out, touching my face.

"Let's hope," I said, but this time I didn't feel alone. This would be different. This time I'd get the goods on the right person. It was just that things had gotten a bit more complicated. One minute, I was looking for a chemical killer, now I'd have to add knifer to the modus operandi. The two didn't fit, not the usual combo. One was sneaky, but this was up front and vicious. Whoever had done in Bath had enjoyed it. So sadist got thrown into the mix. I was glad Candy was around. She could help me deal with all of the possibilities.

Chapter Forty-Three

· ·

"This isn't gonna be so good for you down here," said Pat Reagan, sitting in my office.

"No, no it isn't." Both of us were talking understatement here. It was bad enough that we were drug central, but Murder, Inc. too? That would be a downer for the publicity department.

"Listen, Prof, I've got some facts for you that're strictly between us."

"Gotcha."

"This Bath was a queer; the suspicion is that this is some type of homo-bashing."

"Bath was my office partner; he didn't appear to be gay."

"These days who knows? This is info I got from your Dean, who said he'd had complaints about Bath from the students. He apparently had a rep for coming on, then using the men's can as a love nest."

"The Dean told you all this?"

"He didn't seem all too happy about givin' me the dope, but I got it."

"So this was a sex quarrel?"

"Somethin' like that. Queers run a risk when they start cruisin'. Anyway, you'll probably get some bad publicity."

It flitted across my mind to tell Reagan about my idea of Bath as a killer himself. I decided to button my lip. Bath's killing had a logical explanation; my great idea was based on tasting coffee and thinking there was a drug in it. Maybe all of this was over. Maybe there were two killers. One was Bath, poisoning people to keep his job. The other was someone he'd had sex with who didn't like it, or him.

"We'll get through it," I said, keeping my mind on the points he was making.

"I'm sure you will. Remember, this what I just tol' you is just us two, right?"

"Right."

We shook hands. He left.

I digested what he'd told me. It made sense. Violence was all over the Urban U. It wouldn't take much for someone to take out a professor.

With Bath gone, there should be no more killings. I still believed someone had doped Randall's coffee, but that belief would die with me. Life ahead looked good—me and Candy, no killers to track down, a bed of roses.

Chapter Forty-Four

· ·

Candy and I were lost in Manhattan. At night.

Actually, that was not entirely true, for Candy wasn't lost. She was with me, who was supposed to know where the hell he was going. I did know, however, what I was looking for, which was an Irish bar named Wildes. I'd learned about the place from an Irish bartender I knew named, appropriately enough, Kenny McCoy, who'd opened his own bar and e-mailed his old customers. I thought I'd remembered the address; I was wrong. The two of us had been as far west as 11th Avenue and had seen nary a sign of a bar called Wildes, Irish or otherwise.

While I was standing at a corner, I felt, then saw, a hand come on to my bare arm. The hand had come from the left; Candy Dyer was on my right side. My first thought was that the hand was a bit off the mark for a pickpocket, the second that the hand was too soft for a cop. I looked down to see what was what. As it turned out, it was more a case of who was who.

"How you doin', Professor?" said a soft voice I'd heard before at the college, only this time the speaker was dressed in a skimpy, shiny red outfit, the skirt very short, the blouse barely containing what it was supposed to contain. Sleek black hair had given way to a blonde wig. This was one Carolyn something—I'd forgotten her last name—who'd taken one of my classes.

"Hello, Carolyn," I managed to say. "We're looking for a bar," I added, not knowing what else to say. It's not often you see your students at their other jobs.

"What's it called?"

"Wildes."

"East side," said Carolyn Whatshername.

"East side?"

"Yes, it's down that a way, it's brand new," said the girl, turning and pointing east. I could hear Candy laugh.

Before the conversation could continue, there came a whistle from across the street. I looked but could make out no one in the crowd. The whistle came again.

"OK, got to run. See you two next week," said the student, who wiggled away in her very tight, very short, very red outfit.

"Oh, boy," I said.

"Got to make a living," said Candy. "You on track to the bar now?" she added, smiling up at me.

"I hope so."

"Wasn't that something?" said Candy.

"We know nothin' of the lives of our students, absolutely nothin'," I said, thinking for a moment where I'd come up with that phrase of wisdom, and then remembering it was from Annie Porter.

"But this, this is exceptional," said Candy.

"A first for me," I said, turning and starting us in what I hoped was the right direction to the bar.

"And she was in your class?"

"Yes. I can't remember her last name. I had no clue this was how she paid her way to school."

We made our way through Manhattan's crowded night-time streets.

After a walk in which I'd doubted where I was going at least three times, there appeared a bar with a large sign: WILDES.

"Hooray!" cried Candy Dyer.

"Was there ever any doubt?" I said.

"None, whatsoever."

We were close together on the busy street.

Across the street was a large store window so I could see the two of us, me swarthy but dressed in all white, Candy a blonde in all black.

I put my arms around Candy Dyer, she came into me, tilting her head back as she did so. I moved my face toward hers. Shadows somewhat hid the scar on her cheek.

I could feel the wetness of her mouth and the press of her body next to mine. We were as one. Sidewalk walkers gave us sidewalk space. I heard some applause. It was some time before we parted.

"Well, that was nice," said Candy.

I searched for something witty to say. I could think of nothing, I kissed her again. For me, nothing now existed but Candy's soft mouth. The honking of horns, the to and fro of the city, planes passing overhead, none of it registered on my senses. All that I felt and heard and tasted was Candy Dyer.

This time it was me who spoke.

"Well, that was very nice," I said, proud of myself for thinking of the word "very" all on my own.

"Three is my lucky number," said Candy, putting her slim hands around my thick neck, pulling me down and into her. The kiss took my breath away.

"We better stop or we'll get arrested," said Candy.

"Right you are."

We entered the bar and were greeted by Ken McCoy himself, who had a very thick Belfast accent. Ken McCoy had known me when I had a wife. He smiled and shook Candy Dyer's hand. He led us past the bar to a table in the corner.

The owner of Wildes pulled out the table so we could sit side by side.

"First drink is on me," said Ken McCoy.

"Thanks. Make mine a half and half."

"And you, my dear?" said McCoy to Candy.

She named a white California wine.

McCoy left. The two of us were alone in the dark corner of the bar.

The drinks soon arrived.

"Here's to us," I said.

"To us."

Chapter Forty-Five

. . . .

We walked from the bar back to my car. Crossing the street, I felt Candy pull on my arm.

"It's him," she said, her voice suddenly harsh.

I didn't have to ask twice. Candy had been lucky; she'd found in the sea of NYC the remaining creep who'd ironed her face. There'd been two. One of them was now departed, thanks to Candy. This was the other one. His ass was in serious trouble.

"What'll we do?" I said.

"You get the car, keep in touch by phone, I'll tail him," she said, already moving away from me, the words rushing out.

I went to get the car.

I cleared my mind.

This was going to be some night.

Chapter Forty-Six

. . . .

I was following the creep, who was driving a large BMW. Selling dope pays—big time. Candy was beside me. She said nothing. We'd done it right. With the car, I'd picked up Candy just as the creep was getting into his car. I was now doing a tailjob. I was good at tailing; Dom Mancini had taught me. Even though Candy had spotted me. That was because she was a cop's daughter. Now I was in good form, doing it just right. Ahead of me drove a guy driving to his doom.

He drove 30 mph; I drove 30 mph. It was the law to drive 30 mph. Obeying the law made us the object of contempt.

"Go home, ya slow fuck!" this coming from one car driven by a balding, red-faced, fat man in a Volvo, window down, giving me the finger.

"Learn to drive, ya lane-hoggin' motherfuck!" screamed a thin-faced young man wearing a white shirt and red power tie and driving an SUV. I tried to assess the number of times four-wheel drive would be required in Brooklyn. Not many was my conclusion.

We left Manhattan, used the Battery Tunnel to the BQE. Then deeper into Brooklyn.

The car finally stopped in an area I knew. It was part of crazy Brooklyn. This was half-gentrified, which meant half was livable and half questionable as to the housing of humans. That would be OK. This guy wasn't really human, and in a little while he wouldn't be really alive.

The BMW driver was lucky, for he found a parking place. I had a sneaking feeling his luck was about to run out.

Candy watched as the creep walked inside a brownstone.

"You don't have to come with me," she said, not making eye contact.

"Where you go, I go," I said. Which was true. This would be her show, but I would be there to back her up. She'd done that plenty of times for me, so now I could return the favor.

A half-smile moved over her face. A streetlight made her scar easy to see. This slime bucket and another one had held Candy down, used a hot iron on her, marking her as someone who'd crossed them on a drug deal. Back then, Candy'd also been a dope dealer. She'd made the wrong dope deal. She'd paid a big price. All of her life she had been pretty, but now she was an oddity that made people look twice when they saw her bad side.

We parked, walked toward the apartment house which housed a guy who was spending his last moments on earth.

I gave the area a once-over. Quick-in, quick-out would be the order of the day. This was a crummy area, but someone would be watching. In Brooklyn, there's always a watcher.

"You won't have much time," I said.

"Won't need much," said Candy, her speech even, no emotion to it.

"Silencer?"

"Yes."

Knocking at the door of the brownstone, I was soon greeted by the creep.

"Yes?"

I knocked him back into his place. Candy closed the door.

The SOB was on his back, blood coming down his chin. I'd really laid one on him.

"Take my money, I have money!" he squeaked.

The foyer had light. Candy used it to advantage.

"Remember me?" she said.

The ironer looked at her face. The wheels turned. His memory brought him up to speed. He started to whimper.

"Don't kill me, please, it was…wasn't me used the iron!"

"But you were there," said Candy, who now had a pistol in her hand.

"Please!"

Candy shot him in the thigh. He screamed. I hoped the neighbors had their TV on high.

"You took my face, now I'm gonna take your life," she said, the words even, no yelling.

Candy double-shot, boom, boom, one right after the other, into the gut of the creep.

He writhed, screaming, on the floor. She kicked him in the mouth to stop the noise. He gurgled.

The creep died hard. We weren't "quick-in, quick-out". It takes a while to die from being gutshot. I gave Candy the time; she'd been put through hell, and each and every day when she looked in the mirror she was reminded of what had been done to her. There was a grandfather clock in the place; the tick-tocks went on and on. Finally, the creep stopped moving. I felt his neck for a pulse. Nothing. He was on his way to hell.

"He's dead," I said.

Candy slumped back into the door. Her right hand touched her scar. She dropped her pistol.

While she was recovering, I picked up the pistol, returned it to her purse.

"It's time," I said.

She nodded.

We were soon in the street, moving slowly away. It was luck that had allowed Candy to get the now-departed drug dealer. I hoped our luck held.

This had been some evening—French-kissing, Irish drinks, lover's talk; all of this, plus revenge served cold and red.

A night out in Brooklyn.

Chapter Forty-Seven

· ·

"Ya asshole! Ya fuckin' asshole!" said an intense woman with jet-black hair driving a large Mercedes, with two children, without car seats, in the backseat. I flashed the woman a large, winning smile. The woman flipped me a raised finger which she jabbed, vigorously, in the air. She must've not known me. That I was a professor and a swell all-around fellow.

I traveled through the early morning streets of Brooklyn as its citizens sent their offspring off to school and went to work and sweated and cursed and threatened harm to others, in this case to a contented professor of chemistry.

The populace continued to exhibit a negative attitude toward me. An old couple was crossing the street against the light. I moved my Camry with the green light.

"Ya bastard! We're senior citizens!" screamed the old, white-haired woman holding onto the arm of her old, short, mostly hairless husband.

A car passed on the right. The driver's window was down.

"Outta my way!" yelled the young black man who wore what looked like a woman's black hose over his head. The young black man cut in front; I noted the dents in his Hyundai.

I bore on, driving at the legal speed, driving in one lane at a time, not switching lanes, stopping at stop lights, and, with each new block, encountering intemperate motorists who seemed not to be unhappy and who were not hesitant in their direct stating of their frank opinions of me. I thought it was good that I held a high opinion of me or else this negativity would've been depressing.

I was on the way to the college. So far, nothing had come of Candy's killing. It'd made the papers, but no neighbor had come forth saying he'd seen at the scene a blonde in black and an all-white bambino. She'd had her moment of revenge; maybe her luck was catching, maybe I'd find the bastard who pushed my wife and boy into an incoming train. It wouldn't be a gun for me; I'd use my hands on him. I'd rip his fucking face off, I'd.... I slowed down, I was doing sixty in the city.

Finally, I entered the parking garage. There was a new man on duty, which meant that Beef Patty was still at the 4-12 p.m. shift. I knew the night man, who was a member of the Latin Monarchs, which meant the guard would spend most of his time distributing drugs to the students. Of all the groups in the world who did not need to go through life stoned, the students were at the top of my list. At one time, I'd marveled how the Latin Monarchs managed to dope up the pupils of the Urban U. without running afoul of the law until I'd learned the hard way that the law, in the form of my old pal, Dom Mancini, had cut in on the action.

Today, I did not enter the college itself. I parked and went out onto the Street and headed for the subway. At this hour, the Street was not awash with the less fortunate and those who might require something from me. That was good, for I was not really in a giving mood, unless you call giving grief giving.

I entered the subway a block from the parking garage. I have a less-than-positive view of the New York subway system. Which is to my mind accurate. Being on the subway was being trapped. The brakeman was sure as hell not going to come to the rescue if some shit went down.

I took the Bernie Goetz train into Manhattan. Keeping my eyes fixed above contact level, I stood, back to the door, as the train rolled toward the city. As the train moved along, my mind drifted to thoughts of Candy. Candy naked on her satin sheets, Candy a true blonde, the feel of her skin next to mine, Candy moving rhythmically underneath me.... I felt myself getting aroused. I decided to think of something else other than sex and Candy Dyer. Riding on the subway with a throbbing erection might call unwanted attention. I wanted to be invisible so that some punk didn't give me some unwanted attention.

Off the subway in midtown, I made my way to the main campus of the Urban U. At one time, this had been a familiar walk. That was some time ago.

I showed my I.D. to a security guard.

"You got to sign in," said the guard, who was tall and white and whose uniform fit. I would bet he'd didn't pork coeds during his spare time.

"I'm here for a meeting," I said.

"Put down the room."

I signed. I clearly wrote my name as "Al Pacino."

The guard did not even glance at what I'd written.

I walked into the campus. It was another world from the streets of Brooklyn. The brick buildings formed a quad. There were trees ringing the quad. There was grass in the quad, complemented by well tended flowerbeds. The main campus in Manhattan and the Brooklyn campus of the Urban U. were polar opposites, with my college being used as a depository for professors who were academic failures. Here on the main campus, Ph.D.s were granted in the humanities, MBAs for the business-minded, and JDs for those who wanted to deal with justice. It was a place which took itself very seriously. When I was here, I thought I was hot stuff. Times change. People change.

Sitting on a white bench, I looked at one of the four-story, all-brick buildings. I located the third floor. I focused on the window of what had been, some time ago, my office.

I watched a few students show up for classes. I felt the chill, such as it was, go out of the morning air. Even the air smelled better here. Maybe that just my mind doing the smelling.

I checked my watch. The meeting started at 9 a.m. I'd arrived early, which had always been my modus operandi. I was sure the meeting wouldn't convene on time. Professors never are on time. A lot of them are always late to class; technically that's neglect of duty but no one gives a shit. I used to be Johnny come earlier, now I did like everyone else and came to class when I wanted to.

I now had time to kill.

Chapter Forty-Eight

● ●

Still murdering minutes before the meeting, I stopped in front of my old office. On the door were the names of two professors I didn't know. They were both Tues/Thurs teachers. I tried my old key, which still worked, and entered what had been my office.

In my day, there had been three professors in the office. One had been a man named Burton Franks, the other yours truly, and the third an assistant professor from the English department named Ms. Jill Carmody.

"I have to observe her class," I'd said, pointing toward the assistant professor's desk.

"I'm sure she'll do a fine job of teaching," said Burton Franks, who'd been my mentor. He always wore a bow tie; he had a neatly trimmed gray moustache.

"What do I know about literature teaching?"

"You know about teaching. This is the idea of the Provost, for there to be cross-disciplinary observation." At the time I thought this was a foggy idea, now it seems to make sense. It stopped the campus from dividing into little camps that knew nothing but their own business.

"She told me she's a feminist," I said.

Burton Franks put down the book he was reading. The old professor spent an hour before each class rereading the book which was to be the focus of the lesson of the day. It was a practice to be admired. He was a guy to be admired. I admired him.

"Yes, she is."

"Is that good?"

"Her class will be 'fine.'"

"Why?"

"'Literature illuminates life for those to whom books are a necessity,'" quoted Burton Franks.

"Means?" I said.

"It means there are those who seek out quality in literature and those who are merely provocateurs," said Franks, looking pleasantly at me.

"So she's OK?"

"She is indeed, 'OK'. Her feminist zeal will always be tempered by her love of what's good in literature and what is not."

"Can I leave the woodshed now and go observe her class?"

"Yes, my boy, you can."

I had not talked to Burton Franks in a long time. The old professor had died in his sleep at his retirement home somewhere out West. I had learned of Burton Frank's death by reading his obit in the *Times*.

I thought about Biden, who was a good example of the trendy, yet Biden had failed to get published. He'd been banished to our place in his youth. Biden would be unable to find another job. Biden would be like Dr. Rudolf Randle had been—a target for the Dean.

I noticed my former office had only two desks, on each of which was a CPU. There were 17-inch monitors on both desks and there was one laser printer linked to the two computers. The floor was carpeted (gray), the walls were painted (off-white), an AC unit was mounted high up in a window. From the window, I had a view of the quad and its flowerbeds and its ring of trees. The two professors in the office did not stare out upon an old, masturbating white man who had stimulated himself and earned meal money by observing, and documenting, female elimination practices. Why did I stay at the Urban U.? That was simple; Candy was there, not here. Plus, I'd worn out my welcome at my old department. Hard to believe that a nice guy like me could do that.

I left the office. I went to the restroom on the third floor, which didn't smell and had no corpses for me to discover. I was still early for the meeting.

The restroom mirror reflected a "husky" man wearing a charcoal-gray, pin-stripe suit, a crisp white shirt, and a red power tie that would've passed muster at Ben Benson's. I looked at my socks, which were gray, and at my black Cole Haan shoes.

"If I looked any better, I'd be dead," I said to the man in the mirror. The man did not answer.

The appointments committee meeting would take place in the conference room next to the Chair of the English department's office.

I opened the door. I was not to be the first in attendance. Seated at one of the chairs around the conference table was a leggy blonde who looked, to my mind, a lot like a young and hot Sharon Stone.

"Hello."

"Hello," said Jill Carmody, who moved her eyes up and down me.

"You are no doubt amazed that I am in professional attire," I said.

"No. You always were properly dressed, it's just that most here aren't," said Jill Carmody, who was dressed in a black pants suit. She had on some type of gold jewelry around her neck, and her blonde hair was cut short. She was taller than Candy Dyer, and half of her face had not been ironed.

She laughed a confident, dressed-all-in-black, leggy-blonde laugh.

"This room bring back memories?" asked Jill Carmody.

"Yes."

"I remember your grilling me in here."

"Those were the days." I said, trying to recall what had gone on. This had been the second level of evaluation, an all-campus committee.

"You were the only professor who ever gave me an honest evaluation."

I sat down across from Jill Carmody.

"I was somethin' back then."

Jill Carmdoy smiled. She had full, red lips. Her teeth were even and white and had, no doubt, received the concentrated attention of a toney orthodontist.

"One point. After this meeting, I'd like for us to meet. Is 8 p.m. tonight at The Café all right for you?"

"I'll have to go and take out a second mortgage," I said.

"I'll treat."

"Now wait just a measly minute. There won't be any 'tricks' afterwards, no takin' me back to your apartment to see your etchings, that clear?" I said, not really wanting to go. I wanted to be with Candy. Even she needed some attention after her night of activity. She'd waited for that moment, and it'd been dropped in her lap, but now she had to deal with the aftermath. What is to replace hate after it's been satisfied?

Before Jill Carmody could answer, the door opened and in walked Stewart Bodner.

"Ah, I see that you are here," said Bodner, talking to Jill Carmody.

"Yes, we arrived early," she said.

"Together?" asked Bodner.

"No," I put in. "She came in a limo; I was delivered parcel post."

Bodner turned to face me. He was, like Jill Carmody, dressed all in black. Even his shirt was black. His tie was silver. His skin was sallow, his hair appeared to be dyed a shade of black not really to be found in the natural world. He did not look anything like Sharon Stone.

He looked like Winston Wiant, the head weirdo at our place—the Dean's right-hand man.

"You look nothing like Sharon Stone, you know," I said.

A snort of laughter came from the direction of Jill Carmody.

Bodner smiled at me but said nothing. He took a seat at the head of the table and waited for the rest of the committee members to arrive.

Silence hung in the air.

"Boy oh boy, is this silence ever hung," I said.

Chapter Forty-Nine

• •

"Bodner opened the meeting when all, finally, were in attendance. Thus, present and accounted for were: Vlad the Impaler, Jill 'YumYum' Carmody, and yours truly. Also allowed in the same room were Sidney 'NibShit' Lipschitz (ten minutes late) and Mary 'the moron' Mastoris (12 minutes late)." This I wrote down, to keep my hands busy, so that I wouldn't strangle someone. Academic meetings and me don't mix. Being in a locked room with assholes is not fun.

I stopped my writing and looked toward Mary Mastoris, who was sitting next to Jill Carmody. The close proximity to Dr. Carmody did not work to the advantage of Ms. Mastoris, for she looked like a fat frog. Mary Mastoris, B.A. M.A. Ph.D. had received tenure, and promotion to full professor, for singing, in public places frequented by trendy liberals, the love lyrics of some poet I'd never heard of. By Mastoris's side was a carrying case of some sort. I had attended, with Annie Porter, one of these performances. At the time, I'd wanted to beat up each person in the room. Annie had told me to behave.

I shifted my glance to stare at Sidney Lipschitz, who was old, paunchy, mostly bald, and had written two forgettable articles in 40 years in academics. Bodner's wrangling of Lipschitz into promotion to full professor was one of the great political feats of Western civilization. Bodner had surrounded himself with a ring of incompetents. That in itself was not a good idea, for revolution might stir in the ranks, which apparently was the case with Ms. Carmody. This was always going on. Once the great achievement of becoming chair had been achieved, then life was spent worrying about who wanted to dump you.

"We now come to the focus of today's meeting," said Bodner, who had been reading announcements, in the best tradition of a junior high school principal, for fifteen minutes, informing the committee members of facts they either should have known or could have read beforehand.

"I thought your boring-ass reading was the focus," I said.

"Point of order, point of order, the Chair has the floor," said Sidney Lipschitz, who talked out of the side of his mouth.

"I now come to the matter we must deal with," said Bodner.

"Well, Sidney, since you're the 'floorman', how about a parquet pattern; I'm open to colors." I was, as was evident, a bit pissed off.

"Huh?" said Mary Mastoris.

Jill Carmody said nothing.

"Mr. Biden will soon be brought in. Have we all read his record?" said Bodner.

"Not much to read," said Professor Lipschitz.

"Excuse me, but since you've been twice noted in the faculty newsletter as Most Unpublished, shut up," I said.

"You can't talk to me like that, you…."

"Remember our mission, which is to assess whether or not Dr. Biden should be re-appointed for another year," said Bodner, overtalking Lipschitz.

"We should keep an open mind," said Mary Mastoris.

"But our minds shouldn't be vacuums," I said, looking across the table at Sidney Lipschitz.

"We must remember that today we query but that we will not vote today. We will assemble again at the end of the week to take our vote."

"Were you addressing me?" said Lipschitz.

"I've never dressed a man in my life," I said, smiling at the old fart.

"What?" said Lipschitz.

"Huh?" said Mary Mastoris, who had a limited vocabulary.

Jill Carmody covered her full, red lips with one of her slender, tanned hands.

"I will ask Mr. Biden to come in," said Bodner, rising and walking to the door of the conference room.

I watched as Biden was led into the room. The young Ph.D. from Princeton appeared to have adopted the mode of Ted Bundy as he strolled his final stroll. His head was down, his shoulders slumped. This was not a confident man.

Lipschitz gave Biden what had been known, in former times, in Brooklyn, as the Redhook Brush-off Stare. Ms. Carmody gave him a nod as she assumed the look of an ice princess. Mary Mastoris smiled at him.

To Biden's left, at the head of the table, sat the unsmiling Chair, Dr. Stewart Bodner, dressed in funeral duds with an attending hostile expression on his pale face. Biden looked at the professors like he was looking at an execution squad. In that respect, he wasn't far wrong.

"Hello," I said. Biden didn't reply.

"Sidney, why don't you begin?" said Bodner, calling on Lipschitz who, referring to a file in front of him, launched an assault.

"Why wasn't your book published by _____ Press?" said Lipschitz.

"I don't know," said Biden.

"Sidney," I said, "I've researched the department's records. You're not even a blip on the publication radar screen."

"You shut the hell up!"

"Up I will not shut."

"Make him shut up!" said Lipschitz to the Chair.

"Continue, Sid," said Bodner.

"I've looked at your student evaluations and I see some criticisms of your manner," said Lipschitz.

"Oh, Sidney," I said. "I've checked with the Assistant Provost, you haven't even handed out the student evaluations for your classes for the last 20 years."

"You fuckin' bastard!" said Lipschitz.

"Is it possible to reconsider Lipschitz's tenure, even though it came about in the nineteenth century?" I said, thinking this was going well. Too bad it couldn't be taped and sent to the *Chronicle*.

"Does that conclude your questioning, Sid?" said Bodner.

"No, I'm not done. What's this I hear that you're not collegial?"

"People don't seem to like me," said Biden.

"Not to worry, three-quarters of the English department want Lipschitz dead."

"Thank you, Sid, let us move on. Mary, you're up," said Bodner.

"Why don't you sing Blake when you teach his poetry?" asked Mary Mastoris.

"I don't understand," replied Biden.

Professor Mastoris removed from the carrying case at her side a guitar. I regretted my neglecting to bring my video camera, for a tape of this performance would convince any normal man never to be a professor. She got ready to warble. I decided to pitch in.

"Do you know 'Michael Row the Boat Ashore'?" I asked.

"Oh, yes," said Mastoris, preparing to strum her guitar.

"Mary!" said Jill Carmody, getting Mastoris's attention, shaking her head in "no mode" to amplify her point.

"Oh, OK," said Mastoris, putting down her guitar.

"I have a few questions," said Jill Carmody.

Carmody proceeded to ask Biden direct questions about his scholarship and his teaching. These questions demanded precise, concise, recognizable answers. Biden sweated, stuttered, and stammered. The tall, blonde woman bore in; Biden was a sitting duck.

"Your turn," said Bodner, nodding my way.

Biden stared at the tabletop. His hands were clenched in front of him. He did not meet my eye. He did not meet any eyes.

"I've been told by some of my better students that your lessons on Blake are first rate. Can you tell us why you teach Blake?" I asked.

Biden seemed to have forgotten that Blake was a writer.

"The real reason a delay has occurred in the publication of your book on reader-response theory stems from the fact that you are so far ahead of the curve that criticism of your groundbreaking insights is nearly impossible. Could you expound on your cutting-edge concepts?" I asked the professor, trying to get Biden to defend himself, piling on the bullshit, most of which I'd got from Mac, who didn't seem to mind helping Biden. I wondered why.

Biden had difficulty communicating what his book was about.

"You're certainly one of the most engaging young professors we've seen in this department for quite some time. Could you tell us, as colleagues, how you're able to always be so upbeat and supportive of your fellow professors?" I was getting desperate, trying to get him to stand up and fight for his job, which he'd told me was all-important to his life.

"I don't understand why everyone hates me," said Biden, briefly glancing around the room. I could've answered that one for him. This guy was a world-class loser.

I gave up.

Bodner ended the meeting by picking up the hammer used by Lipschitz and pursuing a line of questioning I was sure the Taliban would've liked. Again, Biden was unable to resist the assault launched against him.

"Thank you for coming in," said Bodner, his tone now neutral.

Biden left the room quickly, stopping only to shake the department Chair's limp, white hand. I wondered if a poster child was needed for the

Stockholm Syndrome.

"We shall meet again at the end of the week. Check your e-mails," said Bodner. With that, he and Lipschitz left.

"Bye-bye, have a good day," I said, waving at them.

No response was forthcoming.

In the conference room were me, Jill Carmody, and Mary Mastoris.

"Did you ever hear of 'four dirty ditties by three naughty nuns in C-flat'?" I asked.

"Huh?" said Mary Mastoris. I was beginning to like her.

"Mary, I'll be with you in just a minute," said Jill Carmody, who stood up from the table.

Mary Mastoris picked up her guitar case and left the room.

"You're not gonna try somethin' with me now that we're all alone and I'm defenseless, are you?" I said, looking at her. She was tall, I didn't really have to look down at her. It was then that my memory worked. She looked like the blonde I'd met at the Spa. I wondered how they were friends.

"Tonight at eight?" said Jill Carmody.

"Well, I'll have to get out of these rags," I said.

"Eight?" said Jill Carmody.

"You know, Sharon Stone herself is now well over 40."

"So eight it is," said Jill Carmody, who left the room.

I was alone in the room. It felt good to be alone. Being around academics I held in contempt was tiring.

"You gon' be in here long?" said a voice from the door.

I turned and faced a Hispanic janitor who appeared eager to clean up the room.

"Make sure you wipe off that chair," I said, pointing to where Bodner had sat.

"Que?"

"The man who sat there was full of shit."

"Que?"

"Are you an administrator here?"

"Que?"

"Adios."

Chapter Fifty

· ·

I was once more alone and in my lab.

Ms. Candy Dyer was not due in until the next day. I let myself into Candy's desk. I searched through the papers. I found nothing such as a lurid diary saying how she'd been swept off her feet by a Sicilian sexual dynamo. I should've felt guilty about doing this, but I didn't. Like Newman said, He who has information has power. I was all for having that.

I went down to my office. No sooner was I in than someone knocked at the door, followed by the door opening.

"Hello, Annie."

Annie Porter came into the office. I could smell the raspberry shampoo she'd used. I looked at her outfit, which consisted of jeans, a loose white shirt, and boots of some sort. I could see her shape. She turned toward me, and I could see her blue-green eyes. She looked good.

"You look good," I said, regretting the words as soon as they escaped my lips.

"Someone die?" said Annie Porter, staring at my suit, tie, white shirt, and matching shoes and socks.

"I had a job to do," I said.

"Sorry, I shouldn't tease. How did Biden do?"

"F-."

"Bad?" said Annie Porter.

"Makes me wonder how he got a Ph.D. He was awful. Never saw anyone worse at making his case. They murdered him." Which was true; he was probably now in some emergency ward, trying to recover.

"But you'll still vote for him," said Annie, concern coming into her voice.

"Why not?" I said, noticing how she kept on task. That was all I now was to her. Useful. Maybe that was all I had ever been.

"Would you lower that?" said Annie Porter, squinting from the sunlight slashing into the room.

I moved to my desk. My new neighbors next door had their blinds down, except for the bathroom, which had its blind pulled down to within two inches of the bottom. I focused. There was something shiny at the bottom of the window. I put down the blinds in the office.

I sat down. I took out a Corona from Honduras, cut it, placed it in my mouth. Annie Porter sat down at the desk of the very young and very unable Dr. Biden.

"I tried to call you last night. There was no answer. Don't you have an answering machine?" she asked.

"I turn off the answering part at night and during the day."

"That's why I couldn't reach you."

"Did you drive to my place and leave a letter in my mailbox or tape a note to my microwave?"

"Please, this is serious."

"Is it?"

I rolled the Corona around in my mouth. Rolling cigars in one's mouth was almost as bad as smoking them. After my tracheotomy, I'd put in steel lips and a copper tongue.

"What did you want?"

"Are you meeting with Jill this evening?"

"Yes, at The Café, no less; I've been bonin' up on fork usage."

"Did she tell you why she wants to meet with you?" asked Annie Porter, boring in, getting to her point. She may have looked like a hippy-dippy, but she was tough. I had a tape which proved that.

"She probably wants to ply me with liquor, then take liberties with my person."

"Not likely. She has a new one, you know."

"What's she look like?"

"Like Jill."

"Like Jill now or like Jill way back when?"

"Back when."

"Back when as in 20s or 30s?"

"20s."

"Our little Jill's becoming a dirty old woman."

"This one lives in the Heights."

"Jill lives in the Heights."

"They're not living together, yet."

"So Jill is on the prowl," I said. So that was who the young blonde was. I felt out of place at the Spa, not being gay and all.

"Nice," said Annie Porter.

"This new one, does she really look like Jill?"

"Yes."

"Does she work out?"

"I don't know the details of her life."

"I think she ogled me."

"She what?"

"At the Spa, a.k.a. Lou's, I was working out, rippling, sweating, being really manly, and there she was, ogling me, then strikin' up a conversation,"

I said.

"What did she want to talk about?"

"Whether or not I was gay."

"What'd you tell her?"

"I said no."

"Will you work all of this information about her partner in over dinner with Jill?"

"I think I might."

"Could you 'work it in' after she tells you her plan?"

"Then I should call you?"

"Would you?" said Annie Porter, smiling.

I liked to see my preconceptions confirmed. Good-looking women see the world as an arena for getting what they want. Annie wanted Jim to stay on the main campus. She'd do what she had to help him. That was all that mattered. I was a means to an end. No more, no less.

"Of course," I said, lighting the Corona. I then blew a smoke ring.

"I know Biden's no good, everyone knows it, but...." said Annie Porter, holding her nose, then laughing.

"Mary Mastoris and Lipschitz, they're good?"

"Jim's in trouble," said Annie Porter, blurting out the words, no longer laughing.

"Is he?"

"Yes. I found out yesterday the college has a new formula for the size of the department."

I gnawed on my cigar and waited.

"The Brooklyn campus is now figured in the total."

"Which means?"

"That Biden and the adjuncts down here must be counted as part of the department...."

"Sorry to interrupt but this higher math is beyond me. We're talkin' about Jim, right? What're you worried about?"

"I don't trust Jill."

"Good."

"Yes. I always considered her a friend, but lately…."

"You're on target. Jill's a friend of Jill. She cares nothin' about you and Jim."

"You're probably right about that."

"I wish I wasn't. What're you worried about?"

"Jim's record is not strong."

"Whose is? Lipschitz? Jim has tenure, he could roll around buck naked on the floor during class, singing filthy songs while pointing to his private parts, and no one would do anything."

"Don't make me laugh, this is serious. Jill's forcing a recall election. She's going to change the department," said Annie Porter.

"Look, don't worry about Biden."

"But all of this is bad for Jim."

"Don't worry."

"Why not?"

"All of this nonsense about votes and maneuvers is academic crap."

"So what's to be done?"

"Let me worry about that."

"I guess I'll have to trust you."

"Yes."

"Don't drink too much tonight."

"I'll be on the wagon."

"Or under it."

"Ouch."

Annie Porter laughed.

"Oh, by the way, I've something to ask you," I suddenly said.

"What's that?"

"You have a good opinion of Candy Dyer, right?"

"That I do. Why?"

"I'm goin' to the Dean to see if I can have her taken on for next year," I said, rushing out the words.

"You'll have your work cut out for you dealing with him. Sorry, I have to run. Jim's waiting," said Annie, who did not this time kiss me.

She left the office.

The room filled with smoke.

Someone knocked at the door.

"Professor, this is for you from Mendy." Mina, Mendy the Cup's assistant, handed me a package.

"Tell him thanks."

"Yeah."

I would've preferred that Mendy himself had delivered the film. Maybe this meant there was nothing to see of note.

I sat down at Biden's desk. I withdrew the contents.

The old man next door had taken many pictures of the office. There were photos of Bath alone, of Randle alone, of me alone. Those confirmed my suspicions about the old pervert. He was looking to get the goods on whoever he could. Mendy had developed 50 pictures. I tore all of the pictures into small pieces, then placed the pieces in a paper bag. One of the pictures I studied. It was of Bath. He was seated at his desk; his white linen pants were down. Bath was looking at someone. The someone couldn't be fully seen, just a leg, in gray pants. The someone wasn't all that tall. Pat Reagan was right; the old boy had been a cruiser. Well, he'd cruised his last cruise. I subtracted a worry from my list. I owed Mendy the Cup one.

I turned off the light. I stood far back in the office, where I could look out the window but could not be seen by whoever was in the apartment next door. Time passed. Five minutes. Ten. The blind in the bathroom across the way went up.

I could see, quite plainly, the small Indian kid who dispensed, and mopped up, coffee for Fat Harry Blazakis.

Fat Harry was asking for it.

I tried to think about Biden. Thoughts of Candy interfered. Images of her flooded my mind. I let my recollection of her in her bedroom surround me. I smoked, in the dark, as I recalled.

Chapter Fifty-One

- -

Night had fallen in Brooklyn. I would drive to the Heights, which was an old but nice neighborhood of Brooklyn. It hadn't really needed to be gentrified.

In the parking garage, I was greeted by the night security guard.

"Got bad news, Prof," said 'Beef Patty' Norwood.

"You do?"

"Yeah, there gonna be trouble down here. I talk it over with Malvina. She think I better get a new job," said Beef Patty.

"We'd miss you," I said, wondering where the big black man could find another job. Sleeping, having sex with teenagers, and eating candy were not really something to put on a resumé.

"You know wha's happenin'?"

"No."

"The Seoul Brothers gettin' in J.P.'s face," said Beef Patty.

"They are?"

"Yeah, it got somethin' to do with that ol' whitey next door who got his dick cut off."

"It does?"

"Yeah, when I get a line on it, I'll fill you in."

"Thank you, Lester." This had, for once, nothing to do with me. This was the coming to a head of trouble that had been brewing for a long time. It was inevitable that sooner or later J.P. and Jimmy Fisheyes would have a showdown. I just hoped I wasn't in the middle when it went down. However, I wouldn't mind to watch.

I left the Urban U. and headed for my rendezvous, or whatever it would turn out to be, with Jill Carmody. At one time, I would have regarded such an evening as entertaining, maybe amusing, but now the time would simply be hours away from Candy. I'd told her about this evening; she thought it was OK if I dined with a lesbian.

Chapter Fifty-Two

· ·

I walked toward the restaurant on the river and noticed those who walked with me. Most of them were young with deep pockets. I had a nice suit on but the pockets weren't particularly deep.

A barge was moored close to the restaurant; the barge advertised itself as having a bar and a ballroom. I could hear singing. I headed toward the noise. At the entrance, a thin, young man with a shaved head and one gold earring and wearing a tuxedo asked me for an invitation.

"Don't have one."

"Say what?" said the young man, not smiling.

The tone suggested that, regardless of the tie and tails, the thin young man still spent his evenings no doubt somewhere in Brooklyn.

"What's goin' on?"

"No invitation, you can't go in."

"I have better things to do," I said. Which I did.

I went into the ritzy restaurant.

"Do you have a reservation?" asked the maitre de at the front desk. He was wearing a tuxedo and had a neat mustache.

"I just want some French fries and a Michelob to go."

"Name, please," he said, not cracking a smile.

"Carmody, party of two."

The maitre de checked his list.

"Ah yes, and you are?"

"Two."

"Follow me." I followed.

The maitre de led the way deep into The Café, passing swarms of the drinking, networking upwardly mobile. At journey's end, I saw Jill Carmody sitting at a table which The Café advertised as having a million-dollar view of Manhattan.

"Good evening," said Jill Carmody, who was dressed in a slinky black dress.

"Your dress is black, and it is slinky," I said. She looked good but nowhere as good as Candy.

The maitre de pulled out the chair. I debated as to saying "You don't think I'm falling for that one. First you question my name, then you make me look out the window at what's left of Manhattan, now you try the old pull-out-chair, sit-down, pull-back pratfall routine."

I decided not to. I was out of my element for such comments to be appreciated.

"I'll bring the wine list," said the maitre de.

"Does Budweiser make a good Zinfandel?" I said to the back of the disappearing maitre de.

"I do frequent this place, you know," said Jill Carmody, her voice husky.

"Oh."

Jill Carmody smiled, parting her full, red lips, exposing her perfect white teeth.

"I recommend the Merlot," said the maitre de, who had re-appeared. He was quick. Probably knew a good tipper when he saw one.

"No, no, my fine fellow, she'd like the Pouilly Fuisse, 1968. I'd like a Jack Daniels drownin' the rocks. She'll probably prefer that wonderful appetizer of grilled octopus and Manila clams. Is that available tonight, or should I wait and ask our waiter?"

"No, it's available. Shall I bring two wine glasses?"

"No, she's a guzzler, is the little woman."

Jill Carmody laughed.

"How did you know that's my favorite wine?" she asked.

"I broke into your townhouse today. I have a full dossier on you. Will it be the Chukar Partridge for your entrée?"

"You are a bit scary, you know," said Jill Carmody.

"I know. At night, I walk two paces back of myself just to feel safe," I said, smiling at her.

The maitre de returned. By his side was a young Hispanic with jet-black, Roberto Duran hair who uncorked. The wine was offered to Jill Carmody to taste. They knew better than to give it to me. I didn't look like the wine-tasting type.

"Lovely," she said.

I drank a large gulp of the Jack Daniels the Hispanic wine de-corker had set before me.

"Lovely," I said.

"I'll send your waiter over."

"Wait a bit, I want to get her pie-eyed."

The maitre de and his wine boy left.

"Success to crime," I toasted.

"Sam Spade?"

"Yes."

"He your hero?" said Jill Carmody.

"Yes."

"Not Marlowe?"

"Marlowe wouldn't have sent over Al Capone."

"And you, you would have sent over Brigid?"

"Yes, but I would've scheduled conjugal visits."

Jill Carmody laughed. I liked the sound of her laughter, but I knew a laugh I liked better.

She ran her long, slim fingers around the edge of the wine glass. She looked at me. I could see her blue-green eyes and her long eyelashes.

"Do you know why we're here?"

"Sin?"

"No, departmental politics."

"Well, that's kinda like sin."

"I plan to take over the department," said Jill Carmody.

"That's nice," I said, taking on more booze. This promised to be a long evening.

"The department is full of deadwood."

"How dast you so speak of Sidney Lipschitz."

Jill Carmody smiled.

"He's what I'm talking about."

"I know, I try to come upon him in surprise, then yell 'HEY, SID, HOW YOU DOIN' in the hopes a coronary will occur."

"This vote on Biden is a chance for me to discredit Stewart."

"Couldn't you just send everyone a photo and tape to it a message which read somethin' like 'Are you kiddin' me?'"

"I could, but I want to use the vote on Biden to my advantage."

"You do?" I said, listening to another woman lay out her plan for power.

"Yes. The department is full of those who either do no work or do no cutting-edge work."

"Biden doesn't strike me as an edge-cutter," I said, hating that word.

Most of this work is about as cutting-edge as a dull lawn mower.

"He's not, plus he's a poor teacher."

"Didn't Bodner steal your thunder by sendin' him down here?"

"That wasn't Bodner. I also serve on the presidential committee. Unlike the one you're on, our committee wasted no time sending Dr. Biden packing."

"Our esteemed President, this one of her missions?"

"Yes, we'll be funded in the future, proportional to our acclaim in the critical world."

"Do you realize what crap all of this is?" I said, unable to resist saying what I meant. Which was a mistake. I decided to control myself. I'm not good at keeping such promises.

"I want to run the department, and the only work done by professors that interests the administration is publication," she said, ignoring my comment.

"Why are you tellin' me all of this?"

Jill Carmody sipped her wine.

"This involves Annie," she said.

"Let me guess, Annie and Jim McDougal don't fit into the department you're going to create."

"No, they don't. Annie's area is now modern drama. Do you know how boring Arthur Miller is to today's English major? Plus she is cross-disciplinary with her art history background. But she does a good job with composition. That'll allow me to keep her on. Jim's a different story. He is a specialist on Hawthorne. Very ho-hum. Jim's also a bit rigid in the classroom. Today's students like to be taught by professors closer to them in age who relate...."

"...and teach by havin' the class sit in a circle to avoid the appearance of authority," I interjected, "then cut them considerable breaks such as not demanding assigned books be read or class be attended on a regular basis and by usin' a scale of grades ranging from A+ to A- while they attend conferences and offer insights no sane person would ever consider." I drained my glass and, holding it aloft, caught the eye of the Hispanic wine boy. He came and poured wine for Jill Carmody.

"I want Bodner to vote for Biden, and also Sidney," Jill Carmody said.

"I seem to recall a meeting in the not-too-distant past at which Bodner seemed just a little bit negative about our boy Biden."

"Correct, but the old guard is now pressuring Bodner to keep Biden on."

"Operating on the principle you should always give tenure to those dumber than you, so they never get wise to you?"

"Exactly."

"Aren't you supposed to be bold and audacious?"

"I try."

"Then I'll vote no. Bodner comes to see me, I'll let him think I'm a yes."

"Perfect," said Jill Carmody, offering her hand. I could feel the heat coming from it. The blonde at the Spa and Jill here would make one hot couple.

"You know, there was a time when I was against you," she said, still holding my hand.

"No!"

"Burton Franks told me you didn't want me kept on because I was a feminist."

"And you replied?"

"That you were a sexist."

"And he then straightened you out about me as he did me about you."

"That he did."

"Here's to Burton."

"Yes."

Jill Carmody released my hand.

We clinked glasses.

"May I take your orders?" said a tall, red-haired woman dressed in a black suit.

I ordered for Jill Carmody. I ordered her appetizer, her salad with her favorite dressing, and her entrée of choice.

"What'll you have, Sir?" asked the waitress.

"The turbon of walleye, a caesar with very hairy anchovies, and the free-range, pan-roasted rabbit which was, earlier today, sadly, run over in the parking lot," I said.

"And you said you've never been here before," said Jill Carmody.

"Do you come here often?"

"Yes."

"Have you ever seen me here?"

"No."

"You may be mink-slinky and have great choppers and sound like Stevie Nicks, but you have your limitations."

Jill Carmody didn't laugh. She didn't even smile. Not as much as a lip twitch. I thought I must be slipping and maybe should try some of my gay Sicilian jokes. Then again, maybe not.

I drank my Jack Daniels. Jill Carmody sipped her wine.

I smiled at Jill Carmody.

"Success to crime," I said.

"Success to crime. So, is your friend, the horrible Dr. McClure, behaving himself?" said Jill Carmody, raising her wine glass, taking on more alcohol.

"Off the record?"

"Off the record," she said, after a hesitation.

"Mac's not changed."

"He's asking for it, you know."

"Hasn't he already got it? He's in Siberia."

"He came this close to being fired." Jill Carmody held up two fingers, showing an inch of measurement.

"But no one came forward."

"No one. We tried, but he had them all under his spell."

"He'll be back to you one day."

"Not if I have my way."

Before the conversation veered into argument, I cut off my comments. What did I care what happened to McClure? Mac was a running buddy, but I disapproved of the other activities. The students might look older, but they were still kids; McClure had no business cultivating his own personal fuck harem at the college.

"Any more changes you have in mind for the department?" I asked. I listened as Carmody revealed her plans. I made a suggestion; she hesitated, then agreed. After that, the topic became boring. But Jill Carmody droned on.

Chapter Fifty-Three

• •

At the college next day, I avoided the elevator and used the back stairs. As soon as I opened the door to the stairway, I smelled it. Dope. Down one flight of the stairs I went, moving very fast, taking care not to fall. There on the steps, two students were sitting, smoking, sampling, no doubt, what the Latin Monarchs had to offer.

"Hi, Prof," said the female student.

"Hi, how are you?" I said, hearing the words slightly echo as I spoke them in the stairwell.

"No class tonight?" said the male student, who took a deep pull on his "cigarette."

"No, if you need to see me, come to my office," I said, making my way past the two dopers. The stairwell was thick with the smoke of heavy-duty marijuana. The Monarchs didn't mess around. They would supply the students with enough pop to keep them mellow for a month. Which was OK with me. Better mellow than hopped up. I didn't need drug crazies in my classes.

As always, I was impressed by the cleanliness of the administrative floor. It was true in college teaching that administrators would not exist in the living conditions they forced upon professors and students. The walls were dust free, and nothing nasty scurried across a dirty floor; I walked on clean, white tiles.

I did not knock at the Dean's door.

At a desk was seated the Dean's secretary, the wizened white woman. I smiled at the secretary. I even removed my dark glasses.

"Yes," said the old woman in a raspy voice.

"I would like to see the Dean."

"Do you have an appointment?"

"No."

"Is this an emergency?"

"Kinda."

"How so?"

"I'm here to help someone."

"Have a seat, I'll see if I can work you in," said the secretary.

"Thanks."

I took a chair in the outer chambers of the Dean's office. The floor was carpeted in a light gray and was clean. An air conditioner blew cool filtered air across the room. This was how the other half lived.

I settled in for a long wait. The Dean did not allow drop-ins. I'd have to endure some time doing nothing.

After I'd read three magazines about academic leadership, I was ushered into the Dean's office. I took a seat in the small green plastic chair directly in front of the Dean's desk. I noticed the Dean's eyes as they swept over me, no doubt taking in the fact that my eyes were not hidden by dark glasses.

"What can I do for you, Professor?" said the Dean, not smiling.

"First, I want to say we made it through the term without the gangs causing trouble," I said, employing a conversational icebreaker.

"That is true. We talked about that situation previously, didn't we?" said the Dean, whose small, plump hands rested on the large wooden desk.

"Yes, we did. It's just that sometimes what we think should happen, doesn't," I said, not wanting to listen to my own forced words.

"That is true," said the Dean, looking directly into my eyes, unblinking, waiting for me to come to the point.

"Nice place you have here," I said, looking around the room, taking in the many pictures on the wall. Over the Dean's head and behind him were frames of his degrees. I wondered if there were from On-line U.

"Did you have a particular reason for this visit?" asked the Dean, showing impatience.

"Well, I did want to inquire about one thing."

"And that is?"

"I want to see if Ms. Dyer will be kept on for next year," I got out, rushing the words.

"Yes, she does an excellent job."

"Yes, she is excellent."

"Does that conclude this meeting?" said the Dean.

"Yes, it does."

"Have a good summer," he said.

I extended my hand.

There was a moment's hesitation, then the Dean briefly shook my hand. I was surprised; his grip was strong, not a dead fish.

I left the office. Yippee!! Candy and I were on for another year. I could tell her; we'd go to a nice restaurant in Brooklyn. Beat up a patron or two.

I again used the stairs, resisting the urge to do them two at a time. The students were gone, but the smell of what they had been intaking lingered. I could've paused and gotten high, but the thought of Candy and me had revved up my motors. Life was going along swimmingly. Bath was dead; there had been no more killings of faculty. The stabbing seemed not to have made a big splash in the newspapers.

Chapter Fifty-Four

● ●

"Watch your step," I said to Dr. Stewart Bodner as we walked away from the college. The day was hot and humid. Heat brought out the worst in Brooklyn. Creatures, human and otherwise, populated the streets.

"Why?" said the dark-clad department Chair.

I pointed toward a tall, shabby, scrawny white man across the Street who was vomiting in a doorway. Some of the vomit splashed out onto the sidewalk but most of it hit a building, running down the brick.

"I see," said Bodner, looking around at the street traffic.

"Oh, it's what we call home," I said, taking off at a fast pace.

Bodner had to walk very fast to keep up. I enjoyed making life difficult for him.

"Today's not a teaching day for you, is it?" asked Bodner, getting the words out quickly.

"Gearin' up for finals, we're almost done."

Bodner and I headed away from the Urban. U.

Finally, we arrived at our destination. In a better area. I had decided not to take him to Fat Harry's. We entered a small corner restaurant with a name I'd always disliked. I found a cozy corner table in the corner restaurant for the two of us.

"This area has certainly changed," said Bodner, looking out the window at gentrification in the raw.

"Seepage."

"What?" said Bodner.

"The sewers of the city are emptying into here."

"What can I get for you?" said the waitress.

I ordered two hard-to-pronounce sandwiches plus a large coffee, all of which would buy a month's worth of food in Guatemala.

"You come here often?" said Bodner, after he'd ordered a salad of mostly sprouts.

"No."

"Let us get down to business," Bodner said with an edge to his voice. He stared directly at me with his dead, seemingly black eyes.

"Let us."

"The department is divided. The whole-college committee you're on perfectly illustrates the division," said Bodner.

The waitress arrived with two coffees. I sipped the coffee down an inch. I added half-and-half. I used the sugar dispenser. I held the dispenser over the coffee for some time. Bodner was looking at me.

"I come from strong stock," I said.

"So this committee meeting is a test of strength between Ms. Carmody and me."

"She's tall, but if you work inside, go to the body. I think you can take her."

"We were having an adult conversation," Bodner said, growing impatient.

"Oh."

"Carmody is power hungry. She's buttonholed the younger faculty, she's pushing for a recall vote."

Bodner must be truly desperate to be having this conversation, I thought. Our exchanges before this point in time had been mostly insults bordering on fuck off.

"What do the numbers look like?"

"I find it difficult to believe I'm talking with you about all this."

"Do you find talking to Lipschitz of value?"

Bodner smiled his Mengele smile, showing uneven teeth. He sipped his coffee.

"Not really, but allies are allies, right?" I said.

"The numbers run against me. Many do not understand our department has a mission...."

"Sorry to interrupt," I interrupted, "but your department has 104 majors out of a college-wide pool of 6,000. Most urban universities of the same size as us have 500 majors out of the same pool size. You're drownin'," I said, showing off my research. I knew of which I spoke.

"That's what Carmody is using against me," said Bodner, whose forehead had started to break out in sweat even in the cool restaurant.

"Does she have a point?"

"Can we speak frankly?"

"Why not?" I was hungry. I hoped the sandwich would be good and well worth the large slice out of my professorial pay.

The waitress arrived with the hard-to-pronounce sandwiches and Bodner's sprout-laden salad.

I took a bite, tried to figure out what had been mixed in with what, chewed, swallowed, then drank more coffee. The sandwich sucked.

"Did you ever check the GPAs of the English majors?" I said, not waiting for an answer. "I have. Their grades on the core classes required of all students are the lowest in the college."

"Yes, but...."

"And to boot, the English majors are a freak show. Look at your classes. It's a parade of misfits and malcontents. What normal person would take one of your department's offerings? The students are dopes, and the professors are worse," I said, making life difficult for him.

Bodner ate his salad. His pallor seemed to worsen. He changed the subject.

"I need you to vote for Biden," Bodner said, blurting out the words.

"For? I thought you and my pal, dear old Sid, were buryin' the boy."

"That was just a ploy."

"A 'ploy'. This sound, Kemo Sabe, very high-level in terms of politics."

"Will you vote yes?"

"OK."

Bodner stared at me. Bodner looked away.

"Good."

He offered to shake hands.

Bodner put his small, cold hand inside my large mitt.

I slowly released the hand of the English department Chair.

We finished our meal.

Chapter Fifty-Five

. . . .

I put on my dark glasses.

"See you tomorrow," said Bodner.

"Right."

Bodner walked toward the Street, where he could take the subway back to the safe confines of the main campus in Manhattan. I wondered if Bodner would survive the subway ride. The English department Chair would make an easy target for subway thugs in search of a dollar, or a little tortuous fun.

I returned to the Urban U.

It was a warm day.

I walked slowly. I could feel the heat of the sun as it beat down on the bricks of Brooklyn. Humidity had come with the heat.

The closer I came to the college, the dirtier the streets became. Power brokers gave way to panhandlers. The heat forced out of the concrete the odors of gasoline and vomit and shit. The humidity was kind to, I could see, the abodes of rats. It was a sight I knew all too well.

"Five dollah, I suck you jus' right," called a sexy voice from a doorway.

"Hello, Bob."

"Sorry, Prof, didn't recognize you."

"That's OK," I said, continuing on my way.

The Teaser laughed a rather sinister laugh.

It was the merry month of May in Brooklyn.

Chapter Fifty-Six

· ·

"Hey Prof, hot day, huh?" said Beef Patty Norwood, who was standing on the front steps of the Urban U. Both armpits of the security guard's blue uniform were stained with sweat. Patty was a heavy sweater. I hoped he drank a lot of water.

"Yes, Lester, very hot."

"You go out for lunch?" said the big black man.

"Yes."

"You go with that lil' fish-face dude?"

"Yes. I did."

"Good thing you was with him, Prof. Dude look like that down here, he askin' for it, know what I mean?" said Beef Patty.

"Yes, I do."

"Say Prof, you 'member wha' I said 'bout trouble down here?"

"Yes."

"Well, we got it."

"We do?"

"Yeah, I tol' Malvina I gettin' too old for this."

"You're a young man, Lester."

"Compare to J.P., I a gran'pa. That one wild-assed young man."

"You got that right."

I took out a cigar, cut it, inserted it in my mouth. The cigar tasted good after the crappy lunch.

"J.P., he got big ol' Harry nex' door."

"He did?"

"Yeah, you knew ol' Harry he was sellin' drugs wit' tha' spick."

"Yes."

"I tol' him not to fuck 'round wit' them Monarchs but he don' listen."

I chewed on my cigar.

"So, J.P., he grab one of Harry's daughters," he said, mopping his large forehead. I noticed that nothing escaped Beef Patty's notice. He probably knew the GPAs of the coeds he fucked.

"Which one?"

"The really fat one."

"Oh, that one."

"Yeah, J.P., he went to where she live, he watch her...."

"J.P. tell you this personally?"

"Naw, that boy think I one useless fat-ass nigger. He think he the one percent, he think I'm shit."

"So who told you?"

"Din't no one tell me, they tol' Malvina," said Beef Patty.

I admired Beef Patty's precision in answering questions. Blacks in Brooklyn knew better than to talk in generalities. Interrogated by a cop, they gave exact answers to general questions. That was the way to avoid being hauled into a precinct building and being questioned under less-than-ideal circumstances.

"Who, exactly, was it who told Malvina about Fat Harry's daughter?"

"Nikki."

"She's a friend of Malvina?"

"Naw, they some type of cousin. Malvina could tell you how they related."

"So, J.P. grabbed Fat Harry's daughter, and then?" I said, trying to direct his conversation so the information came out a bit quicker.

"They got her, snatched her big whitey fat ass off the street outside some club. Shot her full of H. Dump her off uptown."

"She alive?"

"Yeah, but she in the hospital. That H, it fuck you up real bad."

I looked toward the corner deli. I hadn't noticed it was closed when I'd walked by with Bodner. I should've noticed it was closed. Being careless about details is a sure way to stumble into trouble. Especially in Brooklyn.

"So Harry closed down?"

"Jus' for today. J.P. got the Indian kid."

"He did?"

"Yeah tha' dothead, he took over takin' pussyshots of the girls in the bathroom."

"Who rented the apartment for him?"

"Ol' fat Harry."

"So Harry expanded his business?"

"Yeah, he was pushin' for Morales, and he was sellin' pussy pictures," said Beef Patty, who was more observant than outward appearances would indicate.

"And the 'dothead'?"

"He got his joobies kicked in. He ain't gonna be interested in no pussy any time soon."

"So, what's the trouble? It sounds like the trouble is over."

"No, it jus' startin', Prof."

"Jimmy Fisheyes?"

"Yeah, he goin' 'round tellin' everyone that J.P.'s fuckin' wit' his uncle. The Seoul Brothers say they bein' dissed."

"Any more news?"

"Oh yeah, I was gonna tell you. That cop you know, he was lookin' for you las' week. I tol' him the college was closed down."

"What'd he say?"

"Said nothin'. You know cops, they ain't gonna tell no fat black man whas on their min'."

"Sounds like the summer can't come soon enough."

"We gettin' too old for this, Prof."

"If it doesn't kill us, it will make us stronger."

"That a good one, Prof, you make that up yourself?"

"No, it was some German a long time ago."

"That another thing. That lil' Russian broad, she gone. Her ol' man he say he don't want her down here no mo'."

"That's good."

"Summertime, you go up to your place in Canada, don' you?"

"Yes."

"Must be nice up there."

"Very nice."

"When you leave?"

"As soon as school is out."

"After you done with your work, right?"

"Yes, Lester, after the work is done. For now, I've got to go somewhere to get some coffee."

"Why don' you go to the cafeteria?"

"Bad coffee and bad attitudes."

"I hear ya, Prof," said Beef Patty, offering a large hand.

I shook Beef Patty's hand.

Beef Patty went inside the Urban U.

I could feel the hot sun on my neck.

Chapter Fifty-Seven

. . . .

Inside the college were students carrying books on their way to study. The students would need no such books for my finals. I was as basic as could be.

I decided to visit the mailroom. This was becoming a regular occurrence, which I did mostly because Candy told me to. I liked being hen-pecked, although Candy was hardly a hen.

Walking into the mailroom, I bumped into a professor.

"Getting a little pushy, aren't we?" said McClure, who was wearing another *GQ* outfit.

"Dressed in rags, I see."

"You ready for the weekend?" said McClure, flashing his brilliant all-white smile. The big man was deeply tanned.

"Hills and heat. Your ass is in trouble."

"Could it be that you're practicing gamesmanship with your old buddy?" said McClure.

"Don't say I didn't warn you."

"Plus you'll feed me if you happen to win?"

"Yes, I've found an all-you-can-eat sushi restaurant that will allow you to get over losin'."

"We'll see. I've tried a new method of training."

"What's that?"

"Sprinting 100-meter gassers for as long as I can stand it."

"Any improvement?"

"I now pass deer."

We left the mailroom.

A short Asian girl with gleaming black hair was waiting in the hallway.

"Should I go to your office now?" she said, looking up at McClure and ignoring me.

"Yes, I'll be right there," said McClure.

The girl walked away. I watched McClure watch the girl walk.

"See you, I've got to go," he said, offering his big hand.

We shook hands. McClure followed the girl to the elevator. The two of them got on the elevator. I watched as the elevator went up to the seventh floor.

I knew what would go on in that seventh-floor office. McClure was having a last one before school ended. This guy was something else.

I used the back stairs. I took my time climbing the stairs. My mind moved to thoughts of Biden.

In my office, I saw that his green workout bag was there. He must be running. Not the best weather to run in. My bag was also in the room. I had a water bottle in it. The bottle felt warm. I poured the water into a wastepaper basket, where it would stay for months.

I decided to go see Candy, maybe engage in some smooching. That sounded like a good idea.

Chapter Fifty-Eight

I sat alone in the conference room on the main campus. Yesterday's heat wave had been broken by a night and now a morning of hard rain.

The door opened. In walked Mary Mastoris, sans guitar case. With her was Jill Carmody, wearing mostly white and looking good. Mary wasn't in white and she looked less than good. Bad was how she looked.

"Hello," said Jill Carmody in her husky voice.

"Hello," said Mary Mastoris, who must have dressed herself in the dark. Her clothes did not match, plus the individual pieces were odd in design and confusing in color.

"Top of the morning," I said.

Mastoris and Jill Carmody sat down side by side at the other end of the table. No more conversation ensued.

At 9:20 a.m., Bodner and Lipschitz entered the conference room. Bodner was dressed in his customary funeral black while Lipschitz had on an outfit that seemed more appropriate for Boca Raton.

Lipschitz sat across from Mastoris and Carmody. Bodner took a seat directly opposite me at the other end of the table. There were two chairs on my right and two on my left between me and my colleagues. I was sure I'd showered before I'd left the house.

Bodner began to read announcements about matters that should have been summarized and distributed. He read for some time. Lipschitz stared directly at Bodner. Mary Mastoris's eyes wandered around the room. Jill Carmody kept her head down and doodled on the pad in front of her.

"Now, let's proceed to the matter at hand, the re-appointment of Karl M. Biden."

"Call for a secret ballot," said Lipschitz.

"Aren't you rushin' the foreplay just a bit?" I said.

"I've had about enough of you," said Lipschitz.

"Now, Shitlips, I always heard it was you who put what's left of his thing in ewes." I said, giving my temper just a bit of free rein.

"What?" said Lipschitz.

"I don't understand," said Mary Mastoris. These three words were a step up from her usual "huh"; she must've drunk a power drink before she came in.

"There's been a motion for a secret ballot that must be voted on," said Jill Carmody.

"Exactly right, let's vote. All in favor of a secret ballot say 'Aye,'" said Bodner.

"Aye."

"Aye."

"Aye."

"Aye."

"Nyet, nien, nope, no, nibshit, and nutz."

"The 'Ayes' have it. Let's vote," said Bodner.

"I want to go on record that there was no final discussion of Biden's record, not his teaching, not his publications, not his committee work," I said.

"'Go on record,' what's that mean? This more of your guardhouse lawyer crap?" said Lipschtiz, who glared at me.

"Look, Pissdrips, you're the secretary for this meeting so, providing you can still hold a pen, you have to write down any and all of my objections, which will become a part of the recommendation sent to the President."

"What happens if I don't write this down?" said Lipschitz to Bodner.

"No need to talk to your master," I said, "I'll tell you. I'll leave the meeting right now. You won't be able to take a vote and all of this will have to be done over."

"Write down his objections," said Bodner.

Lipschitz asked me to repeat my comments.

"I'll speak slowly, considering that I'm talkin' to the almost-dead."

"I won't stand for any more of...."

"Just take down what he wants to say," said Bodner.

Lipschitz noted the remarks.

"Satisfied?" said Bodner.

"In the Mick Jagger sense?"

"Sid, would you distribute the ballots?"

Lipschitz gave each professor around the table a small slip of white paper, more or less throwing mine at me.

"A 'Yes' means Biden will be re-appointed for a period of one year. A 'No' means he will be terminated as of June 1."

The professors recorded their votes on the small slips of white paper.

"Sid, would you collect the ballots."

Bodner soon had before him five ballots.

"Professor Mastoris, would you please come over here and verify the tally as I open the ballots?"

Since the total votes would equal five, Dr. Mastoris would not have to remove her shoes to aid in the count.

"We have a vote," said Bodner.

"So soon?"

"Point of order, the Chair has the floor," said Lipschitz.

"Will you be buried in that outfit?"

"The vote is three 'no' and two 'yes,'" said Mastoris.

"You backstabbing' sonufabitch!" said Lipschitz.

"I demand a recount!" I said.

"No, it's correct, I counted them twice," said Mary Mastoris.

"Oh, in that case, I withdraw my request for a recount. Have the absentee ballots from upstate arrived?"

"That concludes our business for the day. I will inform Dr. Biden," said Chairman Stewart Bodner, glaring at me.

"Oh, one last point."

"Stop wastin' our time!" said Lipschitz.

"What is it?" asked Bodner.

"Did I hear a formal motion for adjournment?"

"Is there a motion to adjourn?"

"So moved," said Lipschitz.

"Second," said Jill Carmody.

"The meeting is adjourned," said Bodner.

"Stewart," I said, "I have a letter for you from the Dean."

"Let me see it," said Bodner.

I handed the department Chair the sealed envelope I'd received from the downtown Dean.

Bodner opened the letter. His fish-belly white face paled.

"What's the matter!" said Lipschitz.

"This letter, it…it says Karl Biden has died."

I heard Jill Carmody draw in her breath. Mastoris stammered a question. Lipschitz tried to make himself heard.

I removed a Lonsdale from my leather carrying case. I cut the end. I began to roll the cigar around in my mouth.

It was true. Biden was dead. Probably from the heat.

Chapter Fifty-Nine

"Did the letter tell what happened?" asked Jill Carmody.

"Yes. He was jogging. He collapsed on the street. The EMTs said it was heat stroke."

"How awful," said Mary Mastoris.

"He was a young man," said Bodner.

"Yeah, not like Lipschitz, who's older than dirtballs," I said, smiling at the old professor.

"You fuckin' bastard!" said Lipschitz.

"Don't get excited, Sidney, you could be next, you know," I said.

"Please," said Jill Carmody.

Mary Mastoris started to cry.

"I'll have to inform the President," said Bodner. He got up and left, Lipschitz in his wake.

"I'll be with you in a moment," said Jill Carmody to Mary Mastoris, who also left the room.

Jill Carmody and I were alone in the conference room.

"I can't believe this happened," she said.

"Oh, it happened all right."

"An awful thing."

"Yes, to happen to a colleague."

Jill Carmody left the conference room.

I lit the cigar. The room soon filled with the aroma of the Lonsdale from Nicaragua.

"No, no," said the Hispanic janitor, standing in the doorway, pointing at my cigar.

"I'm leavin'."

"Que?"

"You're no fun, you know."

I left the conference room and walked down the hallway, trailing clouds of carcinogens.

Chapter Sixty

. . . .

My shiny black shoes squeaked on the clean gray floor. Ten meters or so in front of me, Jill Carmody turned into a classroom. Ahead and to the right, an office door opened and out stepped Annie Porter and Jim McDougal into the hallway.

They both saw me.

"Hello."

"Hello," replied the two in unison.

"How'd it go?" said Annie Porter.

"Biden's dead."

"What!" said Annie Porter.

"How?" said Jim McDougal.

"Runnin' in the heat."

"What does this mean?" said Annie Porter.

"Did I tell you not to worry?"

"Yes, but."

"Jill will fill you in, but I can tell you things will go your way."

Annie squeezed Jim Mc Dougal's hand.

"I have to go."

"Thanks," said Jim Mc Dougal.

I said nothing.

Annie Porter and Jim McDougal walked down the hallway and into the same classroom Jill Carmody had just entered.

I slowed as I approached the room. I could see, inside the room, professors sitting in the student's chairs. Jill Carmody sat at the desk. She was writing on a legal pad in front of her. I did a quick count. There were more than 20 professors in the room.

I walked past the room. The hallway assumed the odor of the Nicaraguan Lonsdale I was puffing on.

There were 54 faculty in the English department. There had been twenty or so professors in the room. I waited, leaning against a clean wall. Four more professors made their way down the hall and into the room. They were all in their 30s.

At 73, Lipschitz was a hanger-on. I was convinced Lipschitz would be removed from the Urban U. with his boots on. Stewart Bodner was also no spring chicken. Jill Carmody was 40-something. I had been on the college-wide committee that had hired Jill Carmody. I had voted against hiring Bodner. I'd also voted against promoting Bodner to full professor. So had Burton Franks.

"He's a night crawler," had said Burton Franks.

"I can see that, you can see that, why can't everyone else see that?"

"The vote was close; many of us did want him out."

"Close doesn't count."

"Let me give you a piece of advice."

"What's that?"

"Make your peace with Bodner."

"He's a turd."

"That may be, but you will have to spend your career with him. Sid Lipschitz is, as you said, 'a turd,' yet I've managed to remain on civil terms with him for 30 years."

"You're a better man than I am."

"No, I'm a man who takes the world as it is. You're a man who tries to make the world over."

"The world needs makin' over."

"Let God make over the world, you just try and live in it."

Two young professors arrived. I did the math. There had been 20 in the room. Annie and McDougal had made the total 22. Then four more, now these two. Jill Carmody would get her majority. Whatever she had wanted to do with the department, she could now do.

Jill Carmody had not shed a tear over the death of Biden. She had not canceled the meeting that was occurring down the hall. She had kept on task. I admired her control.

Annie Porter had not missed a beat in moving from the death of Biden to what it meant for Jim McDougal. I also admired her control. I believed that it was good to be in control.

I put out the cigar out on the clean floor. The cigar was supposed to be a four-star, yet it had left a bad taste in my mouth.

I left the building. My work was done here.

Outside, I looked across the quad. A light rain was coming down on the college. I would now go back to Brooklyn. It was hard to be clean in Brooklyn. Forty days and forty nights of hard rain could not cleanse Brooklyn, even the new, trendy Brooklyn.

I walked across the campus. The warm rain fell upon my head.

The rain came down harder. The rain came from the heavens. God was supposed to be in heaven. God let what was going on in Brooklyn go on. God needed some talking to.

Biden was just some guy I'd known for a short time. He was really nothing to me. His being dead, I could live with; it was what had killed him that haunted me.

Chapter Sixty-One

. . . .

I drove into the parking garage of the Urban U. There were no more than three cars in the entire garage. The term was nearly over. I had only to turn in my roster. The English exam, which would be given to a herd of students all gathered on the tenth floor, started at 2 p.m. I'd leave the Urban U. today. I'd drive into the night. Next day, I'd be in Canada. I would be 1,029 miles from Brooklyn until the sixth of September. I wouldn't be alone. Candy was looking forward to the trip. She wanted to go fishing, said that she knew all about what to do. I'd give her the job of fixing worms to the hook.

"Hello, Prof, how you doin'?"

"Doin' fine, Lester, how about you?"

"I be glad when this day over."

"Why's that?"

"That little red-haired woman, the one you usta go round wit', she up on the tenth floor." Beef Patty knew more about me than I did. Maybe he should've graded my papers.

"She is?"

"This afternoon she gonna have the One-Percenters, the Seoul Brothers, and the Monarchs all up there on the tenth floor."

"That's true."

"Gonna be trouble."

"That a fact?"

"I got a feelin'."

"Let's hope your feelings are wrong."

"Malvina say my feelin's usually right. She say I ain't no light bulb but my feelin's, she say I right on about them."

"Who'll start it?"

"That Jimmy Fisheyes, he think he can take J.P."

"How so?"

"He think he know karate, don' you know karate, Prof?"

"Yes," I said, fibbing.

"Wha' you think? That gook, he take J.P.?"

"No."

"Why?"

"Hitting J.P. is like slapping a she-bear in the face when she's takin' care of her cubs."

"Jus' piss him off, huh?"

"That's right."

"Ain't good to get J.P. pissed off."

"No, it's not."

"That mick cop, he down here again."

"When did he arrive?"

Beef Patty checked his log.

"An hour ago."

"You tell him about Professor Porter and who was on the tenth floor with her?"

"No."

"That's because he didn't ask you, right?"

"Right."

"Since he didn't ask, you didn't volunteer the information, did you?"

"No, I din't," said Beef Patty, his face opening into a wide grin, exposing at least two gold teeth.

"Trouble starts, Reagan can handle it, right?"

"Right."

"Malvina's wrong about you."

"How's that?"

"You are definitely a light bulb."

The big, black man laughed a big, black man's laugh.

I left the parking garage. I used the back stairs to enter the first-floor lobby of the Urban U.

A small white security guard was watching the Street through the large glass front doors. On the Street itself, one of the panhandlers was mooning the guard, exposing buttocks which were not entirely clean.

At the elevators were two people. I gave them what I considered to be a broad, winning smile.

"Hello, Dr. Carmody, hello, Dean, isn't this a lovely, lovely day in May?"

"Well, it was," said the Dean, looking toward the front doors.

Jill Carmody smiled at me.

Inside the elevator, I pushed the button for the sixth floor.

"Floor?"

"Ten," said the Dean.

"Goin' to assist Professor Porter?"

"Yes," said the Dean.

"Do you want to join us?" said Jill Carmody.

"No, thanks."

I could smell the Opium she was wearing. It was no doubt the odor of that perfume that had set off the panhandler on the Street.

"Well, it was certainly nice sharing a ride with you two. Congratulations on your election, Dr. Carmody."

"Thank you."

I got off the elevator.

Looking ahead, I saw Detective Reagan standing by my office door.

"Hey, Prof, I need to talk to you," said Reagan.

"Shall we step inside to my elegant office?"

"There're two guys in there."

"Are there? How about the student lounge? That should be empty."

"That'll be OK."

We moved away from my office, back toward the elevators, passing empty classrooms.

At the opposite end of the hall was a student lounge where, during the school year, students smoked dope and engaged in god knows what. Now, the lounge was empty.

There was a table in the middle of the room. Around it were four chairs. I sat in one of the chairs. I lit a cigar. Reagan did not sit down. The short detective began to pace the floor and run his fingers through his thinning but still jet-black hair.

I waited for Reagan to say what he had to say.

The room was dead quiet. It would be dead quiet until the sixth of September. All of the students would now be on the tenth floor, some taking a writing test, some aiming to take shots at one another.

Chapter Sixty-Two

● ●

"I don't know exactly where to begin," said Reagan, still pacing.

"The beginnin's always a good place."

"It's about this Biden."

"Biden is dead."

"Yeah, I know."

"You know how many people from the college came to his funeral?"

"No."

"One."

"Prof, I don't get where you're goin' with...."

"He was buried in Williamstown. It's a nice place, ever been there?"

"No."

"His father was a big-shot professor at a real college."

"Isn't this a real college?" said Reagan.

"Kinda."

"Why're you tellin' me this?"

"His old man was able to bury his baby boy and still be proud of him. I went to the funeral and said some good things about him."

"But you thought he was a fuck-up."

"That's what you wanted me to do, stand in front of his father and say 'Yeah, I knew your son, and boy oh boy was he a fuck-up'?"

"I guess not."

"It's true, Biden was a fuck-up. He was goin' to be fired, which meant he'd have gone home to his big-shot father with his tail between his legs, like a beaten dog. Would you like to face your old man like that?"

"No."

Reagan sat down across from me.

"Prof, this makes five professors who died down here. When you start to add them up, there's a pattern."

I smoked.

It was very quiet in the student lounge.

"Hey, Prof, you know me, I got a thing about loose ends. It was bad enough with one prof dead."

"Not quite."

"How so?"

"Randle spent morning, noon, and night grindin' his considerable guts about gettin' back to the main campus. Stress will kill you. I think if you're lookin' for a killer, that's who you're going to find."

"But Biden was no old stressed-out guy."

"No, Biden died because he was a fuck-up."

"I don't get you."

"You work out?"

"Not really. I take the wife bowlin' sometimes."

"Working out isn't for the stupid. You need a plan. You start liftin' weights like a half-ass you'll rip yourself up...."

"That's pretty much what the ME said."

"Biden started running because he was worryin' himself sick about gettin' fired. He went from no running to running in hot weather. You know what the temperature was on the day he died?"

"No."

"Ninety degrees plus humidity. He was a fuck-up."

Reagan stared at his hands. The nails were neatly manicured.

"If I have the ME take a close look at this Biden, what's he gonna find?"

I said nothing.

Reagan took a deep breath.

"You know, Prof, if it wasn't for you I wouldn't be a detective...."

"Correct."

"When I came to college, I was scared. Remember what I told you on the first day I was down here?"

"You asked me if you could sit next to the door so you could cut out if this wasn't the place for you."

"That's right. You helped me out. I owe you, but...."

"There's always a 'but'."

"Yeah, there is. Then I was a piece of street shit, but now I'm a cop, now I got a job to do."

I drew on my cigar.

"If I ask the ME to look in Biden for drugs and he finds somethin', then we got a problem. I checked into this alkaloid stuff, some of it isn't in the drug you gave me. Some of it is bad news."

"How so?"

"Prof, I read your papers. A lot of this points to you."

A voice came over the emergency intercom. It was the voice of a man. The man was trying to sound like he wasn't scared. The man was doing a piss-poor job of sounding like he wasn't scared.

"This is Jim McDougal. I'm on the tenth floor. There's a riot goin' on up here. Send help. Send it now!"

Reagan was on his feet.

"Where's that fat spook?"

"The 'fat spook' had to go to the main campus. You want me to go up with you?"

"No," said Reagan, who left the room.

I was alone in the student lounge.

I got up and pressed the return button on the intercom.

Jim McDougal was still there.

"What's the problem?"

"Is that you?"

"No, this is fuckin' Wyatt fuckin' Earp. What's goin' on?"

"A big black student and a small Korean student are fighting."

"You could get a thousand dollars ringside for that one."

"This isn't funny."

"So break up the fight or maybe send in Annie."

"Is help on the way?"

"A cop will soon be there, but he ain't gonna be very popular with the students. Where's Annie?"

"Right here with me."

"Can you see the kitchen from where you are?"

"Yes."

"Take her there. There's an elevator that'll take you all the way to the garage."

"What about the students?"

"Fuck them, you get Annie out of there," I said, switching off the intercom.

I needed coffee. I'd go visit Fat Harry. By the time I got back, the problem on the tenth floor should be over, but the problem with Detective Reagan would not be over.

I used the back stairs to leave the college.

Chapter Sixty-Three

· ·

"Professor, there is trouble at the college?" asked Fat Harry as he set a cup of coffee on the counter.

"There is trouble."

"Serious?"

"Yes."

"J.P. and Jimmy Fisheyes?"

"News travels fast around here, especially bad news."

I suspected that Fat Harry dripped the greasy sweat from his fat mitts into his coffee. Maybe Starbucks could serve it as "Grecian Formula Blend."

"J.P., I wish he would lose this fight."

"Don't bet on it."

"I have been told that Jimmy Fisheyes knows karate, as I have heard you do also, Professor."

I nodded and, in doing so, again lied. I didn't know squat about karate, but being a hand-killer was not a bad rep to have at the Urban U.

"So, tell me, should not Jimmy Fisheyes be able to defeat J.P.?"

"No."

"And would you tell me why not?"

"My father once shot a spring bear. I was with him. The bear died right in front of me. I was no more than 11 or 12. Just as the bear was dyin', I touched it, right above its paw. I'd always carried a hatchet whenever I was in the woods; I'd thought I could kill a bear with that hatchet. Touchin' the bear's leg was like touching twisted steel. After I felt that bear's leg, I never bothered to take my hatchet with me."

"More police are arriving," said Fat Harry, looking over at the police cars lining up on the Street, ignoring my wonderful tale full of sage advice.

I turned on my stool, swiveling away from the counter. I could see several cops going into the Urban U. I could also see two EMT trucks parked in front of the Urban U.'s large front glass doors. Coming out of those doors was a couple. The man was tall and blonde and well preserved. The woman was Annie Porter. The man had his arm around Annie Porter's shoulders. The couple looked like they belonged together.

Jim McDougal and Annie Porter crossed the Street. They came toward the corner deli. Jim McDougal looked into the deli. He saw me. He brought Annie into the deli.

"Here, Professors, sit in a booth," said Fat Harry.

Annie Porter sat down in the booth. Her face was very white, her hands were shaking.

Jim McDougal came over to the counter.

"Would you bring her a glass of water?" said McDougal to Fat Harry.

"Coming right up," said the deli owner.

"Thanks for your escape route," said McDougal.

"A fox always has more than one way out," I said, watching as Fat Harry served Annie Porter. She began to sip the glass of water.

"That was some scene up there," said McDougal.

"I bet."

"It was J.P. and that Korean James Kim…."

"He prefers to be called Jimmy Fisheyes."

"Whatever. Those two had been after one another from the moment they arrived on the tenth floor. I thought they would get into it before the test started, but they calmed down when we handed out the blue books."

"They both want to pass."

"I guess so, so anyway, I thought we would make it through the test, but this J.P. and 'Fisheyes' finished writing at about the same time. They came up to hand in their essays and then that Dean appeared."

"I assume the Dean added gasoline to a raging fire."

"That's exactly what he did. J.P. hands in his blue book, and next to him is the Korean, so J.P. says 'You askin' for it, slant' and Fisheyes says 'Do you want a piece of me, nigger?' So when the Dean hears that, he tells Fisheyes he's going to have him arrested for using the N word. At that point, Fisheyes kicks J.P. in the face."

"Let me guess, the kickin' in the face didn't seem to bother J.P. a whole lot."

"You're right. Fisheyes kept on with all of his karate and J.P. kept coming at him."

"I take it Fisheyes will need medical assistance?"

"Yes, and it was then that all hell broke loose. The Koreans and the blacks were throwing chairs at one another. Annie and I were in the middle. We were going to get...."

"And the department Chair, the fair Ms. Carmody?"

"She got on the elevator."

"How?"

"When the Dean started to stick his nose in between J.P. and Fisheyes, our esteemed Chair walked over to the elevator."

"Smart."

"That's about it."

"You never mentioned the cop."

"I never saw him. I just did what you told me to do."

"She OK?"

"She's shook up."

"You better go and take care of her."

"I will," said Jim McDougal, offering his hand.

I shook the hand of Jim McDougal.

"Harry, would you give me a regular to go?"

"No problem, Professor."

Jim McDougal sat with Annie Porter.

Across the way, students were now pouring out of the building. Most of them were laughing. In Brooklyn, a race riot is no big deal.

I finished the coffee. Jim McDougal and Annie Porter left the deli. McDougal waved his hand. Annie Porter did not look at me.

"She will be OK?" said Fat Harry.

"Yes."

"You were right about the fight. Apparently, J.P. was victorious."

"Where's your helper?"

Fat Harry started to sweat even more than his usual drip.

"He did not work out."

"He was always nice to me, where did he go?"

"He has required some medical attention," said Fat Harry, who turned and walked away to wait on another customer.

"Harry, what do I owe you for this coffee?"

"On me, Professor, enjoy," said Harry from the other end of the counter.

"I'll see you in the fall."

Fat Harry made his way back toward me, wheezing as he walked.

"I may not be here upon your return."

"Business not so good?"

"My wife, she thinks I should open a place elsewhere."

"There's always a J.P. 'elsewhere.'"

"I have not yet decided," said Fat Harry.

"I would miss you, and our conversations."

"I would miss you also," said Fat Harry, extending a plump, greasy hand. I shook the fat hand.

I stepped into the crowded streets.

Various students shouted at me. They told me of the fight between J.P. and Jimmy Fisheyes. I thanked them for their insights.

Chapter Sixty-Four

. . . .

The parking garage of the Urban U. was being used by the EMT squad. They had a lot to do.

"Hey Professor, que pasa?"

"Hello," I said to the president of the Latin Monarchs, who was also an EMT.

"The gook, he really got it."

"He did?"

"Yeah, they took him away."

"They did?"

"They took him to Holy Name Hospital."

"They have a unit there for paralysis."

"That's why he was taken there."

"Total?"

"Neck down. J.P. broke his fuckin' back."

"J.P. hurt?"

"Nada. Not even a bloody nose. That one tough negro."

"No arrests?"

"No one there to do any arresting."

"No cop?"

He pointed to the back of the garage. Something was under a sheet next to the police ambulance.

"Who's that?"

"You knew him, his name was Reagan."

"What happened?"

"The students made for the stairs. He was in the way. They ran over him."

I chewed on a Robusto.

"Cuban?" asked the Latin Monarch's president.

"Cubans are illegal."

"Everythin' worth anythin' is illegal, Professor."

"No, this is not a Cuban."

"Honduran?"

"Yes."

"Hoyo de Monterey?"

"Yes."

"I smoke only Cubans."

"Cubans are expensive."

"Dinero is no problem for me, Professor."

I stared at what was lying at the back of the garage. Reagan had died trying to break up a dime-a-dozen gang fight brought on by a dip-shit Dean. Reagan had suspected me. Thoughts of loss conflicted with thoughts of relief.

"Adios, Professor, I have to go."

"Adios."

Chapter Sixty-Five

. . . .

The tenth floor of the Urban U. looked like a Florida trailer park the day after a tornado. It was empty of students. Why I'd come here, I hadn't a clue. I smelled a familiar smell.

Behind me, something moved.

I turned just in time to miss a knife thrust at my head. I faced the knifer. He had my way to the elevator blocked. I was really glad I'd been curious.

"You were talkin' to that cop," said the man with the knife.

"He's dead now."

"That doesn't change what you know." The knifer went into a crouch, like he knew what he was doing.

I tried to buy time.

"What do I know?"

"You know about the killings down here."

"Who said there were killings?"

"Don't be coy, Bucceroni, it doesn't suit you."

"What does suit me?"

"Bein' dead," said the knifer, making another move.

He missed again. I still had feet that worked.

"Why you doin' this?"

"You're close to figuring it all out."

"I am?"

"I killed Randle and Biden."

"Why?"

"They were scum, they deserved to die."

"Just for bein' sent here?"

"Just for that."

"And Bath?"

"Bath was my lover. He and I were 'partners'. But he was running scared. He had to go."

"But why Biden?"

"To lead a trail to you."

The knifer tried another cut, I felt something scrape my side.

He got too close, I grabbed him, twisted him, used my big hands to break his neck. He sank to the floor without a peep.

There he lay. A little guy. A soulless creep. And, up until a few seconds ago, the Dean of the college.

I took his knife.

So now the pieces fit. The Dean and Bath, a couple, had read my papers and gone into the chemical killing business. They'd saved Bath's job. Then Bath's nerves had given out, so he'd been removed via a slit job. And the Dean'd planned for me to be blamed. It had nearly worked, for Pat Reagan was ready to finger me.

I looked at the body. Some new cop would find him. Whether a trail led to me or not would be anyone's guess. I provided an answer for the cops by dragging the tiny, deadly Dean to the stairs. I put him air-borne. He landed hard, face-first, at the bottom of the stairs. Which didn't kill him. Yours truly had done that.

Chapter Sixty-Six

. . . .

I left the tenth floor, went to the ninth, opened a window. No one up, down, or dead-on was looking at me. I dropped the knife into the layers of trash below. It'd been wiped clean. It'd take a world-class looker to find the Dean's weapon of choice.

Checking my shirt, I found an air vent. Luck had ridden with me, for an inch closer and I would've been stuck.

That was Brooklyn for you, here an inch, there an inch; here dead, there alive.

Final Chapter

. . . .

Walking down the hall, I could see the light in my office was on. I opened the office door. No one was inside. There were some books on the former desk of the late Dr. Biden. Gone were Biden's effects. Another life had been swept away.

I looked out the window. The blinds were up in the apartment across from the Urban U. The apartment was vacant.

I lit a Robusto.

I smoked and thought about Detective Reagan and about an ME who had evidence of drugs in a dead professor. I came to believe that MEs were not dedicated detectives who worried about loose ends. Truth be told, I didn't spend much time mourning. Life had come at me hard, and I'd struck back. In Brooklyn, that was the only way to handle life.

All of this I would run by Candy. It'd make for trip chitchat on our way to Canada.

The door to the office opened. Into the office came a professor in funeral garb; he was followed by another, older, professor in a wrinkled summer suit. The two professors sat down at two of the desks. They said nothing.

"Hello, Stewart, nice outfit, and hello to you, Sid, nice coat," I said to the former English department Chair and to Full Professor Sidney Lipschitz.

Dr. Bodner did not respond, neither did Lipschitz. Bodner sat at Biden's former desk with a pale hand held to a pale forehead while Lipschitz stared at the desktop of the late Dr. Rudolf Randle.

I rolled my Robusto around in my mouth.

"Stewie, Sid, you two boys seem out of sorts. How about I make the two of you a nice cup of coffee?"

About the Author

· ·

W.J. Reeves labors in Brooklyn. He's happy to offer the second book in the Bucceroni Series, *Banished to Brooklyn,* another turbulent adventure in the stormy life of Professor Richie Bucceroni.

www.ingramcontent.com/pod-product-compliance
Lightning Source LLC
Chambersburg PA
CBHW031253170626
46807CB00001B/130